Alec couldn't—shouldn't—have her. Not now. Not ever.

Oh, who the hell was he kidding? Rory wanted him as much as he wanted her. And Alec had been alone for a long time—too long to resist a woman so willing, so alluring...so *naked!* But with one last, desperate attempt at self-preservation, he tried to look as shocked as he felt.

"What are you doing?"

Rory thrust her hands onto her hips, emphasizing her nakedness by being entirely unabashed about her lack of clothes. Alec swallowed hard, but found his throat parched, his mouth dry, his brain trying desperately to disconnect from his conscience long enough to savor what was in front of him.

Nude and beautiful, Rory captured a part of Alec he now knew wasn't as tamed as he'd believed.

"I'm about to make you an offer I hope you won't refuse," she said, grinning wickedly.

D0423491

Blaze™

Dear Reader,

Blame it on the bubbly...or in this case, on the sangria.
INVITATIONS TO SEDUCTION owes its creation to a
gathering of friends in Chandler, Arizona, a bottle of sweet
Spanish wine and an editor who was willing to listen.

It was there in Chandler that the four of us, five counting our
editor, entertained the idea for a series based on a book of sexy
invitations. You know, the ones you're supposed to share with a
lover? The type that are sealed for secrecy, until you and your
partner can discover the erotic mystery together? At first we
planned just the novella collection, but our editor suggested two
related books within the Blaze series introducing readers to a
naughty book called *Sexcapades* and the sensual havoc and
"happily ever afters" it ultimately causes.

The five of us had great fun linking the stories...and we hope you
have equally as much fun reading them!

Happy reading,

Julie Elizabeth Leto   Vicki Lewis Thompson

Carly Phillips   Janelle Denison

Watch for *your* invitation!

June 2003—*Looking for Trouble*
by Julie Elizabeth Leto (Blaze #92)

July 2003—*Invitations to Seduction,*
"Illicit Dreams" by Vicki Lewis Thompson
"Going All the Way" by Carly Phillips
"His Every Fantasy" by Janelle Denison

August 2003—*Up To No Good*
by Julie Elizabeth Leto (Blaze #100)

LOOKING FOR TROUBLE

Julie Elizabeth Leto

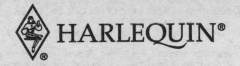

HARLEQUIN®

TORONTO • NEW YORK • LONDON
AMSTERDAM • PARIS • SYDNEY • HAMBURG
STOCKHOLM • ATHENS • TOKYO • MILAN • MADRID
PRAGUE • WARSAW • BUDAPEST • AUCKLAND

To Vicki, Janelle, Carly and Brenda.
See what a little sangria, Bailey's and Arizona air will inspire?
Here's to a fun series with great friends.

And to Kathy Carmichael—thanks for lending me your name
for my characters and your sympathetic ear, whenever and
wherever I needed it. You're the best.

ISBN 0-373-79096-1

LOOKING FOR TROUBLE

Copyright © 2003 by Julie Leto Klapka.

This edition published by arrangement with Harlequin Books S.A.

® and TM are trademarks of the publisher. Trademarks indicated with ® are registered in the United States Patent and Trademark Office, the Canadian Trade Marks Office and in other countries.

Visit us at www.eHarlequin.com

Printed in U.S.A.

1

RORY CARMICHAEL CLOSED HER EYES and tried to block the electric rush of excitement shooting through her bloodstream. By now she should have been accustomed to the tingle, the thrill, the unabashed seduction of learning a secret. The chance to find out something she shouldn't know enticed Rory's gaze away from the employment application in front of her to the enormous round table in the center of the Divine Events reception area.

And the book. The big red book.

What in those pages was so tempting? So irresistible? Every single person who'd crossed the glass-and-brass threshold of Divine Events hadn't been able to resist the allure. Rory had been in the eclectic, chic office of Chicago's up-and-coming leaders in the party-planning business for nearly thirty minutes, and in that time frame, at least four clients had wandered to the table and flipped open the book sitting beneath the floral arrangement. And unless Rory's imaginative and curious nature proved entirely overactive, they had each furtively torn out pages and stuffed them in pockets and purses.

Knowing she should be concentrating on filling out the employment papers that would soon make her a member of the Divine Events staff, Rory tried hard to tamp down her interest in the mysterious contents of the book.

So far, no luck.

A pretty blonde in blue jeans wandered nearer and nearer, seemingly just as drawn by the red leather-covered book. The grand flower arrangement beside it— a Grecian urn, overflowing with birds of paradise, hyacinth, hydrangea and greenery—should have been an overpowering focal point for the room. But as Rory sat at the receptionist's desk—the one she hoped would soon bear her nameplate—she couldn't miss how patron after patron ignored everything else—the wild flora, the crystal bowl of expensive chocolates and the stacks of photo albums chronicling the many successful parties, auctions and receptions planned and executed by Divine Events— in favor of the scarlet leather book.

Just what was in there?

"How's it going, Rory?"

Cecily Divine strode out of the kitchen behind her, a large mug of root beer clutched in one hand, a cell phone tucked against her ear, somewhere beneath her thick raven hair. One of three cousins who ran the business together, Cecily had immediately impressed Rory. She wanted to work for Cecily, learn from her and her two cousins, whom Rory had met briefly when she first arrived. Maybe she could pick up some tips on how to juggle a million things at one time. Heck, Rory would settle for learning how to ignore the book on the table, which neither Cecily nor her cousins seemed to notice any time *they* walked into the room, even when their clients seemed obsessed.

Cecily waved to the blonde near the reception table, who'd paused, frozen, her eyes wide and her hands still, as if peeking into the leather book constituted some sort of forbidden sin.

Rory sat up straighter, but still couldn't see a title, if the book had one. She swiveled to answer Cecily's question, but her would-be new boss had returned her attention to the phone. She watched Cecily maneuver the wrought-iron spiral staircase which led to the second floor offices, the acrylic heels of her thigh-high boots rapping music on the metal. The woman smiled down at Rory apologetically as she chatted with the client on the other end of the line.

Rory gave her a wave that meant, ''Don't worry about me.'' She could fill out an application, particularly when the job promised to be the stuff of Rory's dreams. But she'd sure make more headway if she could sate her curiosity about that darned book.

The minute Cecily disappeared into her office, Rory heard the telltale rip of paper from the center of the room. The blonde had obviously succumbed to the same temptation as the other clients. Rory forced her gaze downward and managed to maintain her discretion for all of fifteen seconds. She really did have a problem with curiosity, though her great Aunt Lil called her affliction plain old nosiness. However, Rory knew her need-to-know tendencies kept her out of trouble more often than they lured her in. And of all the problems that had plagued the Carmichael women over the past two generations, a probing interest in other people's business was, comparatively speaking, a minor offense. And thanks to her intense curiosity, Rory knew the score of living on the edge, even if she never played the game herself.

She clutched the pen tighter in her hand. That was about to change.

When she looked up, the blonde had tucked the pilfered page into her handbag. Gia Divine, a statuesque brunette dressed in slim slacks and a cuffed button-down shirt, appeared on the balcony and beckoned her client up the stairs.

By the time Rory finished filling the application in with her new address, cell phone number, social security number and various other identifiers, Cecily had taken another important call—this one from the manager of a band she'd been trying for six weeks to book for a corporate shindig. She asked Rory to wait. Alone. In the lobby.

Rory tried to remain focused on acing her imminent interview, her final hurdle in her race toward gainful employment. But the stillness of the reception area, quiet except for the piped-in strains of jazz fusion floating over the air, forced Rory to revise that plan. First, she was going to find out what was in that book. Then, she'd complete the process for her job. Afterward, she'd head to State Street and give her wardrobe an update, even before she met her new landlord and moved into her apartment. If she intended to blend in with the chic surroundings, she'd need more than the T-shirts, jeans, conservative skirts and sweater sets she'd packed from home.

She grinned, satisfied with her plan. If there was one talent Rory was particularly proud of, it was her knack for compartmentalization and order. She set her priorities, then dealt with them one at a time—never needlessly worrying about one while she concentrated on the other. And right now, all she wanted was a peek at that book. And once Rory decided what she wanted, she rarely changed her mind.

Glancing at the switchboard on the desk, Rory verified that Cecily was still on the phone. In a dash, Rory scurried to the entrance. Seeing no one on the sidewalk who looked like they were coming inside, she hurried to the table and grabbed the scarlet book.

The leather cover revealed nothing. The book wasn't

hardbound, but a large paperback, the size of a magazine and the thickness of an encyclopedia volume. The leather cover had been added afterward, apparently to cover the racy title, which Rory found by opening to the first page.

Sexcapades: Secret Games and Wild Adventures for Uninhibited Lovers.

Yum! Rory had heard about this book. In fact, she'd caught a quick glimpse of the publication while at a bridal shower, though she couldn't very well peruse it at her leisure since her Nanna had been sitting right next to her. Though twenty-five years old, Rory avoided any and all situations that made apparent her status as a mature, sensual woman—at least in front of her grandmother. Long before she'd hit puberty, she'd come to understand the importance of avoiding conflict or engendering distrust in this regard. She completely understood why her grandmother avoided any topic of a sexual nature around her granddaughter. She'd raised Rory's mother the best way she'd known how only to watch her become the school slut, get herself pregnant with twins at age sixteen, then abandon the babies three months later to run off with some old guy who eventually got her hooked on drugs until she overdosed. No wonder she was so strict with her granddaughters.

Rory had survived Nanna's overprotectiveness by playing the good girl and saving her secret curiosities for her darkened bedroom late, late at night. She dated, but when she did, she willingly chose the laced up choirboys her grandmother nudged her toward. Bad boys were bad news. Heck, some of the choirboys weren't exactly heralds of joy, either. But Rory knew her strengths as well as her limitations, and when it came to men, she was definitely limited. She simply didn't have the experience. Luckily she was a good judge of character, but she suspected that in the city—without the familiarity of knowing at least a hint about someone's family history or neighborhood standing—classifying people into either good and bad wouldn't be as easy. Chicago, like most major metropolises, found its rhythm from an eclectic mixture of people. Woven with centuries-old threads of tradition and mended with laces of current trends and expectations, the fabric of Chicago could envelop, bind or suffocate at will.

Rory had come to the city on a dual-purpose mission. First, to find her twin, Micki, who'd dealt with Nanna's strictness by running away when they'd turned fifteen. Second, Rory wanted to find herself. The real Rory. The unfettered Rory. The Rory she couldn't become under the watchful eye of her loving, but smothering grandmother. The Rory she truly wanted to spend the rest of her life with, bound by skin and soul.

And Rory knew her old self well enough to know she had to explore this book. So she did, though she didn't find much.

The pages were sealed.

Each section had a provocative title, however, and Rory couldn't help but stop at the one that read, Slippery When Wet. When she tugged a little too hard, she realized that each page was perforated for quick removal. Her inadvertent rip went halfway down, but she sighed. The page remained in place. She turned back to the beginning and read the instructions.

Start with number one and work your way toward number one hundred—or pick and choose a title that sparks your fancy. Tear out the section that interests you and give it to your lover. Or keep it to yourself for now, and spring a surprise on your unsuspecting partner sometime soon. Each individualized sexual adventure or fantasy should remain sealed, so even you will experience an element of surprise. Then live and love! Go on, tear one out. Do it. Then, do it. You'll be, oh, so pleased that you did.

Since there were already quite a few fantasies missing from the book and she'd halfway pulled one out already, good girl Rory Carmichael followed the instructions. She ripped out the page that had caught her eye, dashed back to the desk and stuffed it into her purse. She had no time to wonder if she'd done the right thing before Cecily appeared in her office door, declared her phone call successful, then beckoned Rory upstairs for her interview.

Rory grabbed her bag, patted her purse, and pushed away all her guilt. She'd used up more than her share of that emotion back in Berwyn, living with her grandmother and great-aunt, trying without being asked to atone for the sins of her mother and sister. From now on, Rory would look out for her own interests, even if she had to swipe a page from someone else's book to do it.

SHE'D ACTUALLY STOLEN TWO? Rory winced as she withdrew the pilfered pages from her purse. She hadn't meant to be greedy, but, apparently, she'd been a little over-enthusiastic. Well, she couldn't very well return one, could she? It might be true that she'd now have plenty of opportunity to view the book since she was officially the new client services specialist for Divine Events—the fanciest name for receptionist she'd ever heard—but she couldn't deny the fact that perforated pages did not reattach.

Though still sealed, Rory could read the loopy font on the front.

This one was called "Strangers in the Night."

Frank Sinatra. Very retro. Very cool.

She wiggled in the seat of her Jeep, then glanced through the windshield to make sure no one in the parking lot could somehow peek through her tinted windows, spy her taboo activity and turn her over to the virtue police. Good girls not only didn't steal, they didn't read secret sexual fantasies outside in broad daylight. Well, Rory was done with that whole good-girl thing anyway. For the most part. In theory.

And the first way to prove a theory was to experiment, so she slipped her finger beneath the gluey edge and broke the seal.

For a moment, her eyes wouldn't focus. After she read a few lines, she couldn't believe her luck. She'd just arrived in Chicago—hadn't even unpacked her meager belongings from the back of her fourth-hand Jeep Wrangler. New in town and teeming to transform herself, this fantasy drove right up her sophisticated-woman-wannabe alley.

Well, more like cruised. Nothing too drastic, nothing too shocking. The perfect medium to ease her into a new outlook on men and dating and sex.

Find a stranger who excites you.

Not so easy, she thought, seeing as she'd been in the city for going on three hours and she'd yet to meet anyone male, much less anyone exciting.

She shrugged. *Details, details.* But, just in case, she glanced one more time around the parking lot.

Empty.

She kept reading.

Picking up strangers isn't a wise activity, but there's no harm in a little careful flirting. Is your mate around? Smile a little more at a stranger, talk with more animation…. Does this rile his or her jealous instincts? Jealousy can be a very potent aphrodisiac.

Rory frowned. This wasn't turning out how she'd envisioned at all. She didn't have a mate, "around" or otherwise. Disappointed, she continued to read, wondering if she couldn't somehow adapt the fantasy to her current circumstances.

Or maybe your mate isn't nearby. That's okay. Flirting with a stranger will stir your juices, prep you for when you make your next rendezvous with your trusted lover. Be outrageous…or, better yet, be mysterious. And make sure your warm-up target doesn't follow you home!

Okay, this wasn't so bad. Rory could manage this. She definitely considered "Strangers in the Night" a safer bet than the remaining, still-sealed fantasy, "Slippery When Wet." She didn't have a lot of flirting practice, as flirting usually led to dating, and dating usually led to trouble. Not trouble with men, necessarily, but trouble with convincing her grandmother that seeing a movie with the guy she met at school but whose family hadn't been given the Nanna Seal of Approval wasn't going to result in the complete ruination of her life.

Weary of the drama that played out between her and her beloved grandmother whenever the topic of men came up, Rory had chosen instead to pretty much stay out of the dating theatre. But now she was on her own and ready to act out in the way that the wild Carmichael women were so infamous for.

Luckily Rory had in abundance what she figured both her mother and her sister lacked—a strong sense of self and loads of common sense. Despite her sheltered upbringing—or perhaps because of it—Rory considered herself incredibly capable of taking care of herself. She'd developed a sharp mind and a clear-thinking outlook in her quest to keep peace in the house. Her remarkable capacity for spotting liars and frauds, an offshoot of her overly curious nature, made her the go-to girl among her friends whenever they weren't sure whom to trust. Now, Rory had a chance to use her skills for her own benefit. On her own for the first time, Rory relished the chance at freedom, the opportunity to push her limits and test her mettle…and she had the perfect fantasy to lead her way.

2

"SHE'LL BE THERE SOON. This is the least you can do, don't you think, Alexander?"

Alec Manning frowned, all too aware that what his father said wasn't half as chilling as what he didn't say. *For all the women you've ruined, the least you can do is save this one.*

"I don't like to meddle in other people's lives, Pop."

"Isn't that what you're doing every night at that club of yours? Manipulating the patrons into interacting with each other so you can write about them for your study?"

He should have been impressed that his father took the time away from his busy schedule as an oncologist to understand the details about Alec's project, but he couldn't muster more than mild annoyance. His father had always been interested in Alec's academic work. It was the only part of his youngest son's life he could respect.

Or that he could respect until six months ago, when Alec had been canned from his cushy job in Boston University's Sociology department. Too bad he didn't pay enough attention to his own textbooks, or he might have realized that screwing the dean's wife was not acceptable behavior in the academic society, even if the woman had been willing. All the women in his life had been willing and more than aware of his inability to keep out of trouble and away from scandal. Like the one that had him currently unemployed and taking on a boarder until he could secure another university gig worthy of his diplomas.

"My new study is different," Alec countered. "All I do at the club is steer certain women toward certain men and watch them interact. This time, no one gets hurt."

His father chuckled in that all-knowing way that truly ticked Alec off. He wondered if his father had invented the God complex, or if all physicians fell victim to the omniscient mind-set.

"You don't know that, do you, son? You don't follow those people home. But, hey, you don't force them together, either. They make their choices."

Alec pushed away from his desk and stretched his legs and back. "And this Aurora Carmichael has made her choices, too. She wants to find her twin. Who am I to discourage her?"

"You're going to be her friend."

"I'm going to be her landlord, Pop. I don't have time for friends."

"Not even those of the female persuasion? Why do I find that impossible to believe?"

His father's doubts crackled through the phone line. Alec's six months of celibacy wouldn't convince his father, his brothers or his colleagues that the straight and narrow would remain his path for the long haul. Hell, most of the time, he had trouble convincing himself. Some nights, he felt like a testosterone time bomb. Any minute now, he expected some hot little number would dance into his life, light his fuse and blow his libido— and his future—sky-high.

He'd tried everything to avoid that scenario, even conducting this research project—a study of the shift in sexual aggression from men to women—undercover. The sexy sirens who'd once driven him insane with desire and temptation now flirted and fawned over a man that wasn't really him. At least, not anymore. At first, he'd thought himself so freaking clever for picking a topic so near and dear to his personal interests for study. He'd practically patted a callused spot on his back for the smart way he'd turned his weakness for women into a business pursuit. But that was before he'd spent six months doing all his studying from behind the bar rather than in his bed.

Still, he knew the lurid subject matter would catch the attention of the generous and groundbreaking Hensen Foundation. And once he had the Hensen Foundation grant money in hand, his scandal-damaged career would jumpstart, no matter what scintillating topics he chose to study.

So, to that end, Alec had gone undercover. By night, Alec Manning changed his appearance, his attitude, even his name. He became Xander Mann, slick, suave bartender—a killer with the ladies, the envy of men. Only half a year ago, Alec and Xander had been one and the same person. But his bad-boy ways had forced him to leave a job he loved. So, to salvage what was left of his career, he'd decided to recast Alec as the studious professor, dedicated to his work and swearing off women.

All women. Even the sweet, little shy types. Especially the sweet, little shy types, like the one who was scheduled to move into his second-floor apartment sometime this afternoon. It shouldn't be so hard—they'd never been his type anyway.

"Are you suggesting I seduce Aurora Carmichael?"

"Good God, no! I just want you to help her grandmother out a bit. The woman has been through a rough year."

"She's in remission, right?"

"Yes."

"And she's supporting her granddaughter's move to the city, isn't she?"

"Aurora is twenty-five years old. Marjorie can't stop her from going out on her own."

Yet the woman had gone so far as to contact Alec a few weeks ago herself, promising three months' advance rent if he'd agree to take her granddaughter as a tenant. At the time, he'd been impressed by Marjorie Carmichael's supportive attitude. Now he wondered how much of her generosity was concern—and how much was an attempt at long-distance control.

"But Grandma wants to stop Aurora from finding her missing sister—and you want me to be a part of the old lady's plan. Do you think that's fair?"

Alec had known nothing about Aurora's missing twin sister until this call from his father, Marjorie's oncologist and good friend. He couldn't believe his father would make such an uncharacteristic request. He also couldn't believe his father thought there was the slightest possibility he'd get involved in stopping this girl from finding her sister. If anything ever happened to either of his brothers, Alec certainly wouldn't want anyone blocking his efforts to help them. He didn't think his father would, either.

"Marjorie just wants to delay their reunion. I think she may be trying to find the girl herself first. Son, I wish I could explain, but I don't have details. Marjorie gets too upset, and this kind of stress isn't good for her recovery. I just thought that you might be able to discourage Aurora from seeking out her twin immediately. According to Marjorie, Michaela Carmichael is nothing but trouble. Marjorie is certain Aurora's life will fall apart if those two find each other again."

Anger burbled in Alec's chest. He had his own concerns. He wasn't about to be drawn into someone else's daytime drama. "I'm not going to interfere. Sorry."

"Maybe if someone had interfered in your life a little sooner, you wouldn't be in the mess you're in," he said softly.

Alec laughed, but the sound echoed with bitterness, though most of the acrimony he'd once felt had been diluted by time and self-reliance. When he was thirteen, he justified his reckless, indiscreet actions by blaming the fact that he had no parental supervision while his widowed father worked long shifts at the hospital and he and his brothers fended for themselves. As an adult, he had no one to blame for his troubles but himself.

Still, he never could pass up an opportunity to remind his father of his shortcomings, few though they were. "Any ideas who that someone should have been?"

"Me," Dr. Manning answered without hesitation. "I'm not stupid, son. And I don't need you to remind me of what a poor father I was after your mother died, any more than you need me to remind you that keeping your pants on when in the company of your boss's wife might be a good idea."

Touché, Alec thought. But dead-on as his father was, he'd forfeited his right to interfere in Alec's life a long time ago.

"Look, Pop—"

"I don't ask lightly. I truly care about Marjorie's recovery."

He knew his father told the truth. Peter Manning's dedication to his patients overrode everything else in his life, as evidenced by his three wild sons. Even his own wife's death hadn't slowed him down. Maybe if she'd suffered from cancer instead of diabetes... Alec pushed the malignant thought aside. He'd been only ten when his mother died. He had no idea how or if his father had mourned. The only thing he did know was that his father was a good doctor, so good that his family took the back seat to his Hippocratic oath. The double-edged sword cleared a path for hundreds of remissions and recoveries for his cancer patients—and shredded any and all opportunities for normal relationships with his sons.

"I know you care about Marjorie. Look, I'll keep an eye on Aurora, try to steer her away from trouble, as if I have any experience in that area. But if she wants to find her twin, I don't see how anyone is going to stand in her way."

A sigh broke the silence. "You're probably right. Marjorie describes Aurora as a mousy little creature, but I've met her. There's more grit to her than her grandmother acknowledges."

Alec wondered. When he'd spoken to Marjorie Carmichael, he'd heard nothing in her description of Aurora to make him think she was anything but introverted, obedient and boring. If she'd been a man, she'd have been the perfect tenant. For the moment, she was simply the perfect woman to have around. She wasn't his type. Alec had always preferred women with at least as much sexual and life experience as he had. Aurora Carmichael wouldn't tempt Alec back to his bad-boy ways.

But his father classified her differently than the grandmother did. Considered his new tenant as strong rather than shy and inexperienced. Dr. Peter Manning didn't bestow praise, even on the granddaughters of his patients, haphazardly.

Hmm.

"Sounds interesting," he commented, not entirely serious. And not entirely pleased.

His father cleared his throat. "I hope you mean that in the strictest, most professional sense, son. As her landlord."

Alec chuckled, and this time the humor was real. Even in his sordid past, he never messed with virgins, wallflowers or girls who lived with their grandmothers until they were twenty-five. Grit or not, chicks like Aurora usually took the slightest attention from men the wrong way and fell hopelessly in love. And at this juncture in his life, the last person Alec needed in his house was an enamored tenant who might morph into a "fatal attraction."

"I'm not looking for a woman right now, much less an innocent, inexperienced one. Rest assured, Pop. Miss Aurora Carmichael is completely safe from the likes of me."

"MAY I HELP YOU?"

Rory Carmichael never imagined such a polite phrase could have such a double edge. Apparently the innuendo depended entirely on the delivery—and the deliverer. Day-old stubble over a rugged jaw. Chestnut hair just shaggy enough to be sexy for another couple of days before it required a good cut. Sleepy, bedroom eyes. A deep, raspy voice.

Nanna never mentioned that Dr. Alexander Manning was a certified hunk-o-rama. So what if it was daytime? "Strangers in the Night" could be adapted, right?

May I help you? She was about to find out.

She cleared her throat and prayed her long-dormant Carmichael genes wouldn't fail her now. "I'm looking for Alec Manning."

"You've found him."

His grin revealed straight white teeth, and he had a

pinch of red over his strong nose, telling her he usually wore glasses.

She licked her lips lightly, careful not to smudge her newly purchased lipstick in "Prime Passion" plum. She boldly raked her gaze from his bare feet to his broad shoulders, willing herself to follow through with the flirtation, inexperience be damned. She was flirting, not performing brain surgery.

"You're Alec? Imagine the luck."

Just as she was about to note the exact color of his greenish irises, he stepped back, out of range. "Don't tell me you're Aurora Carmichael."

"Let me guess," she said, preparing to do her best imitation of her grandmother. "Oh, Aurora is such a sweet girl. On the shy side, but pretty in the way nice girls are. She'll be a lovely tenant. She's neat as a pin and never makes too much noise."

Too bad that soon none of that description would be true. Yes, in the past—the recent past, as recent as this morning—Rory couldn't have contradicted one item in Nanna's assessment. But as of today, Rory Carmichael would be neither sweet, shy nor nice. Okay, maybe she'd hold on to nice. So long as nice meant considerate of others and generally polite. Those things were too deeply ingrained to undo…and, besides, she liked being nice. But the neat thing? No more. Watch out, carpet, you're about to be covered with discarded clothes. Sink, prepare for a mountain of dirty dishes. And quiet? Ha! Maybe she wouldn't play her radio at deafening volumes at midnight, but at noon? Beware, Chicago.

"Okay, you're obviously Aurora," he concluded, having the smarts not to sound disappointed. In fact, his amazed grin, lopsided and damned cute in a manly sort of way, reminded Rory about the *Sexcapade* in her purse.

Her tummy fluttered.

"I take it you're surprised to meet me. The real me, I mean. I'm afraid the girl my grandmother described is a figment of her imagination."

Not exactly the truth, but her claim did elicit something close to a smile from him. Instantly a flicker of awareness sparked between them. Rory inhaled excitedly. Oh, yeah. Her juices were flowing all right. And his didn't look so dormant, either.

Dr. Manning shook his head and chuckled in that sexy-as-sin way that on any other day might have sent her running. Any other day like yesterday. Certainly the day before. But today? No dice. No retreat for the new Rory.

"Surprised isn't the right word," he explained.

She raised an eyebrow. She just bet it wasn't.

"I expected you...earlier," he continued. "I've got your key in my apartment." He glanced over his shoulder. Then, just as quickly, he turned his penetrating gaze back to her. "You're different than I..."

He pressed his lips tightly together, stopping his speech before he completed his thought.

"Choose carefully what you say next," she warned, emboldened by her wardrobe, her freedom, the *Sexcapade* in her purse. Rory no longer looked like an innocent kid or felt like one. And Alec had most definitely noticed.

"Maybe I should just keep my mouth shut," he suggested.

She shrugged, but only with one shoulder, so that the move appeared ever-so-slightly coy. "You know what they say about first impressions."

She tried to slip her hands into the pockets of the jeans she'd bought just before arriving at her new apartment, but could only manage to squeeze her fingertips beyond the tight denim. Her new wardrobe rocked, even if she did miss the loose-fitting comfort of her old clothes. Well, sacrifices had to be made. Judging by the carefully contained look of hunger in Dr. Manning's eyes, the discomfort was worth her trouble.

"First impressions?"-he asked. "Don't they say they're overrated? Look at me, for example. I haven't even invited you inside your new home, and I'm normally such a polite guy."

He opened the door wide and she sashayed into the foyer. As she looked around, a thrill partly unrelated to the feel of Dr. Manning's gaze on her backside shimmied up her spine.

This was her new home. High ceilings. Carved scrollwork. Wood floors cracked by time, but solid underneath her new, thick-heeled boots. A sanded, waiting-for-polish staircase led to her second-floor apartment, one she'd rented sight unseen on the recommendation of her grandmother. Nanna had been surprisingly supportive of Rory's move to the city—supportive, but still mildly controlling. She'd arranged for Rory's new apartment with the son of her oncologist. She'd even paid the first three months rent, which wasn't cheap, thanks to the prime location in the Lincoln Park neighborhood.

Rory swung around in time to catch Dr. Manning's last lingering look. A surge of excitement shot through her veins. She could get used to having men look at her that way.

"Nanna assured me you'd be very polite," she continued. "The perfect landlord. An intellectual gentleman she could undoubtedly trust with her granddaughter."

Alec shut the door behind him. "That's the impression your grandmother got from one phone call?"

"Apparently. I'm actually surprised she didn't insist on meeting you, maybe having your fingerprints taken and run through the FBI's database. Your father must speak very highly of you. Nanna trusts him with her life.''

''I'll get your key,'' he said, ignoring her reference to his dad's sterling reputation.

He disappeared, leaving Rory to wonder why the glowing description of Alec by his father wasn't a compliment, until she realized that she hadn't taken Nanna's glowing assessment of her as that much of a positive, either. Having a famous oncologist for a father was likely akin to having a saint for a grandmother. Expectations ran high and made living by your own rules nearly impossible.

Though she'd only put an hour's drive between her old neighborhood and her new one, Rory couldn't deny the overwhelming distance she felt between the girl she used to be and the woman she'd soon become. For once, Rory had used her single-mindedness to her advantage. She'd secured an awesome job, all on her own. She'd had such an amazing time shopping for the clothes she'd always wanted to buy. Until she'd pulled up in front of the house, she'd forgotten she was supposed to find a stranger to flirt with—then she'd caught that first breath-stealing glimpse of Alec in the doorway.

She wondered if the *Sexcapade* had anything to do with her attitude. Flirting with this guy was as natural as breathing.

Still, Dr. Alec Manning didn't really qualify as a stranger. For at least the next three months, she'd see him on a fairly regular basis. The point of the *Sexcapade* was to rev up the sensual juices by flirting with someone you didn't know and likely would never see again.

And yet Rory couldn't help but grin triumphantly.

There were worse tortures than encountering a hottie like Dr. Manning each and every day.

No, this would work just fine. She'd never had much practice saying sexy things, throwing enticing looks—but she hadn't done such a shabby job so far. Her Carmichael genes apparently woke from hibernation with a vengeance. *Cool.* With a cocky strut enhanced by her tight jeans and her bad-girl boots, she toured the narrow hallway, checking out the large front parlor lined with dusty boxes, stacks of wood and power tools that had been put aside for renovations and repairs.

Renovation and repair. Very appropriate to her current mindset about the foundation of her own life, her own personality. She would tear down and replace what she didn't like about herself and polish and highlight the parts she did.

Rory made a red-letter mark in her mental calendar and didn't bother to tamp down an effervescent smile, complete with bubbly laughter. Nothing could waylay her enthusiasm today.

"Yeah, this is going to work out perfectly," she said aloud, not realizing Alec had come back into the hall until she heard him chuckle.

"Glad to hear you like the accommodations, but shouldn't you wait until you've seen your apartment?"

She exhaled noisily, amazed that her heart could beat so loudly and yet, apparently, not echo off the undecorated hallway walls.

"My first three months' rent are prepaid. I'm certain that living here will be wonderful."

Besides, the landlord is a god.

"A practical girl, I like that."

She couldn't resist. "Girl? Really, Dr. Manning," she backtracked to where he stood, still close to the door, her hips rocking in the saucy swing she'd practiced for ten minutes in front of a dressing-room mirror before she'd finally shelled out the dough for the jeans. To justify the price she'd paid, she had to be able to produce a decent swagger. "Maybe you should go find those glasses of yours."

She reached up and lightly touched the red mark just now fading off from the bridge of his nose, noting that his eyes were hazel, with rich brown centers spiking into rings of sage-green.

"I can see just fine." His voice dipped into a lower octave before he crossed his arms over his chest and set his jaw in what she'd best describe as a scowl, except that the dark seriousness didn't reach his mesmerizing eyes. "But maybe *girl* was a bad choice of words."

She tilted one eyebrow, hoping the expression came off as cool, yet convincing. "You have no idea."

"Want to see your place?"

She swept her hand toward the staircase. "Lead the way."

She followed behind him to the second landing. A large picture window faced the street. Bright sunlight bathed the hall, irradiating the dust motes that flitted through the air.

He sneezed. "Sorry. I hope the cleaning service I hired did a better job inside than out here."

"Don't sweat the dust. I'm a compulsive cleaner."

Damn. *I used to be a compulsive cleaner* should have been her reaction. Oh, well. She'd done a bang-up job so far at tapping into her inner playful tease. One reference to her housekeeping skills wouldn't ruin the mood.

Luckily he didn't seem to notice.

"Good, because I'm not. Anytime you want to come down to my place…"

Again, his words died away, his phrase unfinished. Not that he needed to say any more. The new Rory had all the proposition she needed.

She slipped into the small space between him, the door and the picture window, leaning with her hands pressed behind her backside so that her breasts thrust forward in her tight T-shirt.

"So…is that an open invitation, or should I call first?"

3

"THAT'S NOT WHAT I MEANT," he clarified, looking askance as he attempted to push the key into place. God, she smelled good. And she looked good, too. Good enough to eat. With whipped cream and chocolate. A cherry atop each nipple, perhaps a third cradled in her navel. How long had it been since he'd had sex?

Oh, yeah. Six months.

No doubt about it, celibacy sucked.

Here he was, giving an innocent tour of his place to his new tenant, entertaining images of kinky food sex with a woman he barely knew. Not that lack of familiarity ever stopped him before, but, damn, he knew better now. Didn't he?

"You sure?" she asked, her tone a soft purr. "I heard a distinct invitation in your voice."

He shifted his stance, attempting to alleviate a growing tightness in his groin. "I don't fraternize with my tenants," he insisted. *Keep telling yourself that, Alec. Sooner or later, you're bound to believe it.*

"I thought I was your first tenant," she pointed out, tilting her head to capture his reluctant gaze. He swallowed. Her irises sparkled, an amazing light blue color ringed with spiky black lashes, expertly curled and coated with inky mascara. Her lipstick, a bold, dark plum color, looked slightly smudged. Like she'd just had a drink. Or had just been kissed.

He turned back to unlocking the door. Funny how slippery a key could get. He'd thrust the metal inside the lock, but couldn't get the thing to turn.

"Right. Well, I don't *intend* to fraternize with my tenant." Or any other woman. Even if it killed him. Judging by the painful hardening of his cock, the denial just might. But Alec had made his celibacy vow not so much to save his career from extinction, but to change the way his mind was wired. Turn over a new leaf. Become a new, better man. Career, first. Pleasure, later.

Much, much later.

Her bottom lip curved into a delectable pout, but the disappointment in her eyes nearly pushed him over the edge.

"Look, Rory, you're a very sexy woman..."

"Sexy? Really?"

She reached just beside his hip, skimming her knuckles over his jeans and hijacked the key, turning it easily in the lock, the sticky connection yielding to her steady hand. The scent of her perfume, floral and sweet, made his nostrils flare.

He snorted. "Yeah, like you didn't know."

"I didn't. You were a test."

"A test?"

That sparked his interest, but, unfortunately, the size of the front room stole her attention before she could explain.

"Good Lord! I've never had this much space to myself in my whole life."

Alec glanced around. He hadn't been in the upstairs apartment for a few weeks, but since his place downstairs was nearly the same layout, he realized she was right about the impressive size. Light flooded in from three floor-to-ceiling windows. The living room boasted a full-size couch, love seat, coffee table, end table, lamps and television, and yet didn't seem the least bit crowded. She dashed around the corner and stole a quick glance of the small kitchen, complete with a quaint, aluminum-legged table and plastic-covered chairs. Through the next doorway, she'd find a huge bedroom, centered with a four-poster bed of heavy, polished cherry.

She practically skipped back into the front room, her delight broadcasting from her eyes like a neon marquee. He stood unmoving beside the door, his arms crossed over his chest, his mind focused on remaining aloof from the barely contained excitement surging through her, threatening to yank him in like a strong current at high tide. When was the last time he'd gotten so pumped up over something as minor as spacious rooms? Although, with a woman as attractive and ebullient as Rory Carmichael around—and in his current state of physical denial—Alec figured she could get him certifiably hot and bothered about the extra wall outlets if she set her mind to it.

"This place is amazing," she said.

"Aunt Sophie had a good eye for real estate," he said noncommittally. Rory's disappointment in his mild response showed on her pixie face. He never would have guessed before today but, apparently, he was a sucker for pixie faces. High cheekbones, a delicate nose. Lips likely smaller than the lipstick revealed. God, was he crazy? She was his tenant! And, besides, all women were off-limits, even saucy little seductive ones with playful possibilities dancing in their eyes. Hell, *especially* saucy little seductive ones with playful possibilities dancing in their eyes.

"Why don't you check out the bathroom?" he suggested, needing a moment of Rory-free space to harness his hormones.

She slipped through the doorway he'd indicated with his eyes and, despite his determination to keep out of her orbit for just a minute and recoup his good sense, he couldn't help but follow when he heard her squeal of delight. Time was when a sound like that was a short prelude to a mind-blowing orgasm. Oh, well. There would be no harm in a vicarious look at the apartment through Rory's shining baby blues.

No harm, he thought, until he watched her twirl around in the center of the room, her arms stretched as wide as her smile.

"I've died and gone to heaven," she said on an awed breath. "Oh, the time I'm going to spend in here!"

Rory sighed, imagining her first bath in the claw-foot tub with the wide-brimmed showerhead and slim brass-and-porcelain fixtures. A pedestal vanity and sink begged for a few of the pretty perfume bottles she'd collected since childhood, now tucked safely in a tissue-stuffed box sitting in her car. Empty shelves and cabinets would come to life once she filled them with the pampering lotions and bath oils she'd bought on sale at Victoria's Secret. And still she'd have enough room to host a dance party on the faded but soft oriental rug.

"I just can't believe the size!" she exclaimed.

She saw Alec open his mouth to respond, but whatever he was going to say died a quick death. He cleared his throat to waylay his laughter and set his face in a serious expression that fit him about as well as she might fit in his jeans.

Which wasn't such a bad notion to entertain, actually. Especially when she remembered the *Sexcapade* titled *Slippery When Wet*. She had no idea if the sexual fantasy required rain or bathwater or just some good old-fashioned body moisture, but wouldn't finding out with Alec Manning be a kick?

Her smile must have revealed her naughty thought, because Alec instantly launched into an ultraserious speech about her new home, his eyes never meeting hers for more than an instant.

"The house has great features. There's a third-floor attic I'm renovating, but it's still a mess. You do realize that I'll have workers in the house from time to time, right? Mostly during the day while you're at work, so they shouldn't bother you too much."

She nodded. "But they won't be in my place, will they?"

"Not unless you try that *test* of yours on them, which I wouldn't recommend. A few of them look like they just got out of prison."

Rory laughed, but Alec didn't seem to follow the joke. Maybe he hadn't appreciated her using the words "test" and "you" in the same sentence. Despite the quirky curve of his lips that lessened the sting of his insinuation, she figured she'd better clear up this misunderstanding. She didn't go flirting with just anyone, but then, he had no way of knowing that, did he?

"Good advice and duly noted. But, for the record, I am fairly picky about whom I flirt with."

"Then I should be flattered that I qualify?"

Skewering him with a shocked expression, Rory shoved her fists on her hips. "Why wouldn't you be flattered?"

"No reason you need to know."

"What, are you gay?" she asked, perplexed by his answer.

He didn't blink. "Not last time I checked."

"Do you check often?"

This time, he couldn't contain a smile at her quick response. "Every night as a matter of fact."

She wondered precisely how Dr. Manning verified his heterosexuality, but figured the test involved a woman, just as her test of her newfound flirtatiousness required a man. Oh, wow. *Wait.* That might mean...

"You're involved with someone?"

He frowned. "No."

He stalked to the thermostat and, before she had a split second to process that information, he was running down a list of instructions for the air conditioner and heating systems. He'd moved on to the stove and oven by the time she recovered her train of thought.

"Why does that make you uncomfortable?" she asked immediately after he demonstrated the quirky operation of the oven's self-cleaning system.

"Dirty ovens are a fire hazard."

She smirked. He knew what she meant.

"I don't discuss my personal life with tenants," he answered.

"Boy, for someone who's never had a tenant before, you've sure got a lot of rules."

He dug into his pocket and retrieved a silver key ring with three keys. "I've been wary about renting the apartment."

"You've never lived with anyone before?"

"*We* aren't living together."

"That doesn't answer my question...or does it?"

The man was a sociologist, which made it hard for her to believe he was normally this uptight and unsociable. She wondered if Nanna had somehow warned him off. However, to do that, her grandmother would have had to have blended, even momentarily, the topic of Rory with the topic of men, all in the same thought. *Would never happen.*

He ignored her innuendo. ''I thought it would be a good idea to have some extra income to pay for the renovations. But I'm a busy man. I have a project I'm working on night and day. When you're home from work and the construction workers are gone, that's when I'll be sleeping. We'll hardly see each other, so there's no need to get too personal.''

Rory lifted one eyebrow, then leaned her weight to one side, watching, evaluating. Definitely more to this guy than met the eye, that was for sure.

''So we can't be friendly?'' she asked.

''I didn't say that.''

''Yes, you did.''

He took a deep breath, then exhaled. ''Look, you don't know anything about me. It's complicated.''

''What isn't?'' she asked, more and more certain that she wasn't as cut-and-dried as she'd once thought, either. Less than a day into her big move to Chicago, and Rory felt dizzy from all the conflicting thoughts and instincts bubbling through her—particularly in this man's presence. He was a stranger, all right—one she wanted to get to know—possibly because he'd said she couldn't. Life simply couldn't be allowed to have this many rules. Not now when she was on her own. But even if rules and edicts existed, Rory no longer had to blindly follow. The time had come to either break the rules—or make up a whole new set, just for herself.

''If it makes you feel better, I already know quite a bit about you,'' she explained, opening her hand so she could tick off the facts on her fingers. ''Dr. Alec Manning, professor of sociology, the youngest son of Dr. Peter Manning, oncologist and miracle worker. New landlord, thanks to a generous, but now deceased, Aunt Sophie. Graduated from U.C.L.A. and did his graduate work at Rice University in Texas. Recently departed from Boston University and now working on some sort of project that keeps him very, very busy." She closed the distance between them. Now she would add the new information she'd gathered all on her own in the last fifteen minutes. "Very concerned with his reputation and decorum and rules. So he'll be the perfect man to keep an eye on Marjorie Carmichael's granddaughter."

"Boy, could you be more off? I don't plan to be your baby-sitter," he said roughly.

She frowned. First girl, now baby?

"Good, because I don't have any kids," she snapped, equally annoyed. This was supposed to be a flirtation. She'd started off well, but was regressing quickly from soar and glide to crash and burn.

A silence ensued, a veritable standoff between her frown and his scowl. After a minute, he shook his head, picked up the keys he'd laid on the kitchen table and jangled them.

"May I make a suggestion?" he asked.

He smiled, and Rory's legs wobbled. He covered the scant distance between them, rooting her in place with no more than his intense presence. When he wiped his palm off on his worn jeans, then reached out toward her waist, she used all her willpower to keep from jumping backward.

Instead she folded her arms. "Sure."

"Why don't we start over? Say hello without all preconceived notions and secondhand descriptions that seem to have tainted our first meeting."

Without allowing herself too long to think, she immediately grabbed his hand and shook it firmly, the kind of greeting she'd learned in the one business course she'd completed at junior college. Show your aggression. Show no fear.

So why was it that the moment the heat from Alec's hand pressed into her palm, terrifying yet thrilling images immediately invaded her mind?

Slow, wet kisses. Enticing, teasing seductions. Wild, sweaty sex.

Rory's New Rules, Number One: Sometimes acting like a good girl will allow you to test your bad-girl ways. She'd back off a bit, give Alec some room. Then, when he lowered his guard... Yeah, this could work.

She slipped her hand gently out of his. "So, despite my little test—which you passed, if you're wondering— are you going to rent me this apartment?"

His smile again threatened to do crazy things to her insides. Crazy good things. The kind of crazy good things that got her mother kicked out of Catholic school.

"If you make one promise."

She raised her eyebrows. "Sounds serious."

He shrugged. "I just want you to be honest. With me. With yourself. For both our sakes."

For an instant, she spied a glimpse of something elusive in his eyes. Something that might have added meaning to his odd request. She looked closer, but found herself distracted by the color of his irises. She'd never realized hazel could be such an unusual blend of colors— greens and browns and golds, warm and rich, like the earth itself.

"Then I'll have to insist you call me Rory, please," she insisted. "No one but Nanna and Aunt Lil call me Aurora. And, usually, only if I'm in trouble."

"Rory it is, then. Though I have a strong suspicion that you're looking for trouble, aren't you?"

She couldn't help herself. She leaned in closer—even the pilfered page in her purse wouldn't have fit between them. The *Sexcapades* burned like brands in her side, nudging her to follow through on the promise she'd made to herself—to change her attitude, her life.

"Trouble is hard to define, sometimes, don't you think?"

Alec's half smile knocked another breath out of her lungs, but she didn't back away. The atmosphere crackled with electricity.

"But I'm right, aren't I? That's what you're looking for." He said it with all the cockiness of someone confident of the answer, so she took great pleasure in proving him wrong.

"Nope. I'm just looking to have a good time. What about you, Professor? What are you looking for?"

"Peace and quiet." His answer came too quickly to be convincing. She figured he'd rehearsed that response, if only to himself, on more than one occasion. Rory had been hiding her own personal desires for too long not to recognize the signs in someone else.

"Bull. It's not easy being good all the time."

"You would know, wouldn't you?"

Damn, but this erudite professor of sociology was an incredible study of the first impression. He'd pegged her in less than five minutes.

She stuck out her hand. "Let's make another deal, then."

His eyes narrowed with skepticism. "What kind of deal?"

Wary, this one. Just like she would have been only a few short hours ago. But Rory now had her own reasons for wanting to make a pact with her new landlord, one that would keep them both out of trouble—or in it, depending on the perspective. "The kind of deal where I promise that what goes on in this house is no one's business but ours."

"You realize there is a very forbidden subtext to that statement."

She didn't hide her confusion. "A what? Pardon me, Professor, but I don't speak any language but English."

He chuckled, but the sound was more self-deprecating than condescending. She liked that. "There's more to your proposal than you're willing to admit."

"A woman should have some secrets, don't you think?"

He wiped his hand on his jeans again, then took her palm in his. "So long as she's honest with herself, I guess a few secrets are a good thing to have."

An instantaneous surge flooded through the veins in Rory's fingers and hands, straight to the tips of her breasts, then lower, where the hot blood pooled deep within her. She caught a gasp before the telltale sound escaped her throat, but from the flush of heat creeping over her skin, she knew she couldn't hide her reaction.

Alec licked his lips, then released her hand, though she saw him glance curiously at his palm, as if he'd felt the charged connection as well. Rory turned quickly so he couldn't see her triumphant smile. Even if she didn't come to Chicago specifically looking for trouble, she'd found it.

"Do you want to know what I'm thinking right now?" he asked.

"Actually, no," she answered. Secrets could be good for both of them. Rory knew firsthand that curiosity was a powerful aphrodisiac.

He eyed her doubtfully. "Sure?"

"Positive," she insisted. "Maybe another time. Right now, I want to move in."

She followed Alec into the hall, watching him shuffle down the steps and out the front door. On the stoop, he stretched, rippling the muscles beneath his T-shirt, and tilted his face to the bright summer sky. Rory jogged in front and popped the hatch on her Jeep, tossing aside the absentminded professor image she'd had of Alec Manning. There was more to this man than met the eye.

Still, when he sidled up beside her and wordlessly grabbed the first box, a warm musky scent simmering off his skin, Rory acknowledged that what did meet the eye was nothing to sneeze at. She thought about "Strangers in the Night." She didn't intend to drop the *Sexcapades* dictate, but flirting didn't have to be overt all the time, did it? She could just work a little small talk, right?

He hefted the box into his arms, assessing her piddling possessions with what she'd best describe as surprise. "You don't have much."

Rory grabbed the carton of groceries Aunt Lil had presented to her as a gift just before she'd left. As often as her family drove her crazy, she couldn't deny either their love or their selflessness.

"I travel light."

"Do you travel a lot?"

Rory laughed. "Not exactly. To be precise, I've gone absolutely nowhere, though I did enjoy a brief six months in a studio apartment near the community college a few years ago."

"What happened?

His interest sounded genuine, so she explained. "Took me a while to be able to afford to move out while I went to school full-time. Then, when I finally did get an apartment, Nanna was diagnosed with breast cancer. I moved back into the house in Berwyn and cut my course schedule so I could help Aunt Lil care for Nanna during the chemo.''

"That's a big sacrifice."

She shook her head emphatically. "Not in comparison to what Nanna's done for me. She took us in, my sister and me, when my mom dumped us on the doorstep and ran off. But it's a long story you don't need to hear. Anyway, bottom line is that the city of Chicago is the most exotic place I've ever been. I think the last time I was here was five years ago."

He grabbed a tote bag brimming with T-shirts and slung it over his shoulder, readjusting the box he still held against his chest. "Five years is a long time."

"Five, twenty-five. Both are a lifetime to me."

He nodded, his mouth pinched as if he'd finally gained understanding of some complex concept. "So you probably figure you've got a lot of time to make up for?"

Rory suspected he was just making conversation, innocuous small talk designed to make strangers into acquaintances in short shrift. But she wasn't so complex and he'd hit the nail on the proverbial head. At twenty-five years old, she'd never been anywhere exciting, had never done anything forbidden or thrilling, nothing she could etch on her tombstone if she died tomorrow.

Not that she planned on dying tomorrow. But if she'd learned one thing as the daughter of Katherine Mary Carmichael, dead at the ripe old age of eighteen, was that you couldn't control when you died, only how you lived.

"You said a mouthful, Professor Manning."

4

ON ANY OTHER DAY, at any other time, Alec Manning would be toasting the heavens for throwing such a prime specimen of carnal curiosity in his direction. But here he was, six months into his self-imposed celibacy, a week behind on his research study proposal, overloaded with hours at the club…and in struts pretty, sassy, sensual Rory Carmichael. So instead of saluting the Big Guy upstairs, Alec wondered if one mistake with the wife of a bitter man was truly equal to the breadth of this punishment.

Here she is—the perfect woman—and you can't have her.

Rory's mismatched combination of innocence and aggression, intelligence and naiveté, set her apart from the scores of women he'd studied—both personally and professionally. The sheer determination in her light blue eyes and saucy walk added to her unique appeal. He backed away from the car to sneak another look at her, but was blinded by the sun emerging from behind a thick, gray cloud.

"Jeez, it's bright out here," he said, squinting.

Rory slipped on a pair of sleek sunglasses, the tortoise-shell blending with her dark hair. "That tends to happen at noon. Particularly in the summer."

He grunted. Alec's current project had turned him into a social vampire—out all night, work during the day, sleep in the late afternoon. He couldn't remember the last time he'd ventured out in the noontime sun, except to talk to the contractor repairing the house.

"I'm usually working right now."

Her sassy boots stopped beating a clicky rhythm on the sidewalk behind him. "I can manage the rest of my stuff on my own, if you have work to do."

"That's not what I meant." He shook his head. He really was screwing up this first impression thing big time. Not that he should care what type of impression he made on his new tenant. It wasn't like they'd see much of each other. But since he'd decided he had no choice but to turn his life around, coming across as a self-centered bastard probably wasn't wise. "I was just thinking that I should see more of the sun, directly, instead of just through windows."

She sashayed past him, deposited her boxes on the stoop, then turned back toward the Jeep. "Sounds reasonable."

"Reasonable?" He grimaced, until he realized that sounding and acting in a reasonable, respectable fashion had been his primary goal. He put down his boxes, then nodded, his fists on his waist.

"Good. Reasonable is good."

She glanced over her shoulder, her crystal-blue eyes flashing with humor. "You just keep telling yourself that, Dr. Manning."

"What?" he asked, jogging back behind her.

She handed him a box that rustled and rattled. Glass in tissue, he could guarantee.

"What do you mean, *what?* You know what I'm talking about."

He remained silent, impressed when she read the insinuation in his doubtful stare.

"Look," she explained. "I know the sound of someone who's trying to convince himself that something he doesn't like about himself is actually a good thing."

She grabbed a second box, which he immediately took from her grasp. "What don't *you* like about yourself?"

"Today?" She smiled, and the grin lit her face with a force that rivaled the summer glare. "Nothing. I'm liking myself just fine."

"Okay, yesterday, then. What didn't you like about yourself yesterday?"

She shook her head, piled the second box atop his first one, then slung another tote bag over her shoulder and grabbed a suitcase. With both their hands full, they started back toward the house. "Are you studying me, Professor?"

"Would you mind?"

"Yes."

Damn.

"Fair enough. Then consider my question to be of the getting-to-know-you variety. Right off the bat, I'll admit I made some assumptions about you before you arrived that are proving to be dead wrong."

He hadn't thought her smile could be any brighter than it had been when he'd confessed that he found her sexy. Again, he'd been wrong.

"Let me guess," he said. "*Yesterday* my assumptions fit."

"Like a glove."

"What changed?"

"Nothing and everything. This move to the city is giving me the ultimate opportunity."

"To?"

"To challenge every idea everyone has ever had about me. To find out who I really am."

She made it sound so easy.

"You don't like being known as a nice girl?"

"I don't like being known as a *naive* girl. There's a load of difference. And can we drop the girl thing? You're starting to give me a complex."

Alec chuckled. He'd only known Rory for a few minutes, but she was a bundle of contradictions and complexities that a man of his profession could really sink his teeth into. Oh, who was he kidding? He didn't need his profession as an excuse to want to sink his teeth into this guileless, attractive woman. It was all about him being a man…and her being a woman.

"Got it. No more girl stuff."

They set the suitcases and packages down on the stoop then returned to the car once more, chatting and laughing and teasing. By the time they had most of the contents of Rory's new life toted upstairs to her apartment, Alec wondered if arranging for a tenant he'd never met before had been a wise decision. Even after his help was no longer required, he caught himself lingering, ignoring his work downstairs in favor of sparring a bit more with Rory, wanting to enjoy the bubbly sound in her voice and her unique perspective on the world around her.

Ignoring work for a woman. Yup, he was back to his old ways again.

"I'll bring up those last few boxes," he said, reluctantly glancing toward the door. "Then I should get back to work."

She stacked a collection of shopping bags just inside the bathroom door. "Thanks for all your help."

"Do you need anything else?"

A secret smile played on her lips. She glanced at her purse and tugged her bottom lip into her teeth. "Not right this very minute."

Her expression, somewhere between furtive and expectant, caused a hot surge in his blood. She was up to something, this Rory Carmichael. Something that might just land her in some serious trouble.

Alec closed his eyes and breathed deeply, forcing his instincts into submission. The potential for trouble, the thrill of the forbidden, rushed like a tidal wave through his veins. Six months hadn't been long enough for him to tamp down instincts bred and honed since puberty. Instincts he had to fight if he wanted his career back—a career he'd pissed away thanks to one fatal mistake with another beautiful woman looking for trouble.

Anne Bledsoe had come to the university in search of the grad student her husband had alienated most. She'd instantly set her sights on Alec. As an adjunct professor, Alec couldn't catch a break from Anne's husband, the hard-assed, tenured department chair. Work had become a drag and Alec had figured his boss deserved a little payback for taking the fun out of Alec's work.

Yet Anne Bledsoe had been everything Rory was not—jaded, angry, conniving. But she'd willingly met—exceeded—his every sexual need. He'd recognized her game from the start and had played with gusto, then watched as his career swirled down the drain when the dean learned of the affair, divorced his wife and sent him packing. His former chair had even called every major university where he had contacts and shared the story of Alexander Manning's irresponsible behavior. So even though an old contact from the University of Chicago had agreed to consider Alec for a position *if* he won the coveted grant from the Hensen Foundation, Alec's professional reputation had been effectively trashed.

His own damned fault, he knew. Nothing enticed him more than a woman looking for trouble and finding him.

His instantaneous, practically Pavlovian response to Rory Carmichael was a prime example.

But while good sense dictated he remain on the straight and narrow until he at least had a job, some habits were too damned hard to break. Alec couldn't deny his charged response to this young, vivacious woman any more than he could stop breathing.

"You change your mind," he challenged, aware he had no business making this offer, "and you know where to find me."

Rory bit back a smile, then picked up the heaviest box and headed back to the bedroom, glancing once over her shoulder and then nearly tripping over the packages she'd set just inside the kitchen. Chivalry overrode his good sense, so he jogged ahead, moved the cartons, then leaned against the archway so she could squeeze through. When their eyes locked, she hesitated.

Licked her lips.

Fluttered her lashes.

Twisted his insides into a mass of taut wire without saying a single word.

He cleared his throat. "In the meantime, may I offer you some advice?" He knew his words would be more for his own benefit than hers, but he didn't give a damn. Some warnings had to be said out loud before they could be effective.

Her sexy blue gaze seemed deceptively casual. "More advice? Shoot," she invited.

He rolled his lips inward, then skewered her with an unwavering gaze. He had the benefit of experience on his side. The least he could do for his new tenant was impart some of his hard-earned wisdom, particularly when it might save him, too. "Making up for past actions or re-

grets can have a sweet taste. But try to make sure you
don't bite off more than you can chew.''

HE'D INTENDED TO WARN HER. Discourage her. Wipe
some of that naughty innuendo from her stare. Alec knew
when he'd been sighted and aimed at, but Rory likely
didn't comprehend the real danger of hunting a man like
him. A man on the edge. A man barely in control of his
own hungers.

Unfortunately his cautionary advice had done nothing
but jack up his already taut libido. Damn, her baby blues
were hypnotic—a mesmerizing combination of curiosity
and willful expectation. She'd listened to his advice, po-
litely nodded and then disappeared into her new bedroom. And with more common sense than he'd thought
he possessed, he'd escaped her apartment before he did
something incredibly stupid. Like follow her.

Alec drained the last of his iced tea and wandered back
to his desk, determined to make some headway in his
proposal. The screen saver swirled with the date and
time—a rather boring choice from the hundreds of pithy
sayings or cool computer graphics he could have selected
to dance around on his monitor when he took a break.
Trouble was, before Rory Carmichael knocked at the
front door, he hadn't taken a break in a long time. Despite
his lack of a paycheck from any university, his routine
had become a predictable schedule of work, coffee, work,
lunch, work, nap, work and then…more work, although
no longer at the computer.

At night, Alec traded his comfy shorts and worn
T-shirts for tight black trousers and a stylish tuxedo shirt.
He slicked back his hair with a darkening gel, left his
reading glasses at home and became Xander Mann, bartender to Chicago's see-and-be-seen crowd. Digging into

his former life, Dr. Alec Manning had created the perfect alter ego to gather fodder for his research study—the kind of man an innocent, fresh-from-the-suburbs dish like Rory Carmichael couldn't resist. Without funding for his project, he'd had to be creative. And careful. One more dalliance with the wrong woman and he could kiss what was left of his academic career goodbye.

As he watched the rainbow-colored numbers twist around on the black screen, the fact registered that he'd finished helping his new tenant unload her belongings in less than an hour. She hadn't exaggerated when she said she traveled light. Two suitcases, groceries, a handful of shopping bags and a few boxes and totes—and none of the nostalgic trappings he'd expected of a woman her age. Not that he was that much older than her. But five years and a sordid past gave Alec an outlook beyond his years.

In six months, he'd experienced a fast and furious aging process. Might have been less painful to take his lumps a little at a time, but he'd never been fond of baby steps and caution. Oh, no. Not him. He was much more sink or swim.

Like his two older brothers, Alec had lived hard and fast since around age thirteen. By the time their father, the doctor and single parent, had finally taken an interest in his sons, they'd already developed questionable habits. Drinking. Smoking. Chasing women of all shapes, sizes, ages and degrees of beauty. Just before Alec graduated high school, Dr. Manning, M.D., had managed to curb some of his son's excesses…all except for the women. Though Alec finally applied his photographic memory and sharp reasoning skills until he'd earned his Ph.D., his weakness for sex and willing women had gotten him in more trouble than he'd bargained for. Which was why the arrival of Rory Carmichael posed a problem.

He'd returned to Chicago on the possibility that his old professor could hook him up with a position at UC. But even Barker's influence hadn't overridden Alec's reputation. The university president balked at even a trial appointment. But with a lucrative research grant in hand from the Hensen Foundation, Alec could get back on the track to tenure.

Of all his pursuits, frivolous and otherwise, only his career had resulted in anything remotely positive in his life. He'd decided to use what had once been his weakness—his charm with women—as a scholarly strength. And with the review committee from the Hensen Foundation due in Chicago in less than a week, he needed Xander Mann, a bartender persona entirely based on the man he used to be, more than ever.

At Dixie Landing, the hottest Southern rock 'n' roll and blues bar in Chicago next to Kingston Mines, Alec studied the time-honored tradition of meat-market mating. As the bartender, he got hit on a lot. But he'd quickly learned that women simply approached him first because he worked at the club. Seemed less of a mystery, less of a risk.

If they only knew.

With only a little encouragement from him, however, Alec redirected the women toward guys he selected at random. Then he watched them, listened in on their conversations, interviewed them afterward in the guise of casual conversation. In doing so, he gathered amazing insight for his proposed project. The Hensen Foundation, infamous for tackling topics like celibacy and safe sex, would likely snap up his idea of publishing a book exploring how men and women on the prowl had changed in the last decade. As Xander Mann, he got an up-close-and-personal view of the man as prey, the woman as hunter. And if the text he'd been working on came out as he intended, his work might curb his generation's tendency to engage in meaningless liaisons that, in his opinion, left few individuals open to healthy, potentially long-lasting relationships.

If only he could ignore the glaring irony.

He wondered what Rory would think of slick, cool Xander with his blended whiskey voice and unabridged collection of come-ons and compliments. Despite her obvious inexperience with living on her own, he sensed Rory would be no easy mark, not even for a cool operator like Xander. And yet he wondered how much time would pass before Rory traded her inherent sweetness for the driven lust he saw every night. For an instant, a picture of a leather-clad Rory flashed in his mind, stalking into Dixie Landing, scoping out the male clientele for a quick kill. Ruby-red lips. Breasts enhanced by a Wonder Bra that she allowed to peek from a black lace top.

Wasn't hard to form the mental image; wasn't hard to find it appealing. Damned appealing. Appealing enough to rethink his self-imposed ban on fooling around. But he pushed temptation aside. Better to keep things friendly between them, but professional. Landlord and tenant. Simple. After all, he'd promised his father that he'd do all he could to steer her away from trouble. He'd start by curbing his own personal attraction. Right here, right now.

He was just about to sit down and prove he could concentrate on work when he heard a quiet knock. After jogging to the door, he found Rory standing in the foyer, looking particularly chic and confident in a slim, black skirt that reached her ankles but had a slit to midthigh, trendy boots and snug lavender sweater vest that did amazing things to what he'd suspected were small breasts.

Small? Nope, not the right word. More like "just right." *Work? What work?*

"Hey," he said, biting back his urge to say something along the lines of, "Hold on while I catch my breath, beautiful." Wasn't it just this morning when he'd thought taking Rory Carmichael on as a tenant would be the perfect antidote for his raging hormones? So sweet, shy and innocent? Opposite to the type of woman he normally pursued? And yet he could slip back into old habits with her all too easily. How easy it would be to lure this lovely woman inside his apartment and seduce her into his bed.

Or could always use the couch. Hell, he'd settle for right here in the hallway up against the door, though he figured she might object.

"Sorry to bother you again," she said, though he wondered from the glimmer in her light blue eyes if she truly regretted her intrusion. "I was wondering if you could tell me the best place to find a parking space near this address."

She handed him a computer printout with directions to a midtown police precinct.

"In trouble already?" he asked.

She answered with a withering look. "I have an appointment with someone."

The missing sister? Only he wasn't supposed to know about that. And even if he did, he remained determined not to involve himself in her private quest, particularly one he'd instantly admired. Nonetheless, he refrained from asking questions. Her business at the police station was none of his.

He read the address, then pictured the location in his mind.

"There's a bank around the corner. They have public parking. Though you might luck out and get a spot on the street."

She retrieved the paper, careful not to allow her fingers to brush against his, and slid it inside the miniscule backpack that doubled as her purse. "I don't want to be late. This detective might help me find my sister."

He sighed. Now, he couldn't pretend not to know. "Your sister is missing?"

Her frown deepened. "For the past ten years. She ran away. She's my twin."

"Wow," he said, unable to contain the reaction when a myriad of emotions, starting with regret, played across her face. "And you've found her?"

"No, but three weeks ago, I learned she'd been arrested for loitering. First clue I've found since I started looking for her, but I had to wait for the arresting officer to return from leave before I could contact her and get details. She wouldn't tell me much over the phone, but agreed to meet me today. I think she wants to make sure I am who I say I am before she tells me about Micki."

"How will you prove you're her sister?" he asked, genuinely interested. He didn't see his brothers on a regular basis with Mitch living in Miami and Ben stationed in Germany, but he'd be the first to drop everything if one of them turned up missing.

"We're identical twins. Convincing her I'm Micki's sister shouldn't be too hard. Detective Walters claims she doesn't know anything about Micki's whereabouts now, but I'm hoping she remembers something that will at least give me a place to start looking."

Alec listened, watching a weariness glaze over her brilliant blue eyes. Had she been looking for long? All ten lost years? And just where did runaways hang out? He had no influence over where Rory went, but he did want her to be safe. The thought of her wandering, a little lost, a little desperate, through tough neighborhoods in search of a runaway sister bothered him. Raised his hackles, like a male lion who catches the scent of hungry hyenas nearby. He'd known her for less than a day, yet his long-dormant protective instincts revved to life.

Imagine that.

The professor of sociology in him found the phenomena interesting. The flesh-and-blood man wondered if he'd finally met a woman he couldn't instantly label and categorize, leaving her a mystery he might be the guy to solve. That thought caused the unemployed sociologist to remind the hardened flesh-and-blood man to back off before he made another mistake.

"Good luck," he said.

"Thanks," she answered, smiling broadly. "After the interview, I thought I'd stroll around the city, maybe check out the shops on the Magnificent Mile, see who's wearing what and shopping where."

Alec couldn't contain a grin. When was the last time he'd done something so purposeless as window-shop or people watch? Of course, people-watching was part of his profession. Window-shopping…he was fairly certain he'd never done that in his entire life.

"Then 'have fun' is in order, too."

Her smile lit her entire face—from those crystalline baby blues to her full, lush lips—as if he'd unknowingly spoken some secret word.

"Fun is what I intend to have from here on in."

She swung toward the door, waving at him with a quick wiggle of her fingers. The multiple gold rings on her hand dazzled in the sunlight. She left, but her crisp perfume lingered, luring him out of his apartment and into the foyer. Through the window beside the door, he watched her strut toward her car. Deliberate steps. Springy. Filled with excitement. Anticipation. Like a woman en route to her destiny.

Safely alone in the hallway, Alec whistled both his wonder and his regret. Here was a truly fresh, unblemished-by-the-big-city woman, ready to discover all Chicago had to offer—and yet, no matter how he frothed at the mouth to show her every side of the city from the seamy to the sophisticated, he'd shockingly managed to act too weary and jaded to tag along. She'd not only tapped into his simmering libido, but she'd awakened his protective instincts. How he'd tamped them down he didn't know. He chalked the phenomenon up to too many years of indiscriminate affairs, which had turned his attraction to most women into a quick flash of lust, followed by unbearable boredom. Add too many nights at the bar watching the female species on the prowl for sex, and his wonder about women had become controllable. And yet one afternoon with Rory had effectively regenerated his once insatiable need to possess, even briefly, the ones who piqued his interest.

And Rory Carmichael most definitely piqued his interest. And more. Which presented him with a puzzle he didn't even bother trying to solve. The answer was obvious. If Rory really turned up the heat, Alec Manning and all his good intentions and moral vows would go up in flames.

5

THE DETECTIVE'S OFFICE was no more than a closet, cleared of mops, brooms and buckets to make room for a small metal desk, a bulletin board with indecipherable notes about working cases and file cabinets bulging with paper. Rory glanced at her watch. She'd been waiting for Detective Barbara Walters—no relation to the television newswoman—for nearly twenty minutes, and yet the nervous roiling of her stomach hadn't lessened one iota since she'd arrived.

Since the cute uniformed officer with the thick gold wedding band had led her into the room, the door he'd shut behind her hadn't moved. The phone hadn't rung. The intercom hadn't buzzed. For at least the twentieth time since she'd been waiting, Rory glanced at the pocket in her purse where she'd stashed the remaining stolen fantasy. Should she pass the time by opening it?

In her estimation, "Strangers in the Night" had been a complete success. Sure, she'd had to make a few adjustments because of the time of day and the fact that her chosen stranger owned her home, but the fantasy had promised to "stir her juices." And it had most definitely delivered. With all the sensual awareness coursing through her veins right now, she considered herself stirred, blended, pureed and served in an icy glass with a fancy garnish. Funny thing was, she didn't really feel like she'd been flirting. At first, yes. The experience had been new for her, throwing out innuendos and putting a spin on her words with pointed glances. But after a short time, she'd fallen into an easy repartee with a man that, just yesterday, would have scared her to death.

But not today. Once Rory made up her mind about something, she rarely backed down, no matter the odds of success. And she'd certainly decided that Alec Manning was the perfect man to share her first sexual experience with—*Sexcapade* or not.

Potent only scratched the surface of describing him. He was also smart, sexy and kind. She'd seen worry flash across his face when she'd told him about visiting the police station in search of Micki. What woman could resist such a combination of sex appeal and genuine concern for her safety?

Apparently, not a woman like her. If the second sexual fantasy she'd stolen from the *Sexcapades* book proved half as delicious and forbidden as the first, she didn't know how she could possibly resist attempting to draw Alec into the game yet again.

And why should she resist?

Even after he'd left, Alec's presence remained in the four-room apartment. The fragrance of his soap had lingered in the air—fresh and green like new-cut grass. His warmth permeated the sofa, from the soft spot where he'd rested after wrestling to move the dresser to the oversize cushions that he'd fluffed before he left. Rory had actually opened a window and hoped the breeze would wash away some of his enticing, intoxicating scent. The last type of man Rory needed was a reluctant one, and Alec seemed relatively determined to keep their interactions exclusively platonic. Renter to rentee. Still, she couldn't deny the strong suspicion that he was just as attracted to her as she was to him, any more than she could claim his reluctance to explore that attraction didn't stimulate her own interest even more.

Once a Carmichael woman, always a Carmichael woman. Challenges made life interesting, if nothing else.

But since the detective who might know how she could find her sister could come in at any moment, Rory decided to wait and open the second fantasy after she returned home. Then she'd worry about whether or not she should attempt to tempt Alec into sharing the sexy invitation, whatever instructions were inside. Compartmentalized thinking had worked for her before and tackling one concern at a time seemed so much easier. So, for now, she concentrated on the questions she'd jotted down to ask the detective about Micki. And afterward she'd focus on Alec. He wouldn't stand a chance.

Rory tried not to raise her hopes, tried not to believe that one interview with a police officer who had only met her sister once during her arrest would lead her to her missing sibling. Rory had wanted to look for Micki for so long, but she'd been little more than a child herself when her twin had disappeared. She'd had to rely on her grandmother, great-aunt and other adult relatives to spearhead the search. They'd done what they could. Posted flyers. Cooperated with the police. The community had even rallied to offer a reward, but since Micki had left a note pegging her as a willing, defiant runaway rather than an abducted missing child, interest in Micki's case soon waned. Nanna and Aunt Lil stopped talking about her, and old childhood friends stopped asking if the family had heard from Micki or if she'd been found. And most of Rory's current friends wouldn't have even known she had a twin unless she'd told them.

But the minute Rory had tapped into the Internet at the public library just a year ago, she'd taken more responsibility for herself. She'd learned about chat rooms for the families of missing people. She'd initiated public record searches, checking for matches to the name Michaela or Micki Carmichael in search engines and newspaper archives all over the world. Then, three weeks ago, she'd found her first reference to her sister. Rory could hardly believe that Micki had been living in Illinois, much less Chicago, all this time. But there she was, in a public record file for a loitering arrest.

As if on cue, Detective Walters strode through her door, a foam cup of coffee in one hand, a stack of manila folders tucked beneath her arm.

"Ms. Carmichael?"

Rory stood, smiled and extended her hand. Detective Walters tossed the files onto her immaculately clean desk, took one good look at Rory and cursed.

"You're identical," she said on the same surprised breath, then apologized for her reaction.

Rory nodded. "I warned you on the phone."

Detective Walters smiled. "Sorry I was so cautious, but I couldn't give out information just because you asked."

Rory had been more than a little annoyed that the detective hadn't wanted to help her when she'd first called, but she did understand her reluctance. "I guess not. But now that you know I am her twin, I need to find my sister. I miss her. And I've missed her for long enough."

Detective Walters tugged at the crease on her slim navy slacks and sat on the top of her desk. Fortyish and petite, the cop wore her thick auburn hair short, but styled in a feminine wave that softened the lines around her eyes and at the corners of her mouth. Her collarless blouse, also navy, but offset with a beautiful, chunky brass necklace Rory guessed had been handcrafted in the Middle

East, added to a style that testified to her womanhood, and yet buoyed the image of a tough, no-nonsense law enforcement officer. Rory spied the clear look of sympathy in her green eyes.

"Your sister could probably stand to hear that right about now. She's got to be tired of the streets. Ten years is a long time to live hand-to-mouth." Detective Walters shook her head. "Actually, ten years is a long time for anyone to live on the streets at all."

"Do you know where she is?"

The detective's frown deepened. "Like I told you on the phone, I lost track of her fairly soon after the arrest. She'd been volunteering at a homeless shelter, taking care of some of the kids while their mothers went on job interviews in exchange for a place to bunk, but she took off again a few days after the arrest."

"Why?"

"None of the other shelter volunteers knew for certain, but she had been hanging around a junkie well-known as bad news."

Rory's memory instantly flooded with the stories of her mother's downfall at the hands of a creepy addict named Dirk or Dack or something. She didn't know much about him except that he wasn't her biological father and that Nanna and Aunt Lil held him entirely responsible for her mother's death.

"A guy?" she managed to croak out.

"No. A girl, about your age, maybe younger. Hard to tell when they're strung out. I would have picked her up the night I busted Micki for loitering, but she was too quick. Took off before I could cuff her."

Rory sat back down in the chair, her stomach fluttering with a colony of moths the size of bald eagles. This woman had seen Micki, talked to her. She'd connected with Rory's twin more in one night during a reportedly routine arrest than Rory had done over the past ten years combined. Suddenly, a gazillion questions not jotted down on her notecard flew through her head. What did Micki look like? Did she wear her hair long or short? Was she too thin? Did she ever smile?

Why didn't she want to come home?

Each query choked her, threatening to unleash the dam of emotions she'd been fortifying for years. After wiping her eyes free of cloudy, shapeless tears, Rory glanced back down at her notes.

"Loitering sounds like a minor offense. Why did you arrest her?"

Detective Walters narrowed her gaze. "Loitering *is* against the law. Besides, she looked like she could use a hot meal, maybe some social services. I brought her in so we could talk."

"Did she? Talk to you?"

"Not much, but enough to stick in my mind. She's got a smart mouth. A real toughie. But that's what happens when you live on the streets. She was clever, though. And could be quite polite when it suited her."

Rory sniffled and smiled. "Nanna would be very happy to hear that."

"You were raised by your grandmother? She wouldn't tell me much about her past."

Rory stared at her lap. "Our mother was a runaway, too. She dumped us on her mom, then took off and overdosed. But we weren't throwaways. Nanna loved us both. But she was, um, *is* super strict. She couldn't bear to have either of us repeat our mother's bad choices, but Micki couldn't take the constraints. She's always been a free spirit, you know?"

The detective nodded, but her expression lacked any

recognition of the whimsy Rory associated with her sister's personality. "I gathered as much."

A silence persisted until Rory glanced down at the card to ask her next question. "Is Micki…on drugs?"

"I don't think so, but who can be sure? We didn't test her. Released her on her own recognizance after she met with social services. She's skinny, but seemed healthy."

Turning to flip through the file folder on the top of her stack, Detective Walters extracted a business card that had been paper-clipped to the top. "I've got a deposition in about ten minutes and need to review my case report. I'm sorry I couldn't be more helpful, but here is the business card of the social services worker who spoke with Micki before she was released. Maybe he knows more."

"Detective…"

"Please, call me Bobbie."

"Thanks, Bobbie. Do you think my sister is still hanging out in the neighborhood where you arrested her?"

Bobbie shook her head. "Doubt it. I haven't seen her, and because it's a high crime area, I'm there a lot. After you called me, I checked around. No one in that crowd admitted to knowing her. I don't think she normally cruised that side of town. Chicago is a big place."

Yeah, huge. Rory had noted that fact after she'd driven through the city on her way to the appointment. She'd seen the Sears Tower on one side of the city, the Hancock building in the distance. Chicago seemed as tall as it was wide, and the sheer vastness of the city had nearly caused her to delay her search at least until she learned her way around. But she'd had this lead, this connection to the detective, so she'd firmed her resolve and entered the precinct brimming with hope. Now, her one clue had gone precisely nowhere.

Rory stood and offered her hand. "Thank you, Bobbie. I can't think of anything else."

Bobbie hesitated, then reached back and pulled the file off her desk. "Don't give up hope, okay? Looking for your sister is the right thing to do. She seemed like she had her head on fairly straight, but I got the impression she was real tired of living the way she was. Why don't you visit that shelter? They're real nice there. I'll call the director and tell her you're going to stop by."

The tightness in Rory's chest eased. "I'd really appreciate that—and I appreciate you taking the time to meet with me."

Bobbie shook her hand. "No problem. Just take a friend with you when you go down there, okay? Preferably a male one. It's not the greatest neighborhood."

Rory wasn't about to tell the policewoman that she didn't have any male friends in the city just yet. After all, she did plan to rectify that situation fairly soon—with Alec. She grabbed her purse and hid a tiny smile, thinking about the fantasy she had stashed in there, wondering about the wisdom of considering her landlord, even for an instant, as a potential sexual partner. Flirting with him was one thing. Joining him in a fantasy called "Slippery When Wet" was something else entirely.

Yet, as she left the police precinct and made her way back to her car, she wondered, why the heck not? She couldn't deny her attraction to him, any more than she could dispute that he harbored at least an inkling of desire for her. He'd been quite the gentleman before, helping her move her stuff without complaint. He'd been the perfect landlord, awarding her with keys and instructions with patience and humor. She couldn't expect a man like him—educated, sophisticated, undoubtedly respectable—

to conduct an unbidden seduction of his new tenant. Though she wouldn't have complained if he had.

Rory didn't know much about men, but her instincts screamed that she'd have nothing to lose in testing the romantic waters with Alec further. The worst he could do was turn her down, which would only make things uncomfortable for a little while. A hot guy like him was probably accustomed to being hit on by wide-eyed ingenues like her.

Still, she'd have to play this carefully. Finding herself on the receiving end of a rejection wasn't the way she wanted to begin her foray into the dating world. As she slid into her car and revved the engine, she thought the handy little *Sexcapade* in her purse might just be the key to success.

ALEC HEARD THE FRONT DOOR in the hall open, then close. Quick, light steps accompanied Rory up the staircase. He listened for her key in the lock, then the not-so-quiet clap of her shutting door. The muffled sound overhead of her shoes tapping on the hardwood effectively destroyed what was left of his train of thought. He hit the Save key on his computer and shook his head in reluctant surrender.

Maybe having a tenant upstairs wasn't such a good idea. Particularly someone female and pretty and full of life and verve. A woman totally unrelated to his past, and yet a living, breathing reminder of how easy it would be to chuck his new serious outlook and return to his free-loving, *carpe diem* ways. A woman whose sugary perfume had somehow managed to creep into his apartment, where she hadn't yet set as much as a foot. He'd suspected she'd brushed against his shirt at some point during the move, but even though he'd changed into a fresh

T-shirt, he could still conjure up her sweet, floral essence simply by hearing the creak of her couch overhead.

With a deep breath, Alec reinvigorated his resolve to concentrate, then poised his fingers over his keyboard and scanned the monitor for anything he might have missed. While Rory had been out interviewing the police officer who'd arrested her sister—he made a mental note to ask her about how that went—he'd received a call from the current chairman of Amelia Henson's Foundation. Dr. Noah Yeager, a noted psychologist, had phoned to inform Alec that Noah and his wife, Miranda—also a noted researcher and self-help radio personality—were heading to Chicago next week and they wanted to hear his presentation. Why wouldn't they when Alec was at least three weeks behind on the précis? Alec wondered if Yeager possessed some sort of panic radar, seeking out the worst possible time for him to drop in for an in-person pitch, but Alec figured it all went back to irony. Didn't it always? Here he was, devoted to a serious lifestyle with nothing to entertain him but work and work and more work, yet he was behind.

So what had he done all afternoon after hanging up the phone? Had he focused on his notes, organizing his interviews, calculating statistics? Had he consulted his theoretical background studies, attempting to draw tighter conclusions than those he'd originally outlined? Or had he spent the bulk of the afternoon wondering if Rory Carmichael would use the claw-foot bathtub his great-aunt had purchased for the upstairs bath, or if she'd prefer the more modern shower with the multipurpose head?

Disgusted with his lack of progress, Alec stalked to the phone he'd left in the kitchen, found the portable handset on top of the microwave and dialed Dixie Landings. Not needing to listen to the prerecorded message about the

,
time of the next show and the newest act booked into the private lounge, he bypassed the voice-mail system by punching in his boss's extension.

"Shaw Thomas."

"Shaw, hey. It's Xander."

"Hey, buddy. What's up?"

With any other employee, Shaw might have assumed the call was some lame excuse to get out of working a shift. But even playboy Xander, Alec's suave alter ego, showed up at work, on time, each and every night he was on the schedule. He was, after all, working there because of the study. Not that the tips weren't another practical way of making a living. While Alec hadn't yet been completely forthcoming with the owner of the club as to his true purpose—Shaw was a study in male prowess himself and Alec hadn't wanted to taint that aspect of his research—he'd been an honest employee in all other ways. He didn't want to lie now, so he chose his words carefully.

"Remember that research study I was working on?"

"The one for your graduate program, right? Yeah, you told me. Something for your Psych class?"

"Sociology," Alec corrected, not really wanting to play semantics with the man. Psychology was the study of the human psyche; sociology the study of culture and its effect on human behavior. The two disciplines were interrelated, yet entirely separate.

"Don't tell me you want to study me or something," Shaw guessed.

Already doing that, man.

"I'm just behind on my work. Since it's Tuesday and the night is normally slow, I was wondering…"

The sound of Shaw's inhale cut Alec off. The man, hailing from Alabama, possessed the personality of a true

Southern gentleman. He spoke with a twang, smoked cigars made of tobacco culled in Virginia and charmed the panties off women with the same swiftness the Southern sun could melt an ice cube. But he also had a notorious temper, balanced only by his incredible sense of fair play.

"Didn't you switch off with Brad last week?"

"No, I just covered his night for him."

"In other words, he owes you?" Shaw asked, his query a gentle suggestion.

"Yeah, guess he does. I'll give him a call."

He could practically hear Shaw's smile through the phone. "That's it. You'll get the hang of the service industry yet, my boy."

The last endearment cracked Alec up. Likely, he and Shaw were close to the same age. But when he donned the persona of Xander Mann, he looked, sounded, acted and strutted like a man at least ten years younger. The color he slicked through his hair didn't hurt, either.

A quick call to Brad's cell phone netted Alec the night off. After making himself a sandwich out of the ham and cheese he found in his fridge, which surprisingly didn't smell rancid or have green furries growing on it, he snagged a beer and settled back into the chair in front of his computer. When he heard the pipes overhead groan, he guessed Rory was preparing a bath. He popped a compact disc into his computer, adjusting the volume on his speakers and hoping a little rhythm and blues would take his mind off the questions that instantly burned past all his theories and sociological hypotheses.

Did she bathe or shower?

Wouldn't he love to know....

6

RORY CLOSED THE DOOR behind her, leaned her back flush to the hardwood, kicked off her shoes and sighed. There. She'd managed to fly upstairs quickly, efficiently avoiding any contact with her landlord for the moment. Until she was ready. Prepared.

While fighting the unending Chicago traffic, she'd tossed aside any reservations about her decision to entice Dr. Alec Manning into sharing her second sexual fantasy with her. Rory may not have had many opportunities to exercise her determined nature in the past, but when she made a decision, she stuck to it. Quitting school to take care of her grandmother. Moving to Chicago. Searching for her sister despite the abysmal odds of finding her. And, now, seducing Alec Manning.

She'd known him for less than a day, but the prospect of seducing him thrilled her completely, as if he'd been the object of her affections for years. The last guy she'd had long-term affection for hadn't been interested in seduction—at least, not by her. But she only acknowledged that disappointment from her past so she could balance it with her new-found strengths. She may have fallen hard into lust with the first hunky male she'd met—one with a knee-melting smile and the intelligence to earn an advanced degree—but except for one lapse, she was now and always had been a good judge of character. She could trust Alec. And, better yet, she could trust herself.

Not that she hadn't screwed up in her romantic past, limited as it was. She'd dated Tom Byrne all through high school, with the guarded but clear approval of her grandmother. The Byrne family had lived behind the Carmichaels for as long as both families had planted their Celtic roots into Illinois soil. And Tom, the eldest and only son, had seemed destined for either the priesthood or fatherhood to a ruddy, raucous brood.

Tom was quick to laugh and joke. He got decent grades, played reliable quarterback for the football team and spent every Sunday morning in church. While in high school, Rory had attributed Tom's reluctance to do more than kiss her occasionally as a direct result of his Irish-Catholic upbringing. Genuinely afraid of the consequences of having sex at such a young age, Rory had cherished the safety of Tom's attitude. But after he'd gone away to college, choosing party school University of Florida over Notre Dame, or even nearby DePaul, Rory had expected—hoped—that their holiday and spring break reunions would heat up. Become more adult. More intense.

No such luck. And when Tom had finally admitted that he'd been doing the wild thing with several girls other than her for years, she'd been angry. When he further claimed that he'd protected her virtue so he could have a pure and untouched bride, she'd done what any self-respecting virgin would do.

She'd dumped his male chauvinist ass.

And while her friends had encouraged her to run out and rid herself of her chaste state as soon as possible, Rory decided she rather liked herself the way she was. Her virginity was likely the only thing about her life that was hers and hers alone. She controlled it. She alone would make the decision of when, where and with whom to award her "first time."

Her decision had changed her life. She still liked men, of course. Still sometimes lost herself in fantasies about some unattainable guy. But she always knew that she retained control over how she conducted herself in matters of the heart and body. She hadn't wanted to repeat her mother's mistakes by yielding to her desires with no control, no power, no sense of consequences. Rory had remained a virgin not because of some moral mantra or paralyzing fears, but because she wanted to be in charge of her own fate. Her hormones wouldn't drive her actions. Neither would real or imagined slights in her childhood. The sad reality that she'd had no father figure in her household while growing up and that her mother had abandoned her would not dictate how she behaved around men.

The decision hadn't been easy, but once Rory decided to delay her personal foray into a sexual relationship, she stuck to her guns, never doubting the wisdom. She'd read the few romance novels she'd managed to sneak into the house after culling a bagful from a friend's extensive collection. She knew how love and sex changed people. The more she learned about mature relationships, the more she'd felt one-hundred-percent certain that until she was independent and completely on her own, she shouldn't take on the dual task of exploring her sexual needs and attempting to keep her head on straight at the same time.

But now things had changed. She was twenty-five, had a good job, a great apartment, friends and family who loved her. She had a purpose for getting up in the morning. Her mother never had any of those things, except for the love part—but only from her family. Micki had had the love, too. But neither Rory's mother nor her twin had

had the common sense to see that the affection their family offered was a gift. And even if they had, Rory guessed that neither woman would have considered that love to be enough.

So when it came to men, she decided love would either happen or it wouldn't. No pressure, no worries. No expectations. In fact, love would likely become a hindrance in her new life, since she had no immediate need to settle down with anyone other than herself. But her naiveté could cause her trouble when a man finally came into the picture. Because she'd never been in love and had never even had what she'd now consider an adult relationship, she was more vulnerable than other women her age to thinking that she'd found love when she'd only discovered intense lust.

Not that there was anything wrong with lust, as long as she kept a firm grip on her perspective. She'd talked to her friends. She'd read the self-help magazines, the relationship books. She'd studied the advice columns, watched Oprah on television and listened to both Delilah and Dr. Laura on the radio. Because of her inexperience, she was a prime candidate for falling helplessly, madly in love with the first man who gave her an orgasm.

And knowing that, she'd decided to alter her plan a little with regards to seducing Dr. Alec Manning. She was going to seduce him all right, but in good time. After she'd stocked her arsenal with the weapons she needed to remain in control.

On bare feet, Rory padded across the worn throw rug, awash in tiny, blue oriental flowers on a field of aged-gray ivory, and dropped onto the couch. She tossed her purse onto the chipped tile-top coffee table, removed her watch and earrings, then grabbed the now-wrinkled, but still sealed, paper from the side pocket.

Slippery When Wet.

Rory drew her legs onto the couch, curling her bare feet beneath her. If she'd had a bottle of wine in her refrigerator, she might have been tempted to delay her curiosity long enough to pour herself a glass, maybe light a few candles, turn on some music. Change into the silky nightie and satin robe she'd bought in Filene's Basement. Set the scene.

But since she hadn't yet made a visit to the liquor store and hadn't unpacked her CD player, she decided to stay put and finally discover if she'd taken a fantasy out of the book that would appeal to her deepest secret needs.

She slid her finger into the fold-over page, a slight pressure cracking the glue. The short blurb on the outside taunted her, but she read with interest, taking her time breaking the seal.

Nothing thrills the body more than a rush of something wet. Slick. Warm. Prepare for your lover with a bath, but this will be no long, luxurious soak. Turn the heat up high—and the faucet on full. Get yourself wet and ready.

Rory's mouth dried. The tiny pulse hidden within the folds of her intimate flesh pounded, and she shifted her position to alleviate the ache. She flipped open the page, her eyes wide as the author described, in complete and sensual detail, how a woman should masturbate herself to orgasm, prime her body, beneath the hot, rushing water from her bathtub faucet.

Glancing over her shoulder toward her new spacious bathroom, Rory bit her bottom lip. The bathroom back in the house in Berwyn had been the only one, shared by her, her grandmother, her great-aunt and anyone else who happened to be visiting. She'd never dreamt, never imagined...

She read the fantasy again, making sure she understood, fortifying her certainty that she'd actually had the outrageous good fortune to choose a page from the *Sexcapades* book that didn't require a man. At least, not immediately. A caveat to the self-gratification existed farther down the page.

Is this mode of masturbation old hat to you? Increase the tidal wave of pleasure by asking your man to watch. Have him adjust the water temperature, invite him to kneel beside the tub and arouse your breasts while the water works its magic. Chances are, he'll carry you to the bed soon after and make himself wet and wild. In fact, that's the final stroke—drowning in the waves of passion you create between the sheets.

Whoa, Rory thought, her mind reeling. She shook her head, deciding the *Sexcapades* book should probably have been divided into categories like "novice," "intermediate" and "advanced." The thought of inviting Alec to take a tubside seat left her dizzy, disoriented. Intrigued. She closed her eyes, not in the least surprised that she couldn't conjure the scenario in her mind.

Definitely "advanced."

Rory wanted to include Alec in her renewed interest in her sexuality, but not the way the book suggested. She couldn't. Could she? *Nah. Not possible.* She jumped off the couch, page in hand, and wandered to the bathroom, marveling at the large, claw-foot tub that had immediately sparked her interest the minute she'd seen it. At the time, she'd imagined the antique porcelain bathtub as the perfect place for a long-overdue bubble bath. She'd even bought a collection of salts and foams specifically for that reason, along with some scented lotions. But as a place for her first foray into self-stimulation?

Wow.

Despite the rumble in her stomach reminding her that

she hadn't eaten since the pretzel she'd purchased from a street vendor in front of the police precinct, Rory ripped off her clothes. She grabbed a few candles and some matches from a box, then shut herself in the bathroom. The single lightbulb in the center of the spacious bathroom cast a golden glow, enhancing the electric shimmy working its way along Rory's spine. She shivered. She couldn't believe she was going to do this.

But she would.

With little thought to aesthetics, Rory randomly placed the candles around the bathroom. On the closed lid of the commode. On the sink. On the far edge of the tub and others on a small wicker shelf she'd probably use for stacking towels once she'd unpacked. *Oh, yeah. Towels.* She dashed back into the living room and found the box she'd labeled Bathroom. She ripped out the largest, fluffiest terry cloth she could find, grabbed some soap and washcloths, then checked once more to make sure she'd locked her front door. She hadn't. *Jeez.* Imagine Alec walking in on her. Imagine someone else walking in on her! He'd said he hadn't yet rented the third-floor attic apartment, but she guessed he could show the place to interested parties at anytime.

Figuring Alec had a master key, she threw the dead bolt for good measure. She expected he was the type to knock, but what if he did and she was so enthralled in the throes of orgasm that she didn't hear? What if he got worried, kicked in the door?

She grabbed a small chair and hooked it under the knob, as a last line of defense. He might break in, but he'd have to make a hell of a racket before he caught her in the act.

After several more trips into the main room for the lotions she'd bought at the drug store and the warm bathrobe she'd thrown onto her bed while dressing for her appointment, Rory leaned against the door and sighed. She lifted the unsealed fantasy from where she'd perched it on the wicker laundry hamper and reread the instructions. Sliding herself beneath the stream of water in the tub was actually the last step in her self-seduction. First, she had to prime her body with a massage, a smooth exploration of her body. She stepped in front of her mirror, grabbed the vanilla-scented lotion, and filled her left palm.

She doused the light, then unable to see herself with only one candle, she grabbed the one from the toilet and placed it on the other side of the sink. When she met her own reflection, she gasped. Her hair, a wild disarray from her frantic treasure hunts for candles and towels and lotions, fell around her face like a gleaming dark brown mane. The auburn streaks she'd always loved glowed fiery red, glimmering like the center of her eyes. In the romantic glow of the votives, the makeup she'd applied for her interview with the police officer deepened, darkened. From the liner around her blue eyes to the plum lipstick she'd swiped over her mouth, bold color drew out her best features while the candlelight shadowed the rest. She smiled, acknowledging for the first time in a very long while that she was undeniably attractive. Particularly in the right light. The promise of the forbidden dancing in her eyes enhanced the effect.

She smoothed the lotion between both palms, warming the slick emollient, releasing the sweet vanilla scent into the air. She lifted her hands close to her nose and inhaled deeply, filling her lungs with a scent she'd forever associate with the potpourri assortments at the tiny lingerie shop two doors down from her last job, where she'd often browse during her lunch hour. She'd never bought more than hand lotion or bras on sale, ignoring their more erotic offerings just as she'd ignored that central part of what made her a living, breathing, needful woman.

With that thought, she lowered her hands to her breasts and applied the silky lotion to her skin. As the paper instructed, she delayed touching her nipples, instead focusing on the weight of her breasts, the sensitivity of her skin. Her eyes drifted closed as she focused on the sensations shooting through her. Her senses reeled from the flare of warmth licking down her torso. Even without touching them, her nipples tightened. Peeking, she watched them harden into light pink pearls. Curious, she dabbed a bit of lotion on each one, then rubbed. Softly, slowly, until the heat turned to fire. Until her nerve endings quaked, needing more.

She glanced at the tub, curious to the point where she considered skipping the next part of the directions she'd found in the *Sexcapade* fantasy. She was supposed to rub herself with lotion, wash it all off in the water, then ask her lover to reapply. The object was to learn her body completely, to gauge where she liked to be touched, for how long and how hard. Determined to do this right, she slipped over to the commode, moved the candles and sat down.

She squeezed a long stream of lotion along her leg, then rubbed upward from her toes to her ankles to her knees. The essence of vanilla and the flickering light from the flames cast a drowsy haze over the room. Again, she closed her eyes, but this time she imagined Alec's hands on her. Would he be as gentle? She dug in deeper, nearly yelping when she met a sensitive point behind her knee. Had she been standing, she would have lost her balance.

Shaking her head clear, she attended the other leg, then drew her knees in and drew swirling patterns of lotion

over her thighs. She forgot precisely what she was supposed to do—or not do—during this portion of her self-
massage, but she decided to wing it. She'd left the *Sexcapade* on the sink on the other side of the room and the
mood was too delicious, the atmosphere too relaxed for
her to retrieve it. By now, she knew her body's rhythm,
could anticipate her private needs. So after rubbing her
thighs hard, biting into the muscles she'd developed from
walking everywhere before she got a car, she applied a
touch more lotion and then dipped her hands, simulta-
neously, to her inner thighs.

With each circular, massaging motion, she inched
closer and closer to her vulva, closer and closer to the
moist pink flesh pounding in time to her heartbeat. She'd
touched herself before, but never like this. Even when
she'd woken up in the middle of the night, sweaty and
aroused from some erotic dream, she'd satisfied her
throbbing need by squeezing her legs together tightly,
allowing the mad tingle to heighten, then subside. She'd
always wondered what would happen if she slipped her
fingers between the engorged folds, but she'd never tried.
Never dared.

And she wouldn't today. The *Sexcapade* had been very
clear on this point—only the water would touch her so
intimately, until her lover took over. After that, her sexual
pleasure would be out of her control.

Rory wondered what she could possibly have been
thinking. What did she plan to do, dash down to Alec's
apartment sopping wet? Give him a quick rundown of
what she'd just done and then invite him upstairs to finish
the job? She tossed the scenario aside. This was just a
practice session. A dry run, so to speak, a thought that
made Rory laugh because even before she'd slipped into
the tub, she was anything but dry. She'd worry about

Alec later. After she knew what it felt like to climax. After she had some handle on how her body would react to the intimacies of sex.

With that thought, she slid her hands into the tight, damp curls. Electrified, she gasped. Her body had released a lotion of its own, musky, slick and warm. She cooed as her body throbbed. She needed more. Much more.

Slowly she rose and walked to the tub, her gaze determined, her skin alive with pure sexual need. She grabbed the cold water handle and tugged, but the polished brass fixture hardly moved. A drizzle of water pinged on the porcelain. She tried turning the handle upward, then down. She wiped her hands on the towel and tried again. She turned her attention to the hot water, but the stubborn thing wouldn't budge.

She knelt down, wondered if there was some sort of trick Alec had forgotten to show her in his initial tour of the place. She cursed, stood, pulled her full weight into breaking whatever secret seal existed around the pipes. She muttered to herself as she pulled and tugged, then dashed to the drawer in the kitchen where she'd seen some tools, ignoring the drapeless window and apparent draft, which instantly cooled her skin. Muttering additional expletives, she grabbed a wrench, flew back into the bathroom and tried to manipulate the clamp around the handle without damaging the metal.

After a long, torturous attempt to work the plumbing, a skill she'd learned to best leave for professionals, Rory slid onto the floor and started to laugh. She'd finally found the courage to break a few rules and she'd been foiled by rust. Her giggles turned to chuckles, but before she reached hysteria, she heard a knock on the outer door.

"Rory? I heard a bunch of banging. Do you need help with anything?"

Alec. Rory's chuckles renewed even as she grabbed her bathrobe and dragged it over her chilled and decidedly *not* aroused body. She needed help, all right. And wouldn't he be shocked to find out exactly what with?

7

IN HIS PRIME, ALEC had used some lame excuses to justify his behavior, but this one had to top his list. His new tenant had been banging around upstairs. So what? She was probably hanging a picture. Yet the sound had reverberated off the pipes in his kitchen, leading him to believe maybe she needed some help. He loved this old house, but the plumbing had been an issue since the day he moved in.

Besides, he hadn't needed much of an excuse to seek Rory out. He'd only been moderately successful in keeping her off his mind all evening, particularly since the topic he explored in his study dealt with the often painful initiations of neophytes into the club scene. He couldn't help but lose himself in a few daydreams about how Rory would fare in the competitive sport of late-night clubbing—any more than he could help himself from considering how he'd savor the chance to initiate her into the fold himself.

When she swung open the door wearing nothing but a plush white bathrobe and a frustrated frown, he figured he'd guessed correctly about the plumbing. The monkey wrench in her hand sealed his suspicion.

"Hey."

He swallowed the rest of whatever he'd planned to say. The haphazard knot she'd tied at her waist had slipped, revealing a flash of bare thigh.

"Hey, yourself," she answered. Leaning against the half-open door, the wide lapel of her robe gaped. Pale, rounded flesh caught his eye. His mouth filled with a wetness he longed to spread over her body. Promptly he remembered Pavlov's dog again.

He swallowed. "Did I come at a bad time?"

Her frown slowly transformed into a small, secretive smile. "Actually, your timing couldn't be better."

The raspy sound of her voice caused an instantaneous tightening from Alec's chest to his groin. To any other man, the effect would have been purely personal, intimate—but Alec couldn't help but theorize about why he hadn't felt such a lightning strike of lust in such a long time. At the club, he charmed and flirted with beautiful women every night. And though they attempted to charm him right back, none had succeeded. From the green little good girls to the jaded femme fatales, none of them had cracked the wall of Alec's wariness.

Not like Rory had. And, most likely, she wasn't even trying.

He dutifully reminded himself to back off, remain aloof.

Eyes on the prize, Alec. Eyes on the prize.

Yet Rory Carmichael had somehow bulldozed through his protective walls, with only her secret smile and a tiny dose of concentrated flirting, and had established herself as a coveted laurel all her own. She deserved his study, his attention, though Alec's expertise didn't cover chemistry. At least, not academically.

"Timing *is* everything," he answered in a sultry voice more Xander than Alec by a country mile. He straightened his spine and cleared his throat, determined not to add to the electric vibe crackling between them. Didn't take much but a flash of flesh for this woman to entice the one part of him he wanted most to keep contained. "Problem with the plumbing?" he asked.

Her grin quirked into a sardonic smile. "In more ways than one. Is there some secret to turning on the faucets in the bathtub?"

Alec relaxed. Rory wasn't on the make. She just needed help working the faucets.

"The bathroom up here hasn't been used much. I think they're just a little tight."

"Tight, huh? I know the problem." She winked. "Intimately."

Alec knew his eyes had widened the minute he caught the glimmer of amusement in Rory's eyes. Maybe Miss Aurora Carmichael wasn't as innocent as he'd first surmised. She had a playful streak she employed at will.

As an invitation, she swung the door open and held out the wrench. "Maybe you'll have better luck."

With a tingle of apprehension, Alec crossed the threshold into Rory's apartment. Even though he'd lived in the house alone for over six months, Rory's meager collection of boxes and bags scattered throughout the room created a warmth missing from his own space downstairs. Inhaling, Alec figured the effect resulted not so much from the sweaters and blankets dotting the armrests or scattered on the floor, but from the alluring scent of vanilla wafting through the air.

She didn't follow him to the bathroom, instead detouring toward the kitchen. "I guess I'll fix something cool to drink. Want something?"

"That'd be great," he answered. Despite the ham and cheese sandwich and beer, Alec's stomach growled. So before he dealt with the faucet, he followed her to the kitchen to propose they order in some food. That was safe enough, right? A quick take-out meal as reward for his fix-it skills?

"Have you eaten?" he asked.

She opened her refrigerator. "Not since I grabbed a pretzel around lunchtime. Unfortunately the groceries my aunt sent with me don't include anything interesting. Unless you have a craving for boxed macaroni and cheese?"

From her doubtful expression, he guessed she'd prefer another suggestion, no matter what he wanted.

"Pizza or Thai?" he asked.

Rory thought a minute, her lips in a pouty purse, her eyes narrowed into thoughtful slits. The question had seemed simple to him. Today was Thursday, and on Thursday he had Thai food, or on the nights he worked, munched fried gatortail swiped from the Dixie Landing kitchen.

"If this is a tough question—" he said.

"It is!" she insisted, smiling apprehensively as she swung the refrigerator door closed. "This is my first night here, remember? I'd like to make it count, you know? Celebrate a little."

He tried to turn fast enough so she didn't see him roll his eyes, but apparently, this time his timing was off.

"What?" she asked, incredulous.

He swung a full three-sixty to face her. "Ever consider that you're taking this 'first time in the big city' thing a little too seriously?"

She jabbed her fists onto her hips. "Ever consider that you're a big stick in the mud? How long have you lived in Chicago, Dr. Manning?"

He ignored the stick-in-the-mud comment. "Six months."

"Where did you live before that?"

"Boston."

"Okay, so you grew up in Chicago, moved to Boston, then returned to Chicago. I'm betting big money here you haven't been trapped in the suburbs for more than a half day over the past ten years."

"You forget I grew up not far from where you did. There are worse places to live than the 'burbs."

She frowned, her shoulders shaking in a shimmy Alec read as barely contained annoyance. "I know that. But you can be a real spoilsport. Doesn't being unaffected and jaded get boring?"

Spoilsport? Boring? Stick in the mud? Boy, his new persona was a real hit with the ladies.

"Ouch," he said.

"You wanted me to be honest, remember?"

"Yeah. I may have to rethink that request."

"Too late," she answered.

Story of his life. Alec couldn't count how many times he'd wanted something, did what he could to get it, then regretted indulging his desire when the consequences came to bear. However, he suspected he wouldn't regret anything associated with Ms. Rory Carmichael, so long as he kept his pants zipped. A task that was getting harder the more her robe slipped off her shoulder.

"You win," he conceded, flipping the wrench and catching it. Better to concentrate on the activity that would solve a problem, not create one. "Throw on some clothes and once I'm done in here, I'll take you down to the Loop for some real Chicago food."

Her smile lit her face like a roman candle on Venetian Night, which Alec noted was only a week away. His mind flashed with an image of him and Rory cuddled on a blanket at North Side Beach, watching the parade of sailboats and yachts, sipping cheap wine until the sun set behind them and the fireworks burst into the sky over Navy Pier.

When he walked into the bathroom, however, all sappy romantic images popped out of his brain, replaced with the kind of fantasies that normally got him in deep trouble.

Candles glimmered from every corner of the spacious bathroom from behind the commode to the top of the sink and the wicker hamper in the corner. They were new, barely melted, yet fresh with the scent of vanilla that had haunted him since he'd entered Rory's apartment. He inhaled deeply. The smooth, sugared scent seeped into his lungs, warm and inviting.

He spied her clothes, tossed in a pile in the corner, the silky strap of her bra peeking from beneath the soft pool of her lavender sweater. He noted the bottle of lotion, the top askew, perched on the toilet tank. From the tiny white flowers and vanilla beans on the label, he wondered how recently Rory had applied the emollient to her skin, and how much more he could take of the sensual scent before he went insane.

The old Alec Manning, tucked safely away in the temporary persona of Xander Mann, wouldn't have wasted another minute speculating. Xander would have grabbed the lotion, sneaked into Rory's room and proceeded to smooth more lotion over her flesh, from her enticing, slim arms to what he suspected were her incredibly round breasts.

Xander wouldn't have thought twice before seducing his tenant, wouldn't have considered how satisfying his need for sex would play against Rory's emotions or vulnerabilities. The old Alec would have seduced her, maybe broken her unsuspecting heart, then would have either found a reason to evict her, or would have rewarded her sexual curiosity with such coldness that she'd move or come to hate him. Luckily he'd managed to contain Xander to behind the bar—even logical Alec couldn't completely destroy who he'd been in the past.

But he did feel confident he could keep his old instincts under control—until he spied a sheet of paper on the corner of the sink.

Sexcapades?

His eyes widened and, after leaning out the bathroom door to make sure Rory wouldn't catch him peeking at her personal belongings, he read down a little further.

"*Sexcapade* 21. Slippery When Wet."

He scanned the teasing blurb, his tongue thickening with each word he read. Adjectives like *glistening* and *hot*. Verbs like *rub* and *flick* and *massage*. Intrigued, he flipped open the page, noting that the glue seal had been broken. He'd heard about this book, though he couldn't remember where. Probably while eavesdropping on one of the countless conversations he heard between girlfriends sipping Cosmopolitans at the bar at Dixie Landing, pretending they were Carrie and her pals from *Sex and the City*.

He expected the prowling females who ponied up on his bar stools to buy books like that, to be experimental in their sexual preferences. But Rory?

Great. Just great. Not only was she beautiful and honest and alluring, but she was sexually curious, too. *Wonderful.* How the hell was he going to remain on the straight and narrow when the perfect woman lived in the apartment just above his?

"I don't hear any—"

Rory's comment died the minute she cleared the threshold and caught him with her fantasy in his hand.

He laid the paper down gingerly. "Sorry. I shouldn't have snooped."

She pressed her lips together and swallowed.

"That's okay," she said, contradicting her forgiveness by folding her arms tightly across her chest.

"No, it's not." He knelt beside the tub, his wrench poised on the washer on the faucet's base, his eyes focused on the work he should have been doing.

"I wanted you to read it," she volunteered.

He glanced over his shoulder. "You left it there on purpose?"

She smirked. "No. Not consciously. Or maybe I did. I'm not sure. But now that you've seen it, what do you think?"

"Do you really want to know?"

He'd asked her the same question earlier and she'd wisely backed away from hearing the truth. But something had definitely changed since this morning when they'd first met on the stoop. Little by little, she'd dashed each and every preconceived notion he'd entertained about her. Where he'd first spied exuberant innocence in her baby blue eyes, her gaze now brimmed with temptation. He'd sensed her militant determination to spread her wings from the beginning, but now suspected her pertinacity had thrust her into new, uncharted territory.

"Yes," she said, her tone resolute. "I really want to know."

"Why?"

"Why not?"

"You're playing with fire," he warned.

She stepped forward and flicked a corner of the paper with her polished nails. "Actually the *Sexcapade* fantasy is all about water."

"But the result will still be heat."

"Not until you fix the pipes, it won't."

Slowly, complete understanding dawned. Alec had interrupted something when he'd come upstairs, all right. Something personal. Intimate. The candles. The lotion. Rory had been in the middle of making the masturbation portion of the *Sexcapade* fantasy real when he'd heard her attacking the pipes. She'd been frustrated all right…in more ways than one.

He swung completely away from her, trying with every fiber of his being to concentrate on his work. "I'll get right on it. I'm good at this."

Her tinkling laughter added naughtiness to what he'd meant to be an honest appraisal of his handyman skills. The double entendre had been inadvertent. Right?

"I'm counting on that, Alec," she purred. "More than you know."

RORY RETREATED TO HER bedroom, yet even before she shut the door, she wondered why she'd left. What should she do? What did Alec mean he'd *get right on it?* Was that an invitation? A suggestion? A hint? Dang, she was so useless in situations like this. She wished she could grab her phone, call Lisa or Roxanne or Sharon. Any one of her buddies had way more experience in such seductive situations, but she couldn't risk the chance of acting like a whimpering high-school girl in the presence of a man like Alec. He was older. Educated. Sophisticated. She'd just have to work this out on her own.

She listened to him grunt and curse, wondering how much of his frustration was focused on the plumbing and how much was because of her. When she'd caught him reading the pilfered page from the *Sexcapades* book, her heart had lodged in her throat. For a split second, she'd almost succumbed to her prudish instinct and snatched the page away. Luckily her new determination to broaden her sexual experiences overrode her brief mortification. The *Sexcapade* started as an instruction in self-gratification, but the second part, the best part, required a trusted lover.

She'd already decided that role should be filled by Alec. She just hadn't anticipated the opportunity would arise so soon.

His rumpled professor persona tugged at the foundations of her favorite fantasy—*Lolita*, with a twist. She was no child, but still younger, still more naive, her personal experiences limited to the realm of her daydreams.

She had to do this. Her breasts tingled, her body thrummed just thinking about enticing Alec to become her *Sexcapades* partner. He had no agenda, hadn't pursued her, had no reason to hurt her, so long as she kept her head on straight. She might be inexperienced, but she wasn't stupid. What man would turn down experimental sex with no strings attached? And she knew he wanted her—she'd witnessed the signs of his attraction just a moment ago. His dilated pupils. Raspy voice. Jeans growing tighter and tighter by the minute.

The instant she heard the rush of water in the other room, she made her decision. With one forceful yank, she untied the sash on her robe. She wanted Alec Manning. And, from now on, Rory Carmichael got exactly what she wanted.

8

ALEC WATCHED THE WATER RUSH from the faucet, tested the temperature, adjusted the handles, then turned off the flow, satisfied that his job was done. Just to make sure, he turned the water back on, the brass and porcelain knobs swiveling with ease. He glanced over his shoulder at the *Sexcapade* page still lying beside the sink, then concentrated on watching the last of the water twirl down the drain. Even after the last trickle sounded, he didn't move, wondering if the stuck faucet had really interrupted what he suspected it had.

His hands dripping, he reached for a towel, only to find one draped over his shoulder on a vanilla-scented breeze.

"Thanks," he said, sensing Rory behind him.

"Don't thank me yet."

Her odd reply, saucy and seductive, had him turning, determined to set her straight. When the rotation ended with him facing her bare thighs, he nearly fell backward into the tub.

The quickest war in history ensued as Alec battled to keep himself contained. He'd suspected she was perfect before, based only on her outlook and personality. Now that he saw her naked, he knew for sure.

She was flawless.

And he couldn't—shouldn't—have her. Not now. Not ever.

Oh, who the hell was he kidding? He would have this woman soon because she wanted him as much as he wanted her. Because he was a man with insatiable wants and needs that had been suppressed for too long. Too long to resist a woman so willing, so resourceful, so incredibly alluring. So naked. But with one last, desperate attempt to remain true to his personal vow, he tried to look as shocked as he felt.

"What are you doing?"

She thrust her hands onto her hips, emphasizing her nudity by being entirely unabashed about her lack of clothes. Alec swallowed hard, but found his throat parched, his mouth dry, his brain trying desperately to disconnect from his conscience long enough to savor her loveliness.

Her breasts really were excellence in female flesh. Round and plump, with a slight scoop that emphasized the tight points of her nipples. Her slim belly and tapered waist smoothed into hips ever-so-slightly flared in that natural feminine shape that drove him insane. Softly downy curls veiled the triangle at the base of her thighs, but didn't sufficiently hide the pink folds of skin he longed to touch, to taste.

Nude and beautiful, Rory captured a part of Alec he now knew wasn't as tamed as he'd believed.

"I'm about to make you an offer I hope you won't refuse," she answered.

He forced his gaze aside, but when that wasn't enough, he scrunched his eyes completely closed and blindly handed her back the towel. He hoped she'd take his hint and cover up. She only laughed. When he squinted his eyes open, she unfurled the hand towel. He hadn't given her enough material to cover more than a quarter of her nakedness at a time and he had no idea which part she should cover first—those amazing breasts his palms longed to cup or the sweet lips his tongue begged to part.

"You don't have to do this," he said. He knew what she wanted, of course. Sex. Why else would she approach him without a stitch on? But he had no idea why him…or why now.

Not that he cared.

Care, dammit!

Alec had to care. Alec was the responsible, upstanding, academically respected professor of sociology. If he backtracked, dipped his toe in the man he used to be…he didn't know if he'd ever rein in his basic instincts again.

"I don't have to do what—seduce you? You see, that's where you're wrong. I do have to."

He met her gaze. She looked sane enough. And determined. Maybe even a little stubborn. But not crazy. She hadn't been the first woman to corner him while naked, intent on initiating wild monkey sex. She was, however, the first one he felt compelled to turn down.

"Why?" he asked.

"Why not?"

He shook his head and stalked past her. He thought leaving the closed quarters of the bathroom had been a good idea, until he saw her drape herself sensually against the doorjamb.

"It's the book that's making you do this, isn't it?"

She lifted her shoulders in denial, causing her breasts to bob softly, which in turn tightened the seam of his jeans.

"Seems like a perfect place to start. I'm about to enter the intense social world of the big city, right? Sooner or later, some smooth-talking, gorgeous guy is going to hand me some lame line that I will probably fall for because I don't know the first thing about sophisticated men and sex and seduction.''

Dry-mouthed, Alec didn't know which part of that confession to tackle first. However, the status of her sexual experience seemed the most pressing.

''You're a virgin?''

Her eyebrows drew tighter together, emphasizing a tiny frown. ''Didn't you guess?''

''I do not speculate on the sexual experience of everyone I meet,'' he said, knowing his claim was a bald-faced lie. He spent his days and nights contemplating other people's sex lives as part of his research study. ''At least, I try not to.''

With a disappointed sigh, she grabbed a larger towel from the hook behind the door.

''You didn't once wonder about me?'' she asked after tucking the corner securely into a haphazard cover-up that didn't do a damn thing to alleviate the throbbing in his groin.

''I didn't say that,'' he admitted. One lie was enough for the afternoon. Any more and he'd be slipping into Xander territory again. Of course, Xander wouldn't have been so stupid as to deny a naked woman a little sexual experimentation.

Her frown loosened, revealing the hint of a smile. ''So you do find me attractive?''

''I'd have to be gay not to find you incredibly attractive, Rory.''

''You're not, right?''

''Not what?''

She laughed, which lessened the blow of her clarification. ''Gay?''

''Didn't we cover this? No, I'm not. But thanks for asking. Again. You're doing wonders for my ego.''

She rolled her lips together, sufficiently chastised. "I didn't think you were. But dammit, Alec, if you're straight and male and attracted, then what's the problem? You've got a naked, willing woman here."

"Where do you want me to start?" he asked, grumbling a curse to himself. She had to be kidding, right? What was the problem with him allowing his innocent, brand-new tenant to seduce him?

Everything!

And nothing at all.

"We're both consenting adults," she said, her voice the epitome of reason and logic. "I find you attractive... you find me attractive. I'm not asking you to lower my rent or anything."

Good, because he felt quite certain that if she dropped that towel again, he'd allow her to stay for free for as long as she wanted.

"We hardly know each other," he answered, hoping she wouldn't recognize the weakness of that argument. What more did he need to know about her? She wanted sex and, dammit, he wanted to oblige.

"Is there a better way to get acquainted?"

This time, he couldn't contain an outburst of laughter, no matter how hollow and humorless the sound. "I don't know. Maybe we could talk, go on a date or two."

"That's so old-fashioned," she complained.

"I can't believe I'm having this conversation with a beautiful, naked woman. I can't believe I'm having *any* conversation with a beautiful naked woman."

She grinned. "I'm not the one who wanted to talk."

Not sure if his instincts were on target, Alec followed them anyway, grabbing Rory's hand and tugging her away from the bathroom and then swinging her onto the couch. He remained standing—pacing, actually—while she watched him with way too much wicked delight dancing in her eyes.

"Stop that!" he ordered.

"Stop what?"

He jabbed a finger in her direction. "You're reckless," he accused.

She threw her head back and laughed. "Wrong! I'm a twenty-five-year-old virgin, Alec. Reckless is hardly a word I'd associate with me. I've never been anywhere. I've never done anything worth writing home about."

A chill crept along the back of his neck. "You plan to write home about this?"

At the mere idea, her face took on a look of horror and she shivered. Visibly. With a sassy little shimmy that only made the situation worse.

She tilted her head in thought. "Would make an interesting entry for my diary, though. Which, by the way, is essentially empty. No secrets scrawled in the dead of night by the glow of a flashlight tucked beneath the tent of my sheets. No naughty fantasies or wicked daydreams to take the edge off my nonexistent love life." She shrugged. "If you don't want to make love with me, hey, that's fine. I'm sure I can find some man who will."

"No doubt," he spat, not liking that idea in the least. He didn't understand the territorial instinct that had crept beneath his skin, but figured that, once again, chemistry had something to do with the phenomenon. He really should have paid more attention to that discipline. Then maybe he'd know how to counteract the effect. From the moment she'd shown up on his doorstep, he'd experienced an interest in her that, frankly, blew his mind. The polar opposite of every woman he'd ever seduced, Rory boiled his blood to tropical temperatures. And the heat was driving him mad.

She sniffed. "Then I'd better get dressed and go out looking. My brazen attitude might not last long."

She attempted to stand, but Alec reacted, blocking her. "I hope you intend to wear more than a towel."

Her mouth quirked into a playful smile. "I dunno. So far, this Lady Godiva thing has worked fairly well. You may be saying no, but you don't want to."

"You don't know what I want," he insisted.

She glanced down at his erection, clear as day through his jeans. "Oh, yeah?"

Innocent, my ass. Rory Carmichael might never had made love to a man, but she seemed to understand the species incredibly well.

"Why did you pick me?"

She turned her face away, rolling one shoulder in an unconvincing shrug. "You were here."

"Liar."

She skewered him with an angry stare and dropped whatever pretense she might have attempted next. "You seem safe."

He laughed. "You don't know anything about me."

"My grandmother likes you."

"Your grandmother likes my father. She doesn't know a damned thing about me, except what she's heard. And I bet she's heard plenty. The Manning boys were pretty wild."

"You turned out okay."

"You don't know that, either. Did you know I was fired from my last job because of an indiscreet affair with my boss's wife? And that, so far, I haven't been able to get another job? Or that I have to keep my nose clean and my pants zipped or I might lose any chance at ever reestablishing my academic reputation?"

Rory rolled her lips inward and slowly shook her head. "I don't think your father told Nanna any of that."

Alec clucked his tongue. "Respected doctors don't air their son's dirty laundry."

He watched the slim line of her throat undulate as she swallowed. His confession frightened her. *Good*. She should be frightened. She couldn't go around propositioning a guy just because of some false sense of security.

"Let me get this straight," she said, hands on hips. "You won't sleep with me because of your job?"

Alec leaned his head back and stared at the lacy patterns on the ceiling. "Not exactly."

"Good, because there are so many holes in that line of logic that I could drain pasta. You do remember that I promised discretion, right?"

He slung his hands into his pockets and shook his head, chuckling. "How could I forget? I just need to be careful not to make another mistake. Especially one I'd eventually regret."

She slid her arm across the back of the couch, then leaned her cheek against the sweet-smelling, smooth flesh of her shoulder. "Me, a mistake? Not very likely. But I understand your reluctance. Don't agree with it, but I understand. You've cut down on fun and frolic cold turkey. But now that I know what you don't want, I'm even more interested in what you *do* want."

He paced behind her so he could no longer see her lounging in her towel. Easily, he conjured the image of her as she'd appeared in the bathroom. Naked, willing, warm. He'd quit sex cold turkey, as she'd said, after the incident in Boston. From the minute he'd watched Dean Bledsoe's cruel smile while he'd listed every university he'd contacted with the tale of Alec's affair with his wife,

Alec knew he either had to concentrate on his career from that moment on or risk losing everything he'd ever worked for, everything he'd ever truly wanted. Sex, in the past, had been nothing more than a pastime. Something he did for no other reason than because he enjoyed the sensations, the illicitness, the challenge of tempting a woman into his bed.

Until he'd tempted the wrong woman and nearly imploded his career.

"What I want and what I should have are two entirely different things."

"Do they have to be?"

Suddenly he wasn't so certain. Rory wasn't one of his students, wasn't even connected in any way to the university or his study.

"No, I guess they don't."

She nodded and stood and, surprisingly, held tight to the towel. "Good. That hurdle's out of the way. But, unfortunately, you lost your chance. I'm too hungry right now to do anything but eat. Is that offer for a real Chicago dinner still open?"

Despite a quick flash of disappointment, Alec smiled. "Absolutely. And dress up a little. Let's make this a night to remember."

She swung toward her bedroom, an added sauciness to her step that had him hard and throbbing all over again. "That was my intention from the beginning, remember?"

He laughed. How could he possibly forget?

As Rory and Alec exited the restaurant onto busy Chicago Avenue, she couldn't believe how light she felt. After enjoying calamari and martinis at Harry Caray's, they'd taken a short cab ride to Eli's for a tender filet mignon, incredible Shrimp De Jonghe and the smoothest, most delicious cheesecake she'd ever enjoyed. Rory figured she'd added at least ten pounds to her slim frame, but still guessed a stiff breeze in the Windy City might lift her right off the sidewalk. All because she felt "lighter than air," as the expression went. Unfettered. Free. For the first time in her entire life.

Wisely, Rory had listened to Alec when he'd suggested she wear comfortable, low-heeled sandals with her short sundress. Gently taking her hand, he steered her toward Michigan Avenue, Chicago's world-famous Magnificent Mile, where they could walk off some calories and enjoy the sparkling city up close and personal.

"Do you walk this way often?" she asked, wondering if the gleam and glitter of the city would ever lose its shine to her. To her right, the Hancock Building stood like a dark monolith in the midst of shopping heaven, the uppermost lights shining red, white and blue in reverence to the upcoming July Fourth holiday. To her left, the limestone on the world-famous Water Tower glittered over old-fashioned street lamps. A man at the base played his guitar and sang with a surprising lack of talent, yet adults still let children toss coins into his hat. Tuxedoed drivers atop gleaming white and ebony carriages snapped the reins above surefooted horses, pulling tourists around the city, totally unaffected by the cabs and cars speeding by. When she spied the Ghirardelli chocolate shop to her left, she felt certain just thinking about an ice-cream sundae caused her to gain another two pounds.

Two pounds she intended to work off as soon as they returned to her apartment.

"I hardly ever come down Michigan, actually. Seems so touristy," Alec answered.

"I like tourists," she said. "Probably because I've always wanted to be one."

"Where?"

"Anywhere!" she shouted, swirling around in a circle and eliciting a few perplexed stares from passersby. "But this is an awesome place to start!"

Alec looked around, his stare endearingly begrudging. The man held tight to his jaded, unaffected persona with the same stubbornness as she intended to cling to her enthusiasm. If he wanted to miss out on life because he was too cool to see beyond his past, that was his problem.

"Chicago is a great place," he admitted.

"It would be ten times greater if you'd submit to an attitude adjustment."

"What's wrong with my attitude?" He dug his hands into the pockets of his khaki slacks—ones that Rory noticed did particularly amazing things to his tight runner's butt—and stopped walking.

"Like you don't know?"

"I have a great attitude."

"Compared to Attila the Hun, sure."

"Are you saying I'm cranky?"

She skipped back to him, and when she couldn't dislodge his hand from his pocket, she latched on to his elbow and tugged him forward. She wanted to see the lake at night and figured they only had a few more blocks to go.

"Cranky isn't the right word."

"Then what is?"

She leaned her head on his shoulder, inhaling the musky, spiced scent emanating from his warm skin. She thought hard about how she would answer, condensing and sorting all the things he'd told her about himself over drinks, dinner and dessert. How he was one of three wild sons raised by a single-parent doctor father. How he'd nearly blown his chance at a successful future because he'd tangled with the wrong woman—and the wrong man, her husband. How he'd never been in love, since love required he put someone else's needs above his own, a sacrifice he'd so far been unable or unwilling to make.

Alec claimed to have sworn off relationships and women, except to study both as part of the sociology project he hoped would turn into a lucrative grant opportunity and, subsequently, a job, some time next week. Rory understood the importance of this academic pursuit to Alec, beyond the paycheck. Alec Manning had incredibly expressive eyes. He'd probably never be able to hide any truth from her, as long as she had a clear view into those seductive hazel irises.

She finally settled on a word to describe him. "Sexy."

"You find Attila the Hun sexy?"

"No, I find you sexy. Forget the Attila stuff. I was kidding."

"Didn't you hear any of what I explained at dinner?"

She snuggled even closer and noted that he made absolutely no move to break their body contact. "I heard every word."

"Then you know I don't want to get involved with anyone right now."

"I do."

They waited for the light at Chestnut, then crossed, leaving the splashing sounds of the Hancock building's fountain behind.

"And that doesn't change a damned thing about what you want, does it?" he ventured.

She smiled. The man caught on quickly. "Nope."

His sigh was an invigorating mixture of surrender and humor. "If I hadn't spent the entire evening listening to you describe your childhood and young adulthood, I would think you were crazy."

So baring her soul to him as he had to her hadn't been a waste of time. She'd told him everything she could think of that would have been mildly interesting to him, starting with her mother's abandoning her, to her sister's running away, to her grandmother and aunt's insistence that she toe the line as the other Carmichael women had failed to. She'd revealed a little about her broken engagement, her personal decision to wait until she was on her own and independent before she explored another relationship. Or at least had her first fling.

With Alec, she hoped.

When they curved around another building, Rory realized that they had quite a bit more walking to do before they'd reach the shore of Lake Michigan, including walking under the overpass at Lake Shore Drive. Despite her comfortable shoes, her feet were starting to burn a little. And she'd much rather expend her energy in a more interesting way.

"Sorry," she said, not meaning her statement as a true apology. "But I am *so* incredibly sane, I know that I don't want to walk all the way down to the lake."

"Want to grab a cab?"

"Yes."

"Want to go down to Navy Pier? Great view of the lake from there."

"Not tonight."

"What do you want to do?"

She noted a definite hesitation in his voice before he'd asked her that, and the reluctance made her smile. He knew what she wanted, just as she knew he was delaying what she considered inevitable by being gallant and protective. Since returning to Chicago, the man had somehow transformed himself from pillaging pirate to valiant white knight, much to her chagrin. Yet thanks to the *Sex-*

capades page she'd tucked in her purse before they'd left—in case she needed to consult the instructions at some point during dinner—she figured she'd lure the dark plunderer out of hiding soon enough.

"First, I want you to kiss me. Then flag down a cab. The rest we'll play by ear."

9

ALEC REMEMBERED HIS FIRST KISS. He figured most men wouldn't give much significance to such an event. But then most men hadn't been like him—eleven years old when he was French-kissed by a high-school senior who'd been dating his oldest brother and fancied herself a femme fatale in training. Thus began Alec Manning's wild foray into sexual experimentation, particularly with older women who took great pleasure in teaching him everything they knew. By the time he was twenty, there wasn't a man on the planet who'd mastered any technique better than he had. So why, with his plethora of successful seductions in his past, did kissing Rory scare the hell out of him?

"Don't you want to kiss me?" she asked, his hesitation apparently kicking her own set of fears to the forefront.

"Absolutely," he admitted, then decided to go for broke. He couldn't deny how Rory fired his blood into a raging river of lust, unlike anything he'd ever experienced. She appealed to both sides of his personality. The bad boy renegade couldn't resist her bold, adventurous spirit, and the controlled intellectual couldn't deny her strong sense of self and clear common sense. With both halves of him enthralled, he had no way of fighting her allure. No way at all. "But how does a man kiss a woman whom he wants to protect and make love to at the same time?''

Her gaze shot heavenward, her exasperation cutting a cynical edge into her expression. ''You don't have to watch out for me, Alec. I'm perfectly capable of protecting myself. Even from the likes of you,'' she added, punching his shoulder lightly.

Cut right to the heart, didn't she?

''You're so sure of that?'' he asked, his pride feeling the sting. In the past, he would have taken that claim as a challenge, a reason for conquest. But Alec didn't want to conquer Rory. He just wanted to kiss her.

''Why shouldn't I be sure? I've managed to keep my virginity all these years and, believe me, many have tried to convince me otherwise.''

''Then it's a good thing we didn't meet as teenagers,'' he quipped.

She twirled around playfully. ''Might have been fun. You probably needed a smart girl who could take you down a notch.''

He chuckled. Intelligence wouldn't have helped, but his life might have taken a decided turn for the better earlier on had he met a young woman with such sheer determination to tell him no.

But he sure as hell didn't want that from Rory now.

Still, he needed her to be entirely certain that their affair was everything both of them wanted, and nothing either of them didn't. He couldn't afford anything more distracting than a brief encounter right now, and he needed to be sure that she completely understood the ground rules.

''Actually, I'll be eternally grateful that we never met back then,'' he answered. ''We would never have been friends and I probably would have hurt you in one way or another.''

She waved her hand, unconvinced. ''We'll never know. Maybe I would have been the one girl to break *your* heart.'' Before he could protest the unlikelihood of that scenario, she continued, ''But the only way you could hurt me now is if you don't kiss me. Soon.''

His doubtful look elicited a revision of her claim. ''Okay, you could hurt me if you kissed me, made love to me and then I fell in love with you and you didn't return my feelings. But I'm not looking for love, Alec. Love means commitment and compromise and sacrifice and, frankly, I'm just starting to take my life into my own hands. From you,'' she said, wrapping her arms around his waist again, ''I'm looking for pleasure and fun and, I hope, friendship.'' She glanced over her shoulder at the city they'd just enjoyed. ''We've had both the friendship and the fun tonight. So right now I'd settle for some pleasure.''

He slid his fingers into her hair, palms braced on her cheeks, enthralled by the glossiness of her crystalline-blue eyes, the quivering pout of her russet-red lips. She was lovely beyond words, honest beyond logic.

''Don't ever settle, Rory.''

Drawn like a connoisseur to a rare, valued wine, Alec leaned forward until their lips touched. The first taste intoxicated him, blurring the sounds of the city beeping and blaring around them. With drunken need, he swiped his tongue across her teeth, bidding her mouth open. She instantly complied, her arms snaking completely around him and up his back, her body melting against his as if the heat emanating from the concrete sidewalk fused them together—her breasts to his chest, her hips to his thighs. Even her mouth seemed a mysterious extension of his own, full of flavors and textures he was experiencing for the first time, yet somehow knew like the back of his own hand.

Rory didn't falter, didn't shy away. She matched his exploration touch for touch, her hands skimming his back, her belly flush and pressing against his erection. They finally broke when a crowd of pedestrians, trying to cross the street while they still had the light, jostled them from behind.

Alec smirked when he heard someone snarkily suggest that he and Rory "get a room."

With a reticent glance downward, Rory shifted her weight and waited until they were again relatively alone on the corner. Then she lazily traced his swollen lips with her index finger.

"Wow," she said.

He couldn't help but puff up a bit, until he realized that Rory's lack of former lovers didn't give her much to compare him to. But if things went as planned, every lover she ever took after him would have to live up to his memory. That satisfied the egotistical part of him he couldn't seem to wrangle—and, at the same time, freed the conscience he'd worked so hard to build over the past six months.

Rory wanted him. She knew the score, knew the rules and still wanted to play.

Pressure eased out of him like air in the pinprick opening of a week-old balloon. For the first time in he didn't know how long, Alec relaxed, his arms still cuddled around her vanilla-scented skin, his nose buried in her soft dark hair.

"I intend for you to follow that *wow* with several others," he said.

A smile lit her entire face, her blue eyes darkening with desire. "Promises, promises."

"You don't believe me?"

"So far, you're all talk."

Alec hailed a cab with one arm, holding her tight with the other, close so she could feel the increasing length of him against her stomach. "Don't worry, Miss Carmichael. I assure you that I'll live up to every word."

She shivered in his embrace, but the warm shimmy acted like a heat-activated lotion all over him. Lotion. Like the bottle she'd left uncapped in her bathroom—the bathroom where he intended to begin his seduction. After all, it was because of the poor plumbing at his house that she had been unable to act out the page from the *Sexcapade* book. The least he could do was to finally make her fantasy come true.

Rory dropped her keys on the table beside the couch, then felt a fiery spark of awareness the minute the door clicked behind her. On the cab ride over, Alec had done everything he could think of to seduce her without a single touch. He'd teased her, taunted her, primed her with sultry words and heated looks. Whether or not they followed the dictates of the *Sexcapade,* she knew without a doubt that sexual satisfaction was only a short time away.

She knew without a doubt—until he yawned.

Not a polite little stretch, either. This was a full-out, wide-mouthed, eyes-watering gasp for air.

"Tired?"

"Sorry," he said, removing his glasses and wiping the moisture from his eyes.

It's the damnedest thing, being a nice girl. One yawn, and Rory immediately remembered how Alec told her that he normally slept during the late afternoon. He hadn't hit the sheets for over twenty-four hours. Instead of catching a few z's, he'd spent the evening wining and dining her. Now she expected him to seduce her, too?

With her luck, he'd fall asleep halfway through.

No, this wouldn't do at all.

"You're exhausted."

He crossed the room in two broad steps and snagged her around the waist. "I'm sure I'll catch a second wind."

"No," she said, resolute. She attempted to push against his chest, but her resolve took a nosedive the minute her palms met his incredible pecs.

Unfortunately her denial was enough to make him stop.

"No?"

Boy, the man wasn't kidding when he'd said he took his women seriously. "It's just, well, you probably haven't slept a wink since yesterday."

"I haven't. Are you afraid I'll zonk out before we're done?"

She grimaced, but nodded. That had been exactly what she'd been thinking. Embarrassing or not, she decided to come clean. "I'm afraid that's the danger of being a woman's first lover." She wrapped her arms around him and leaned her head on his shoulder. The lack of eye contact made what she had to say a little easier to admit aloud. "She has all these romantic, idealized notions about how awesome the first time will be…and falling asleep in the middle doesn't fit my ideal scenario."

Alec laughed, then yawned again, which made them both laugh even harder. "I guess that would ruin the fantasy," he concurred.

When she pulled back to look up into his hypnotic hazel eyes, Rory suspected her expression was nothing less than dreamy. So, what? Dreamy was a perfect reflection of how she felt. "You won't ruin the fantasy. Not if you leave now, rest up and promise to meet me tomorrow."

Alec shook his head, smiling, as if he wanted to deny the logic of delaying their liaison, but he couldn't. "I promise. But a sleepy woman like you should at least be tucked into bed properly, don't you think?"

Alec swiped a tempting kiss across her lips, then nibbled a path from her ear to the center of her throat. She reveled in the sensations of his hot mouth against her cool skin, languishing in the currents of awareness that traveled the length of her body. She wanted what? When? Tomorrow? No, she couldn't wait. What had she been thinking? That she wanted him fresh and energized so they could go all night? Virgins probably couldn't go all night, anyway, could they? They should probably space things out. A little quickie tonight wouldn't take much time.

Anticipation coiled in her belly, then arced out to every nerve ending in her body. She knew he couldn't read her thoughts, but her actions spoke loud and clear. When his deep-throated chuckle broke her silent reverie, she had one leg wrapped around his waist and a sheen of perspiration coating her skin.

She swallowed, inhaled. Stepped back. "You must be thinking you're pretty hot stuff right about now," she quipped, trying to cover a tinge of embarrassment.

"No matter how hot I am, darlin', you're hotter. Go get ready for bed. I'll come tuck you in."

Rory shook the sensual fogginess from her brain. Her mouth opened to argue, take back her insistence that they wait until tomorrow, but he silenced her with a soft-padded finger over her lips.

"Before you change your mind, I suggest you consider, for a moment, all the sensual ways a man could tuck a woman into bed."

She almost skipped into the bathroom. She'd doused all the candles before they'd left for dinner, but the scents of sweet vanilla and smoke teased her nostrils, taunted her senses with what might have been. Too late now. But the candles weren't going anywhere...neither were the lotions or the water or the tub. She wasn't so sure about Alec, but she had to trust he was a man of his word, a man who made good on his tempting promises.

By the time she shrugged into her bathrobe and entered her bedroom through the connecting door behind the hamper, she'd started to wonder. She couldn't hear any movement in her apartment, making her suspect he'd changed his mind and gone home. Or maybe, somehow, she'd misunderstood. How did someone misunderstand something so blatant? She pulled back the covers. The light from the moon, streaking through the high casement window, gleamed silver on the white sheets.

A second later, she sensed Alec's gaze. He stood in the doorway, hands hooked above the threshold, his arms taut, his hip slung to the side in a pose that stole her breath.

"I thought you'd left," she admitted.

"Not a chance. Climb in."

She stared into his eyes, but in the darkness she saw nothing but shadows. Moonlight reflected off the sharp planes of his cheeks, the rugged square of his chin, the blondish highlights in his chestnut hair. She traced her mouth with her tongue while her gaze separated the powerful outline of his body from the darkness in the kitchen behind him. Her lips dried with each breath she took.

"I can't tuck you in until you're between the sheets."

She set her lust aside long enough to do as he asked. She removed her robe, wishing she had more light to see if her nudity affected him as strongly as it had only hours ago. She climbed onto the bed, satisfied when a sultry groan traveled the distance between the doorway and the bed.

The crisp cotton felt cold against her hot skin. She turned, fluffed the pillow beneath her neck, fanned her hair, then lay still as a stone, her feet tucked into the folds of the sheets, her legs and belly and breasts exposed to the cool breeze from the ceiling fan.

"Now, close your eyes."

Rory leaned her cheek against her pillow. "Come closer."

"I will."

"Now."

"Demanding?"

"I don't intend to only have things done to me, Alec. In fact, I didn't plan to have anything done *to* me at all tonight."

"Ah," he answered knowingly. "You're talking about your *Sexcapade*." He tugged a folded paper from his pocket. The flash of white caught the silverish-blue glow from the moon.

"Hey!" she protested, sitting up. "How did you get that?"

He shrugged and stuffed the paper back into the pocket of his khaki pants. "I stole it."

Despite his unapologetic tone, her anger died quickly to mild annoyance. She had to admit that thought of him taking possession of the sexual fantasy intrigued her.

"I just want to make sure you don't get restless. and go looking for someone else to explore this fantasy with before tomorrow night."

"What if I memorized it?" she countered.

"What if I did, too?"

Threads of excitement crackled through her. If Alec took his promise to fulfill her fantasy this seriously before they'd exchanged so much as a palmful of lotion, she could only imagine how intense tomorrow night would be. How could she possibly sleep now? She wasn't the one who was tired, anyway. She should be tucking him into his bed, poking around in his stuff, learning a secret or two to keep her from being completely at his mercy.

"Lie back, Rory. Close your eyes."

After one last huff for good measure, she did as he asked. She squeezed her lids tightly, then incrementally, with each creak of Alec's footsteps over the bare floorboards, she relaxed. She concentrated on breathing, on molding her body into the soft, feathery mattress. She lured herself into a dreamy state between expectation and complete relaxation. A gentle breeze teased her thighs when he grabbed a corner of the sheet. She couldn't help but adjust the position of her leg. One inch. To the right. The cool wind met with the sweet moisture lingering on her intimate flesh.

The rustling sheet quieted, now covering her knees. She heard Alec's breathing, labored, deep. She felt the heat of his hand hovering just above the skin on her thigh. She nearly leaped upward when the gentle rasp of his fingertip struck against her like a match.

"Shh," he commanded. "Maybe I shouldn't touch you. You're wound so tight."

She peeked with one eye. "And you expected…"

He chuckled. "…that you'd be wound so tight. That's good. The edge is a great place to be, for a short time." Tugging the sheet higher, he covered her skin with maddening slowness, his stare focused, intense. "The catch is not to stay there too long."

She'd already learned that Alec had lived on the edge long enough to experience cuts deep enough to change his life. But Rory had already acknowledged that her chosen path into sexual exploration could be lined with danger—particularly the risk of falling in love with the first man who exposed her to sensual satisfaction.

But like Alec had said, the catch was to not stay on the edge too long. They'd agreed to a brief, intense interaction. And that would be all they'd have.

With a quick flash, Alec tugged the sheet over her, skimming her breasts, covering her all the way to her neck. He bent close for a moment while he slipped the edges of the sheet beneath the mattress and stood.

"There," he announced. "All tucked in."

She peeked one eye open. "That's it?"

His expression was downright wicked. "Oh, did you want something more?"

"If you want me to be more specific," she insisted, "I'm pretty sure I can work out a play-by-play."

"Like writing your own *Sexcapade*, huh?"

"I could."

Before she had the chance to think up a clever title for the teaser page, Alec climbed onto the bed. He straddled her, but because he'd folded the sheet so tightly around her, she could barely move.

"So could I. Let's call this 'Cocoon of Craving.' I don't know…" He ran a finger along the line of fabric that stretched across her neck and shoulders, binding her beneath him. "Too cheesy?"

She shook her head as much as she could, unable to think of anything more clever while Alec hovered over her naked body with nothing more than a thin layer of cotton separating them. The sheet—and his clothes, she amended. But even if she did want a chance at freeing the buttons on his Oxford shirt, she couldn't move her hands. Or her feet. Or any other part of her. Not unless she struggled and she saw absolutely no reason to do that.

He balanced on his knees above her, careful not to crush her with his weight. "Close your eyes, Rory. Consider this a prelude, a taste of what we'll do tomorrow night with no barriers between us."

She obeyed his command, too overwhelmed by need to argue when he promised to give her exactly what she wanted.

He started with a kiss, just below her shoulder and above her breast. His hot breath permeated the sheet, spreading over her skin with such concentrated softness that she didn't recognize the fire until she gasped at the heat.

"Imagine that sensation on your breasts, Rory. On your nipples. They're going to get so hard."

Going to get? Who was he kidding? Her nipples pearled at just his words, chafing against the soft cotton, reaching for his touch.

Instead, he lowered his lips to the subtle swell of her right breast and kissed her again just above the dark arc of skin surrounding her nipple, sucking air from beneath the cotton into his mouth and then blowing the intense heat onto her flesh.

"I can practically taste you. So sweet," he said, sitting up. "Now I can see you, but can I touch you? Taste you?"

Moments passed before Rory realized he'd actually meant for her to answer what she'd assumed were rhetorical questions. She nodded, knowing now why he'd chosen "Cocoon of Craving" as the title of this spontaneous, original *Sexcapade*. With each kiss, she wanted him. When he moved, the tight sheet magnified the sensations, vibrating with each movement so the cotton acted like a thousand feathery fingertips skimming each and every inch of her skin.

"This is your *Sexcapade*, Alec. You can do what you like."

"I want to do what *you* like," he insisted, his voice husky and weighty with need.

She smiled, her breasts full, her thoughts clouded by desire and weary of talk. "I think we'll like the same things."

His grin reached his eyes, sparking with a flame that licked her from the inside out. He lowered his mouth over her, forming an O with his lips that outlined her areola. He suffused the sheet with his hot, moist breath before he suckled her hard nipple with his tongue.

She arched her back, dizzy from the sensations, shocked by the instantaneous response of her body, seeking more. Part of her wanted to tear away the sheet; part of her reveled in the way the cotton soaked up the torrid wetness from his mouth and held the humidity close against her. She thought she'd lose her mind in the sensations, but he moved away. The respite didn't last. In an instant, she was tossed back into the tempest when he tended to her other breast.

Rory had no idea she'd be so sensitive, so responsive to his muted touch. He kneaded and caressed her through the cotton and her involuntary writhing loosened the edges beneath the mattress. With the sheet slackened, she could move her legs just enough to accommodate Alec when he slid lower, his mouth poised above her.

If she thought his breath over his breasts made her crazy, feeling the moist air as it teased her hot center drove her close to insanity. When he flicked his tongue across the sheet, over her flesh, she cried out, shaking. Tiny shivers of sensual awareness changed into intense, bone-deep vibrations all of their own accord. One more lick and her entire body locked, exploded, imploded and then trembled into sated quiet.

The entire time, Alec didn't move. Or if he did, Rory lacked the awareness to notice. The fog started to clear only after she felt his weight lift from the bed and, with a brief swipe of a kiss across her temple, he retreated toward the door.

"What will you dream about tonight, Aurora Carmichael?"

From the sound of his curiosity, she guessed he meant the question for himself, not for her. A tiny smile played over her lips and, with a sigh, she burrowed herself further into the mattress and pillow.

Let him wonder, she thought. She, for one, couldn't wait to find out.

10

JACKS. SHE'D DREAMT ABOUT JACKS. And not some sexy pair of men named Jack, either. Little pointy metal game pieces. A chalk-drawn circle. A bouncy ball in a bright shade of red.

Punching in the code to transfer the Divine Events phone system from live answer to voice mail, Rory flashed back to waking in the middle of the night, her brain bursting with images of two girls, both brunette, both eight years old, playing jacks on the front porch of Nanna's house.

She'd wanted so desperately to dream about Alec, or at least about something sensual and forbidden like the way he'd tucked her into bed. She experienced a wonderful rush of sexual sensations, but she couldn't go as far as to call it full-blown orgasm. That she would feel when he was inside her, joined with her, body to body. As she would tonight.

Instead her subconscious had reminded her about her search for her sister. Her catalyst for coming to the city in the first place, though she hadn't done much to pursue Micki, had she? She'd interviewed the detective, got a name and location of the shelter where she might find someone who knew something more. Yet, distracted by her new job and her new flirtation, she hadn't followed up. Still, she couldn't shake the reality that her sister, like her, was twenty-five years old and more than capable, apparently, of taking care of herself. Rory wanted to find Micki and help her get off the streets. She desperately needed to reconnect with her twin, start making up for all the time they'd missed. But Micki was an adult. If she wanted Rory's help, Rory's love, she wouldn't be hard to find.

Rory straightened the items on her desk, tamping down the resentment and anger she'd thought she'd had under control. About a year after Micki had run away, the fear and sadness had subsided, though apparently they hadn't disappeared. Sixteen-year-old Rory had experienced a range of horrible emotions, topped with rage at the selfish weakness of her sister. Why couldn't Micki tough it out until they turned eighteen so they could venture out on their own together? Why couldn't she just adapt, accept the love they'd been offered by their grandmother who'd taken them in when their own mother didn't want them? Why did Micki have to be so damned stubborn? So much like their mother…who was dead and gone, her memory little more than a grainy image in a dusty photograph.

But in the years that followed, Rory had transformed her anger into acceptance, though the rage emerged every so often, mainly when she had fears of her own to face. Alone. She'd had her friends, but she'd wanted her sister.

Now, she had Alec, too. And soon, tonight, she'd have him in the fullest sense, real and in the flesh. Her conscious mind had been dealing with that possibility all day, alternately causing chills to race up her spine and coating her skin with a sheen of perspiration from anticipatory heat. Knowing she'd soon make love with Alec ruled her reality, banishing the thoughts of her sister to her dreams, subtly reminding her that she was no closer to finding Micki now than she'd been three weeks ago when she'd found out about her arrest. And since guilt was an emotion Rory excelled at, she considered what she should do between now and ten o'clock, her designated rendezvous time with Alec. Follow up with the homeless shelter where Micki had once volunteered, or return to her apartment to reset the stage for the seduction?

"So, how would you rate your first day?"

Cecily Divine jogged halfway down the spiral staircase, hopped onto the banister and allowed the slick material of her knit skirt to propel her the rest of the way. She made a solid landing, despite her slim stiletto heels.

Rory smiled. Cecily only slid down the banister when no customers were in the shop, but Rory guessed it had to be tough for her boss to squelch her rebellious impulses the rest of the time. Somehow, Cecily had managed to meld her wild child persona with that of a competent businesswoman, but Rory wasn't a fool. Such a dichotomy came at a price, a price Rory had only now begun to pay.

"*You* tell *me,* boss," she answered. "How did I do?"

Cecily crossed the room to Rory's desk, then ran her short, polished fingernails over the tabs of the file folders Rory had spent all morning organizing, following up on and sometimes closing out. The firm had several vendors who hadn't confirmed contracts, but Rory had handled those before lunch. One folder caught Cecily's eye, so she carefully pulled it from the stack and read Rory's notations.

She slapped it closed. "You booked Jack Sullivan to shoot the Mordecai *bar mitzvah?*"

Rory shrugged, but her humility was hard to tap into. Jack Sullivan was a nationally known photographer. Enticing him to work an event as potentially mundane as a child's party—even one with a one-hundred-thousand-dollar budget—hadn't been easy. But she'd done it. "I'm good on the phone. And I don't think it hurt that I happened to call when his newborn son was screaming at the top of his lungs. The man seriously needs a vacation.''

''For what the Mordecais are willing to pay him, he can fly first class, bring his whole family, stay at the Intercontinental and still make a tidy profit. Good job, Rory. We really needed someone we could trust to take care of some of the details. The business is growing faster than we realized.''

''That's what happens when you're good at what you do.''

Cecily didn't seem entirely convinced. Though wild in the way she dressed and downright wicked in the way she talked, Rory sensed Cecily wasn't always as confident as she led others to believe. It could have been that Rory just wanted to find a kindred spirit, or maybe her perception came from her own personal experiences.

''Whatever, as long as we can keep paying the bills. And speaking of paying the bills, I have a band to check out on the south side tonight. Very bluesy and very cheap. Just what we need for that charity event in two months. Livia was supposed to tag along, but she's got some trouble with a dress she's designing for that opening tomorrow night. How 'bout you? Wanna hang? I'm buying. Though, frankly, I'm not sure if this bar serves anything but beer.''

Rory glanced at her watch. Just after five o'clock. Rory surmised that Alec was deep in his afternoon slumber. According to a note she'd found tacked to the inside of the front door before she'd left, he planned to work all day on his project, crash around four o'clock after the contractors left, then meet her at ten for their rendezvous. So she had five hours to kill, and why primp and pamper herself getting ready for their tryst when she'd be plenty pampered during the execution of the *Sexcapade?*

Besides, she'd made a great first impression on her inaugural day on the job. Shadowing Cecily would not be a bad idea if she truly wanted to work her way into a managerial position, which she did. The business was growing faster than the cousins had ever anticipated. Sooner or later, they'd need to start delegating the important stuff. And from what Rory knew, she had just as fair a shot at a higher level position as any of the other employees, new or not.

At the same time, the shelter she'd wanted to visit was on the south side. Maybe Cecily could at least point the place out if they happened to go past?

Cecily frowned at her hesitation. "Or did you have plans?"

"No, I'd love to go." Rory dug into her purse and took out the business card Detective Walters had given her. "I was just planning to maybe stop by this place. I can go this weekend, but I think it's on the south side. Maybe close to this bar?" She held out the card.

Cecily looked at it, then eyed her skeptically, the frown deepening on her ruby-red lips.

"You looking to do volunteer work? Cause I know places a little more suited to your background. Not to offend you, Rory, but this is a tough neighborhood."

Rory shook her head. "No offense taken." She gently retrieved the card. "Street-smart, I'm not. At least, not with city streets. But, hey, I probably shouldn't involve you in this anyway. This is for my personal life. Divine Events is my professional life. I'm sorry."

Cecily grabbed the card back, scooted the files over and propped herself on Rory's desk, legs crossed at the ankles. "Don't worry about that corporate shit here,

Rory. This is a family business. And now you're family. And since the Cousins Divine are also Italian, we will probably end up being involved in every aspect of your life, personal, professional and otherwise. It's inevitable."

She waggled her eyebrows and Rory relaxed. "That's okay by me. I'm used to intrusive relatives."

"Good. Now, tell me about this place. Where'd you get this card?"

"From a police detective. My sister used to volunteer there, which is very odd to me, since she's homeless herself."

"You have a sister?"

"A twin. Her name is Michaela. I called her Micki. She ran away from home ten year ago, and a few weeks back I found out she'd been arrested for loitering in the city. I didn't even know she was still in Chicago. Anyway, the detective who busted her gave me the card, told me Micki used to work there in exchange for a place to crash. But she's disappeared again."

"Why did a detective arrest your sister for loitering? Why not a cop in uniform?"

Rory didn't know. She'd never even questioned the scenario. "Wow, I don't know."

Cecily had obviously some direct knowledge of the workings of police procedure. "Something else must have been going down. Loitering is a bogus charge."

Rory tried to imagine Detective Walters lying to her, and she couldn't. The woman seemed completely on the up-and-up. But maybe she'd had to omit details for the sake of her case. "The detective told me she ran Micki in because she looked like she could use a hot meal and some social services. I never asked why the detective was out there in the first place."

Cecily mulled over the possibility, then nodded. "Could happen. But this street ain't the Magnificent Mile. You shouldn't go there on your own."

"I know. I was going to get my landlord to go with me," Rory started to explain, but Cecily cut her off with a wave of her hand.

"Landlord, shmandlord." Cecily snagged her cell phone out of her pocket and hit the speed dial. "You need someone who knows the streets." After about ten seconds, Cecily's eyes brightened. "Yo, Vincenzo. How's it hangin'?"

In less than a minute, Cecily had made all the arrangements. No wonder she was in the planning business. Armed with only her cell phone and her saucy personality, she'd wrangled her cousin Vincent into meeting them at the "L" stop. He'd escort them to the shelter, take them by this new pizza place he had just discovered for a quick bite, then drop them off at the club.

Cecily locked up while Rory dashed to the bathroom, touched up her makeup and prepared herself for an interesting evening. Staring in the mirror, she couldn't believe she was about to embark on such an adventure. Maybe to anyone else, an afternoon hopping around town was expected, normal. But to Rory—who always went straight home after school or work for dinner and who usually spent her evenings either watching *Jeopardy!* with Aunt Lil or hanging out at the mall or the movies with her friends—tonight would be epic.

And that was even before she'd meet up with Alec.

Was there a word to describe something better than epic? Mammoth? Colossal? Sublime?

At that thought, a rush of keen satisfaction surged

through her…then propelled her out the door. She loved her new life. Rory absolutely, positively adored being on her own.

AT MIDNIGHT, ALEC USED his key to let himself into Rory's apartment. She'd called at a quarter to nine, explaining she wouldn't be back as early as she'd planned. The first set for the band her boss had taken her to check out didn't start until nine o'clock and Cecily Divine had expressed interest in hanging out for both shows. Rory had apologized for not calling sooner—but he'd insisted she had nothing to apologize for. Sure, he didn't like waiting, but what man did? What woman did, for that matter? The bottom line was, Rory had opted to put her job ahead of her pleasure.

And this, in his estimation, was a good thing.

Just as he'd suspected, Rory was nothing like the woman he'd pegged her to be before their first meeting. She had her priorities straight. She wasn't about to let him or her sexual interests override the commonsense decision to stick it out with her boss and earn some points on her first day on the job.

Work first, play later. Taking a well-needed lesson from her, he'd used the extra hours to completely catch up on his proposal. This research project wasn't complete, but if the representatives from the Henson Foundation showed up tomorrow, he'd be ready to pitch. And with no hours scheduled tonight behind the bar at Dixie Landing, Alec had the rest of the night to concentrate on Rory and Rory alone.

As soon as she decided to show up.

He couldn't help laughing at himself once or twice as he set the stage for her seduction. He'd brought wine—a fine merlot he'd been saving for a special occasion. He found matches, lit the candles in the bathroom, checked to make sure the faucet he'd repaired yesterday was still in good working order. By the time he'd uncorked the bottle and eased into the cushions of the couch, the scent of vanilla had permeated the room again. Satisfied that he'd prepared as best he could, he relaxed on the couch and sipped a glass of wine.

After ten minutes of silence, he wondered what the hell he was doing.

He was about to deflower his tenant.

With a thick gulp, he downed a glass and refilled. What an archaic thought. Deflower? Did anyone use that word anymore? That's what he got for spending so much time with his academic texts, studying the sociological aspects of dating and mating in the past; he'd needed to be able to compare them to the new trends he tracked in the here and now at the club. At Dixie Landing, most patrons would likely define *deflower* as what you did when the cute waitress in the black minidress offered daisies for sale, a buck a piece.

But no matter the terminology, Rory Carmichael had never had sex before. He'd introduced her to some pretty intense sensations last night, but he knew from experience that nothing compared to full body-to-body contact. She hadn't even slept with the man who'd proposed marriage to her. Luckily she'd had the sense to dump that loser while the getting was good. Still, he'd known her for just over twenty-four hours, had spilled some of the most private aspects of his past with her—and had agreed to be her partner in an outrageous sexual fantasy.

He'd read and reread the *Sexcapade* so many times over the course of the day that he'd frayed the folds of the page. But just as he'd promised to Rory, he'd committed the details to memory. The scenario was intensely intimate, arousing in its simple yet personal eroticism.

Even with his long history of sexual liaisons, he'd never watched a woman manipulate herself to orgasm before— at least, not when she knew he was watching. He got hard just thinking about Rory touching herself, learning herself, washing herself beneath the hot water, allowing the water to press on her, forcing a hot, wet explosion of sensation.

This wasn't the typical way a man initiated a woman into the pleasures of sex. But then Rory wasn't a typical woman. She was young and naive, but smart. Strong, possibly in ways she didn't even realize. Good thing, too. Because if she was foolish or weak, she'd fall in love with him. Then he'd find some stupid-ass way to either disillusion her or take her entirely for granted.

Despite the difference in their ages, they both stood at the threshold to new lives. Alec was finally getting his act together and Rory was finally discovering what she wanted for herself. A relationship would only get in the way, allowing them less time to concentrate on what really mattered. Academic respect for him. Real independence for her.

Or was he just making excuses? Heading off his own emotions before they snared him in an inevitable trap?

Damn. He finished a second glass of wine and decided not to pour another. Alcohol only intensified his mood when he was feeling particularly dark and dour. Every time he thought he had a healthy handle on forgiving himself for all his years of screwing around, wasting time and energy, his regrets pushed their way back to the forefront.

What had he said just yesterday to Rory about regrets?

Making up for past actions or regrets can have a sweet taste. But try to make sure you don't bite off more than you can chew.

His chuckle held no humor. Some sage he was, giving such bogus advice. Especially when he couldn't even follow his dictates himself. Was making love to Rory a way to purge himself of regret? And why did he have so many regrets, anyway? Because he'd spent the magical, young, free part of his life darting from one meaningless physical relationship to another, never learning, never growing, never allowing anyone inside his heart...or because he'd fucked the wrong woman, gotten caught and nearly murdered his career?

The answer didn't matter. The question, in fact, was moot. His reasons for being here, waiting for Rory in her quiet, dark apartment, were inconsequential compared to her motivation. Rory had consciously chosen to make real her sexual fantasy. He couldn't deny they'd experienced a rare connection from the first moment they'd met. He liked her. Respected her. Hell, he admired her. And, for whatever reason, she trusted him. The one thing he was sure of was that he wouldn't disappoint. Not tonight. Not ever.

And he wanted this night with Rory, because if he had any chance at keeping both their lives on track, tonight might be all they'd ever have.

RORY ALLOWED HERSELF ONE YAWN, but the minute she turned the key to her apartment, all fatigue deserted her body. The sweet scent of vanilla wafted from the bathroom. Candlelight sparkled from votives on the coffee table, throwing a golden glow about the room, broken only by shafts of crimson sparkling through two goblets filled with red wine. Music teased her—something jazzy, but soft, instrumental—playing in the other room. Her bedroom?

She snagged a glass of wine, sipped, tensing with the

GET FREE BOOKS and a FREE GIFT WHEN YOU PLAY THE...

Lucky 7

SLOT MACHINE GAME!

Just scratch off the silver box with a coin. Then check below to see the gifts you get!

YES!
I have scratched off the silver box. Please send me the 2 free Harlequin Blaze™ books and gift for which I qualify. I understand I am under no obligation to purchase any books, as explained on the back of this card.

FIRST NAME	LAST NAME

ADDRESS

APT.#	CITY

STATE/PROV.	ZIP/POSTAL CODE

7	**7**	**7**	Worth TWO FREE BOOKS plus a BONUS Mystery Gift!
🍒	🍒	🍒	Worth TWO FREE BOOKS!
♣	♣	♣	Worth ONE FREE BOOK!
🔔	🔔	🔔	TRY AGAIN!

Visit us online at www.eHarlequin.com

(H-B-01/03)

icated himself not so much to family, as she had, but to the family business.

While she'd enjoyed Cecily and her cousin's company, her mind had wandered almost exclusively to Alec—the academic who would always have more book-born knowledge than she ever would, the traveler who'd studied and explored on all four borders of the United States when she'd never left Illinois. The man who'd made love to countless women, making her wonder why the heck he was interested in her.

But he was. He wanted her. Evidence of his interest glimmered in the candlelight, flavored the wine he'd selected and poured. All for her. All for tonight.

"I don't think it's possible to be late for your own seduction," he assured her.

She smiled, relaxed, catching the gleam of humor in his eyes. "I'm more than just a couple of hours late for that, don't you think?"

"It's not my job to think, Rory. It's my job to watch."

He stepped back into the bathroom, out of sight, his body merging with the firelight that danced in orange-and-gold waves over the ivory tile and gleaming white porcelain. Rory entered the bathroom as if passing into another world.

And even though she'd walked this sensual path just the night before, Alec's presence evoked incredible wonder. Newness. Just as she had, he'd placed candles everywhere. He'd stacked a soft tower of towels beside the bathtub. The lotion she'd used on her breasts was perched on the edge of the sink, the cap removed. He'd brought in one of the metal chairs from the kitchen and had placed it in the corner, turned backward. He swung his leg over the seat and eased down, bracketing his arms along the back, his chin perched on his hands.

"You've set the stage," she said. "Thanks."

"Don't thank me yet," he answered. "I may have set the stage, but you're the one who has to perform." His eyes gleamed with anticipation. "Undress for me, Rory."

Biting her lip, Rory popped the top button of her blouse. "And you're just going to watch?"

Rory heard the desperation in her voice, the unspoken plea that he remain where he was. If he moved closer, if he touched her, if she could see more than the desire flickering in his eyes, she might not last. She knew her role, knew what she had to do, but her primed body could easily jump directly to the climactic finale if she didn't proceed with caution. If Alec skimmed even a fingertip over her flesh, she suspected she wouldn't have the stamina to follow through on the complete fantasy—of pleasuring herself before he repeated the process.

"Don't worry, babe. I'm not leaving this chair."

She twisted the second button free, then the third. She closed her eyes, inhaled, then slipped her arms from the silky top. The slick softness caressed her skin. Her breasts chafed against the lace of her bra and she twisted her arms around her back to unhook the lingerie, the fire from the candles teasing her with its heat.

"Wait," he instructed. "Open your eyes."

She complied, but paused, her arms still twisted behind her, thrusting her breasts forward. "Why?"

Alec grinned. "So you'll see my reactions. So you'll understand how hot you are."

Rory's breath caught before she shook the thought away. "I don't want to think about that. I just want to feel the sensations."

He shifted in his seat, stretching out his legs. "That's only *physical* sensation. I want you to know the sensations of the mind. Desire is powerful, Rory. Desire can

make us do things we'd otherwise never do. Test bound-
aries. Throw away everything we've ever learned, ever
known. Does that frighten you?''

She didn't hesitate, not when the truth was incontro-
vertible. ''Yes.''

''Good,'' he replied. ''Now undress and watch me
want you.''

11

"BRACE YOUR HANDS ON THE showerhead."

As she had since she'd entered the apartment, Rory followed Alec's instructions. Her lungs ached, her skin zinged with such need, such want, she could barely breathe. Slick with lotion and hot with desire, she stood naked in the bathtub, her slippery fingers clutching the metal pipe like a lifeline. Alec swung his leg over the chair and stalked toward her. Like a wolf, feral and hungry. And she could do no more than pant, like prey that had lost the fight.

Only she wasn't nearly through—and she most definitely wasn't fighting. Despite his sudden nearness, Alec had stuck to his vow to do no more than watch, even if he had added his own nuance to the simple promise. As she'd applied the lotion over her belly, her breasts, her legs, he'd narrated. Quoting from the *Sexcapade*. Adding commentary. Voicing his observations of her reactions, his response. Instructing and demanding. At the same time, he repeatedly claimed she was the most alluring, intriguing and powerful woman he'd ever met.

And she believed him. In her compliance, she'd gained control. He'd already unsnapped and unzipped his jeans. His upper lip glistened with perspiration and the more he spoke, the raspier his voice became.

He wanted her. But he couldn't have her. Not yet. Not until she'd fully pleased herself. For his eyes only.

"The water will be cold at first," he warned.

She glanced down between her upstretched arms, to where he crouched at the side of the tub, his hand on the faucet, his eyes level with her bare thighs.

Her tongue, dry and thick, swelled in her mouth. Thirsty for water. For him. "A cold shower might not be a bad thing right now," she quipped.

"Oh, it won't douse your arousal, Rory. Imagine the iciness sliding down your body. You think your nipples are hard now? Just wait."

He did his best to test her patience. Five seconds? Ten? Twenty? She had no clue, but the instant she finally heard the squeak of metal turning, she braced herself.

The rush nearly catapulted her into sensory overload. The frigid temperature was a shock, but nothing compared to the sensation of the lotion as it mingled with the water and sluiced down her body, creaming over her skin in thick, transparent rivulets. Slowly the water warmed as Alec adjusted the other faucet, but as the surprise wore away, she realized he had barely tapped into the pressure she knew this showerhead could unleash.

"Look there, on your breast."

She fluttered her lashes. Droplets dribbled around her flesh, a tiny stream trickling off her erect nipple.

"God, I want to lick you," he admitted. "I want to drink right from that spot."

"Do it," she commanded.

"No," he answered. "Not yet. But I will, sweetheart. I will. Turn your face to the water."

She did as he asked. Whatever makeup had been left on her face was now completely washed away. The droplets played on her lashes, splashed down her cheeks, danced down her neck and breasts and belly. The muscles in her shoulders slowly unwound, relaxing so much that holding them aloft caused a cramp in her hands. She let her hands drop to her sides.

"Wash yourself, Rory. Wash all the lotion away, so I can put it all back on when you're through."

Again, she did as he requested, marveling in the difference between massaging herself with the lotion while dry, and then now while wet. The silky, vanilla-scented emollient became slick as oil. Instead of disappearing into her skin, it bubbled up and coated her with an extra layer of sensation. And while she washed the lotion away, she coaxed the flesh beneath to new heights of sensitivity.

She washed her breasts clean, barely touching her nipples, afraid the stabs of sweet pleasure might cause her to orgasm too soon. She washed her belly, her thighs. She turned, her back to the water and allowed the milky water to drip off her backside.

"All done," she whispered, her eyes fluttering against the hypnotic state caused by the lotion, the candlelight, the steam.

"Not quite."

Firelight flickered over the hard, masculine planes of his face, but his eyes reflected nothing but passion. His smile reassured her, beguiled her. He quoted from the *Sexcapade,* which he'd taken the time to memorize. How could she not finish what she'd started? How could she deny the most forbidden part of the fantasy? Alec made this right. Alec made this exciting and sensual and liberating.

She wanted this. She wanted him.

She lay down in the tub, as if preparing for a bubble bath. He flipped the metal switch and turned the faucets to full power. A hot stream of water drove out of the main spigot, awaiting her pounding flesh.

As he instructed, she raised her feet over the rim of the tub. The lotion left a slippery residue at the bottom of the basin, easing her way to sliding her bottom closer to the rushing water.

"Do you know this is how most girls first masturbate?" he asked.

She shook her head. She didn't want to talk now. She didn't know what she could possibly say. How could she do this? With him watching? The one thing she'd always wanted but never had the fortitude to try.

"Do it, Rory. Take your pleasure. Make it yours. Let me see the release on your face. Your sweet, beautiful—"

Before he could finish his compliment, she pressed her buttocks forward. The water slammed against her vulva, sought and found her clit in seconds. A roaring rush echoed in her ears. The water, her panting, his urging words. Pressure and passion built to a painful crescendo. No. She couldn't do this. She couldn't. She pushed back, but Alec stopped her, his hands on her knees.

"Do it, Rory. This is so amazing. You're so amazing."

She swallowed deeply and closed her eyes, allowing herself a split second to imagine she was alone. She shifted no more than a quarter inch, and the madness began anew. Pounding. Rushing. Charging through her, hot and clear. Hard, yet ultimately wet and soft. She lost her breath. She groaned. Moaned. Maybe even shouted. She couldn't hear anything. She could only feel the waves of intensity clutching to hold her body together while her soul tore apart into a million fiery pieces.

At last, she could stand no more. She pushed away, then curled onto her side. She was barely aware of the water stopping its rush. Of a towel floating and fluttering over her. Of Alec's unintelligible words teasing her ears.

Only after he'd lifted her out of the tub and carried her to the bed did she regain some semblance of her senses.

"I can't believe I let you watch me," she said, sighing. Her muscles quaked as if she'd just run a marathon. And won. She turned her damp face into the pillow to hide her smile.

"I can't believe you did, either. I thought you'd change your mind."

That caught her attention. She turned, watching him undress while she asked, "Why? Didn't think I was brazen enough?"

He tore his wet T-shirt over his head, then tugged off his jeans and boxers. She willed her eyes not to widen at the sight of him. Glistening, damp, hard. While she succeeded in stopping her eyes from betraying her reaction, she failed with her mouth. She was aware that she'd tugged her bottom lip into her teeth only after a dart of pain shot to her brain.

"I wasn't sure," he answered. "Most women act brazen because they don't care what other people think of them. You behaved with brazenness because you care about what you think of yourself."

"I don't want to be naive forever."

"Do you feel naive?"

"Not anymore," she said, aware that an uncomfortable laugh punctuated her statement.

"Do you feel different?"

"I'm...scandalized."

He chuckled, grabbed the towel and began to pat her dry. "Is that good or bad?"

"I haven't decided."

"Good, because the night isn't over. According to the *Sexcapade*, we're down to the last step." He quoted from the stolen page, "*Chances are, he'll carry you to the bed soon after and make himself wet and wild. In fact, that's the final stroke—drowning in the waves of passion you create between the sheets.* Are you ready, Rory?''

She grinned. She'd never been more ready in her entire life.

ALEC STOPPED DABBING her skin with the towel long enough to reach above the bed and adjust the blinds so that the moonlight streaked across her skin like shimmering pearl bands. She'd turned onto her belly, snuggling a fluffy pillow beneath her, offering him an unhampered, delicious view of her delicate feet, curved calves, slim thighs, round backside, arched back. From the side, he spied the pale roundness of her breasts. Her hair, damp and disheveled, spiked and curled around her face, still flushed from the heat of the water and the fullness of her release.

She was beautiful. Captivating. No longer innocent, but totally untried.

Once certain she was dry enough that the air conditioner wouldn't chill damp skin, he discarded the towel and grabbed the lotion he'd brought from the bathroom. The second part of the *Sexcapade* directed him to reapply the emollient to her skin, to massage her back to arousal. Who was he to argue?

He squeezed a dollop, warmed it between his palms, then climbed onto the bed and began his rubdown on her shoulders.

"Must be a lot of pressure for you," she said softly, "being a woman's first lover."

"I wouldn't know. I've never made love to a virgin before."

This apparently shocked her. She pushed herself up onto her elbows, displacing his hands.

"Really?"

He laughed, pushed her back down and continued smoothing the lotion down her spine, fanning his fingers across her back. "Why is that so unbelievable?"

She shrugged. "Law of averages."

"Most of my lovers were older than me. Even when I was younger."

That confession injected a tightness into her muscles, but she hardly hesitated before she said, "Tell me about your sexual past. I mean, we're supposed to do that, right? Exchange information about our sexual histories."

Her tone turned serious, formal, more than a little like the voice he heard from his colleagues rather than his lovers.

"How responsible of you," he said, not without an edge of sarcasm. He couldn't argue that discussing his sexual past was the responsible thing to do, but he didn't like dredging up his sordid history. Not with Rory, since she couldn't match any of his tales with her own.

"You're the only lover that matters right now," he answered.

"Very smooth, Dr. Manning. You do know your way around diplomacy."

"Only in the bedroom," he said.

"Only place that counts," she concluded. "But really, I'm not being nosy. Okay, yes, I am. But I'm just fascinated by a life so unlike my own. Your vast experience is something of a turn-on."

"Ooh," he murmured, impressed. "You know your way around diplomatic pillow talk yourself." But since she had asked in such a seductive way, he answered. "You already know about Anne."

"Yes, she was your last lover. But not your first. Tell me about all the other lovers in between."

"You want details?" he asked, not in the least willing to share any of that with Rory, no matter how badly she thought she wanted to know.

"No," she answered reluctantly. "Just a general overview, I suppose."

He groaned, but complied. "I've made love to a lot of women, most older than me or at least equally sexually experienced. I've always used a condom and I've been tested for AIDS and other STDs on a regular basis. I'm clean."

She glanced over her shoulder again and licked her lips, which were curved in a tiny smile. "Glad to hear it. But I don't know, all those sexually experienced women...maybe I should be intimidated. Maybe I won't measure up."

A light danced in her blue eyes—the fire of naughtiness, irreverence. She wasn't really intimidated. And she had no reason to be. She offered him something none of the other women ever had—and it had nothing to do with her virginity and everything to do with who Rory was in her soul. A woman honest about her sexual curiosity, unbound by expectations of the past. A woman who would give without wanting in return anything beyond his ability to bestow. A woman who had a clear goal of what she wanted from her life—and she didn't need him to get it. She wasn't a grad student falling into bed with him because her boyfriend needed a good dose of jealousy. She wasn't an older woman seeking out his more youthful prowess to prove she was still desirable, still vital. She wasn't a scorned wife seeking revenge on a cold husband. No, Rory wanted Alec because she trusted him to make love to her, then let her walk away when the time came.

He spread his hands over her buttocks, kneading the

fleshy mounds, parting her so the cool air would seep between her thighs. "You have no reason to be intimidated. You're unlike any other woman I've made love to, Rory. It's sort of a first time for me, too."

She obviously liked the sound of that, cooing as she lifted her backside while he slathered more lotion in his hands, then explored her legs completely. He turned her over and worked his way back up her body, allowing the tips of his fingers to dip into the damp, warm curls. Sweet pink folds of flesh teased him, but he resisted. No matter how hard his cock strained to delve inside her. No matter how much his soul desired a taste of this delicious, intriguing woman.

In due time.

The slim camber of her belly enthralled him. The roundness of her breasts held him captive. Her nipples pebbled beneath his touch and he watched her squeeze her thighs together, hold her breath. He couldn't hold back any longer. He had to taste her. All of her.

The minute he covered her breasts with his mouth, her hands forked into his hair. He flicked her nipple with his tongue, his teeth. Blood raged in his ears louder and louder with her every coo, her every gasp. She arched her back, offering more. And he took.

Shifting so that he lay between her legs, he blazed a path down her belly. The scent of her arousal intensified with each kiss.

He looked up. She watched him, her eyes wide, her mouth parted, her breasts rising and falling with her quick pants.

"Oh, Alec," she said on a disbelieving sigh.

"There's no sheet to block me this time," he warned.

"I'll come again," she declared.

He arched a brow. "Possibly."

"I can't!"

He grinned. She could, but she didn't want to. He didn't blame her. He wanted to be inside her when she came again, too. He wanted to feel her tight heat around him. He wanted his mouth on hers when she cried out his name.

"Okay. I'll just take you to the edge, then. Let me?"

She nodded and fell back into the pillows. He guided her legs further apart, raised her knees. With an exploratory flick, he tasted her. Clean and moist and sweet. With his fingers, he drew the outer flesh away, found her clit with his mouth and suckled until she nearly jumped out of her skin.

He grabbed the condom from the bed table where he'd left it, put in on quickly, then tore back the covers and tossed the damp towels to the floor.

She grabbed his shoulders and pulled him back over her, then splayed her hands on his cheeks and pressed him down for a long, luscious, hungry kiss. He was lost in the feel of her mouth, absorbed by the breadth of her desire, her need. She reached down, touched him, stroked him with bold passion.

"I want to be inside you," he whispered, his mouth nuzzling her neck.

"Be inside me," she commanded.

He parted her with his fingers, placed the tip of his sex within her. She was wet, slick with want. But still tight. He entered her slowly, teasingly, stretching her, waiting until he could no longer wait to break past any last physical resistance.

She bent her knees, lifted her bottom, clearing the path with instinctual invitation. She grabbed his hips, pulled him deeper, crying out as his body melded completely into hers. He held still for a long minute, bewitched by the sensations of her muscles constricting around him, stroking him, squeezing him until the moonlight and the darkness blurred into a pewter haze. He wanted this. He wanted her. He wanted her release as he'd never wanted anything before.

He rocked inside her slowly, but she demanded more. His thrusts fired her. She grabbed and clutched and moaned with complete abandon. He matched her rhythm, stroked and pumped until nothing existed but his body inside hers, his pleasure inside hers.

He came with her name on his lips. Only after lying in her sweet embrace for a few minutes did he realize that he had no idea what she'd said, if anything, when climax rocked her. Why that mattered, he wasn't sure. But now she didn't have to say anything. Her heartbeat spoke volumes, her tight embrace told him even more. Alec simply wondered if what her body confessed was what he wanted to hear.

12

SOMEWHERE IN THE DISTANCE, Rory heard chirping. She peeked one eye open and noticing the sunlight, guessed some bird decided her alarm clock wouldn't do the trick, so he'd trill extra loud. She hated birds. Okay, she didn't really, but right this minute, she hated anything that forced her to wake up from a night filled with luscious dreams and even more tantalizing realities.

With a yawn, she checked the clock. Eight-thirty. She sighed and closed her eyes, relieved. Divine Events had Saturday hours, but the shop didn't open until half past ten. While she didn't have a lot of time to spare, she wouldn't have to bolt immediately out of bed, either. She felt too delicious to abandon the warm sheets and comforter anytime soon. Turning onto her other shoulder, she groaned, sore and achy from head to toe. But sweetly so. Her muscles protested, but like the hot tightness she experienced after a vigorous workout, the pain was nothing to regret, but something to be proud of. She'd made love with Alec. The sensations washed over her again, easing the dull pain in her neck, back and especially between her thighs. If she never made love again, she'd be satisfied.

After replaying that thought, she snorted. *Yeah, right.* Like she'd never make love again. Ha! Twenty-five years of self-denial had been more than enough. Sex was good. Very good. She intended to do it again. Soon. Hopefully, with Alec, but after reminding herself of her bold confidence last night, she knew she could find someone else if she needed to. If she wanted to.

Which, for now, she most certainly didn't.

All grown up and ready to take on the world.

She blinked against the intruding daylight, catching a glimpse of her rumpled bed in the mirror across the room. Who was she kidding? She'd been all grown up and ready to take on the world for years. Now, she'd just had sex. Great sex, but she couldn't let one or two glorious orgasms turn her into someone she wasn't—or, at least, someone she couldn't allow herself to become.

The kind of woman who became obsessed with a man. The kind who fell in love too easily. Though how hard would it be for even the most jaded woman to fall head over heels for Alec Manning? He was handsome, caring, inventive, intelligent, funny. He loved adventure, flaunted his disregard for rules, even as he tried to follow them. And though she had no one to compare him to, she believed with one-hundred-percent certainty that he knew his way around a woman's body better than most. Never once had he allowed her to feel unsure, frightened or inhibited. He drew out the best of what she'd kept hidden in herself for far too long.

Before she could think about where he was or if he was up for another round before she went to work, Alec appeared in the doorway, a cup of coffee in one hand, her cell phone in the other.

"It stopped ringing, but now it's blinking."

Ah, the chirping. Rory was tempted to roll over and ignore the phone, but mindful she was now employed and the call might be from Cecily or one of the other two Divine cousins, she accepted the cell phone and checked the LCD screen.

Her friend, Lisa, had called. The voice-mail icon blinked.

"That's odd," she said, sitting up, allowing the sheet to fall naturally, glancing away from the phone soon enough to catch Alec's eyes darken with desire.

Alec took a long sip from his mug of coffee. Leaning with one hip on the foot board, he seemed completely comfortable in his skin, all of it showing except for the important parts, covered with loose cotton boxers.

"How do you take your coffee?" he asked.

"I don't. The coffee and the coffeemaker were gifts from my great-aunt, who is addicted to the stuff. Usually, a diet soda is my morning pick-me-up."

"I saw some diet Dr. Pepper in your fridge."

"My libation of choice."

"I'll get you one. In a glass with ice or just in the can?"

Rory smiled. She'd learned last night that Alec was an incredible pamperer. He'd catered to her every need, anticipated and fulfilled each of her desires before she'd had to ask. She'd thought he'd just been a thorough lover—but, apparently, he was just a thoughtful guy.

Man, oh, man, but she could sure fall hard for a guy like him.

She waved her hand. "Don't worry about me. I'll grab a can on the way out the door."

"You've got to work today?"

She watched the way his lips curled as he sipped his coffee, the way a lock of his dark hair fell across his forehead, the particular angle at which his hip cocked as he leaned against the bed.

She groaned, suddenly very disappointed that she had to be at work in two hours. "Saturdays are a big day for party planners. I have tomorrow off, and Monday. What about you?''

"Saturdays are a big night in my business, too.''

"I thought you were unemployed. And caught up on your project.''

"I am, but I've taken a job as part of my research study.''

Something in his eyes, maybe the furtive way he glanced aside, prickled her skin. He didn't want to talk about this. *Hmm.* Why?

"Really? Where at?''

"I'd rather not say.''

"Why not?''

He took a long draft of coffee. "I'm not sure.''

"But you'll try to figure it out?''

"If you want me to,'' he answered, his voice husky.

Her belly fluttered. "Will you do anything I want you to?''

"Looks that way,'' he answered, sliding toward her with dark desire in his eyes, in his smile. Yet he stopped the minute her cell phone rang again.

She checked the LCD. Lisa again. That really was odd. Her friend was never this persistent. Not unless something was wrong.

"Do you mind?''

Alec's grin was lopsided. "Yes, but take it anyway. Must be important.''

Worried, Rory pushed the talk button and said hello. Lisa was an old friend from high school, a transfer student she'd met her junior year, just after Micki had run away. Rory had been in desperate need of a friend then, particularly one who hadn't known her sister. She'd needed someone who wouldn't tell her how much trouble the teen had been, or how Micki had a mind of her own and no one or nothing could have stopped her from running away once she had made her decision. Instead Lisa had listened, asked a few questions, then kept Rory's mind off her sadness while they tested the waters of high-school life. They'd turned sixteen together in style, throwing a double birthday party at the local VFW hall, courtesy of Lisa's parents and Rory's grandmother. Their birthdays had actually been a month apart, but both in the summer. So even though Micki had run away, Lisa made sure Rory never celebrated a birthday alone.

After Lisa went to college and excelled in the field of accounting, they didn't hang out so much, but they talked every few weeks if only for a minute, exchanged e-mails regularly, and met for lunch whenever they could. They hadn't seen each other in person in probably six months, making this phone call on a Saturday morning jack up Rory's alert mechanisms.

"Rory? You okay?"

"Yeah, Lisa, I'm fine. What's up?"

"That's what I'm calling to ask you. What happened last night?"

Rory swallowed, twisting and shifting pillows so Alec might not notice the blush blooming over her body. She and Lisa had been close, but they hadn't spoken since last week, before Rory had met Alec. Before she had stolen the *Sexcapade*. Long before she'd lost her virginity in the most incredibly delicious way. How did Lisa know about last night?

Rory racked her brain. Had she forgotten a date to meet Lisa last night? "What are you talking about?"

"I'm talking about you blowing me off."

"Did we have plans?"

"No, but do you have to have plans with someone to say hello when you see them at a club?"

Rory scooted to the edge of the bed, her back to Alec, and slipped her legs over the side. "What are you talking about? If you were at Cody's last night, Lisa, I didn't see you. I would have talked to you. But I was there with my boss, working out a deal with the band. Maybe I was so caught up—"

"Cody's? What are *you* talking about? I wasn't at Cody's last night. I don't even know where that is. I was at Martini Joe's."

Now she was really confused.

"Martini Joe's? That's in Wrigleyville. I was on the south side. Cody's didn't even have beer on draft, much less drinks in real glasses. I didn't blow you off, Lisa. I wasn't there."

"No way," her friend insisted, and Rory knew the sound of her friend's certainty well enough to know Lisa hadn't been mistaken. "It was you, Rory. I mean, your hair looked different, darker, and I thought maybe you'd lost a little too much weight since I saw you last..."

Rory felt the phone fall from her hand, felt her heart smash against her chest with the force of a sledgehammer. In an instant, Alec had crossed the room, but he didn't say anything, do anything. He was simply there, ready to help, concern clear in his hazel eyes.

She scrambled to grab the phone before Lisa disconnected.

"Lisa, I'm sorry." She pushed her hair away from her face, aware that she must look like a complete wreck. "Where are you?"

"I was at Martini Joe's."

"No, I mean, where are you now? Can you come over?" *Shit*. She had to be at work in two hours! She didn't have time to go out to Lisa's apartment near Wicker Park.

"I'm at home. Where's your place again?"

Rory gave her directions, and Lisa promised she could make it there in forty minutes, if traffic cooperated. "Rory, what's wrong?"

"Micki," Rory said, her throat dry, her eyes moist. "You didn't see *me* last night. You saw Micki."

FORTY-FIVE MINUTES LATER, Rory verified her suspicion. Alec had left the apartment. She'd hardly noticed what he was up to as she'd showered, dressed and applied her makeup. She'd operated on sensory and emotional overload, forcing herself to focus on getting ready for work and nothing else. She couldn't worry about Alec right now. One thing at a time. And now that Lisa had arrived, she had to figure out her next move. And there was nothing to worry about with Alec anyway. There had been no promises between them, no plans.

Still, she hated to think, even for an instant, that their relationship, such that it was, was now over. He'd helped her bring the *Sexcapade* to life with complete accuracy. Would that be all?

"I go to Martini Joe's every Friday night," Lisa added from her perch on the couch. She'd poured herself a cup of coffee from the pot Alec had brewed and now watched Rory pace with patience in her eyes. "What are the chances of your wayward sister showing up this one time?"

"Probably a million to one. But it only takes one, right?"

Lisa nodded.

"You've never seen her there before?"

Lisa smirked and shook her head. "I think I would have noticed, Rory. She looks exactly like you."

"Exactly?"

"Okay, not exactly. Her hair is longer, darker. Like she uses a blue wash or something. And she's really thin. I mean, not like you're fat or anything, but she looked…"

"Malnourished?"

This time, Lisa's nod was sad.

"At least she's alive." Rory paused, then continued stalking from one side of the room to the other, wondering what to do next. She could call Detective Walters and ask her advice, but she didn't want to bother the police-woman until she had something more solid. She was tempted to call Cecily, explain the situation and ask for some time off, but she knew that no matter how much her new boss liked her, she had a business to run. Rory would be unemployed in no time if she followed that route. No, she had to stop, calm down, think logically.

"What are you doing tonight?" she asked.

Lisa shrugged. "No plans. With Rico teaching that law school class, I limit my socializing to Friday nights with the girls. You want to go by Martini Joe's?"

"Do you mind?"

Lisa pursed her lips with worry first, then grinned in the way only friends with limitless patience and loyalty could. "Of course not. But, Rory, just because she was there last night doesn't mean she'll be there again."

"No, but someone who knows her might be. Did you get a good look at who she was with?"

Lisa shivered, shaking her hands as if they'd gone numb. "I didn't need a good look. I might have chased 'you' down if Rico or any of the guys had been with me. But it was just me and some friends from the office and the crowd she disappeared into wasn't a group of per-fume testers from Marshall Field's, if you know what I mean. Martini Joe's is a nice place, Rory, but this group in the parking lot looked rough.''

Rory couldn't let that deter her. She considered asking Alec to join them, but she knew he had to work. She hated the empty feeling suddenly overpowering her. The feeling that keeping something like this from him was wrong. Yet she lacked the confidence in their relationship—if she could call it that—to burden him with something so personal.

Maybe she'd mention her plans, see if he seemed interested. But, either way, she was going tonight to check things out. She didn't believe in coincidences. Though Lisa was engaged to her high-school sweetheart, who taught law classes in addition to working at a high-pressure firm, Lisa socialized regularly. She went to clubs all the time, but until last night she had never seen anyone fitting Micki's description. Rory couldn't let this chance to find her twin pass, not if there was a remote possibility that someone in tonight's crowd might know where to find her sister.

And she would check with Cecily once she got to the office. More than likely, her boss knew someone in management at Martini Joe's. The bouncers. The bartenders. The guy who booked the bands. An inside connection wouldn't be unwelcome right now.

''Be home by eight o'clock,'' Rory instructed. ''I'll come out to your place. Maybe this is a long shot, but I've got to do this. For Micki.'' She let out a shaky breath. ''And for me.''

ALEC CURSED. Watching Rory dance down the steps toward her Jeep ground into his chest like a ten-inch drill bit. He hated that he had to work. He hated that he couldn't go with her to Martini Joe's. But, mostly, he hated that after work she'd doll herself up and hit the club scene, where some guy with more brains than Alec had might snap her right up. Some guy who didn't need to waste time figuring out how wise it would be to leap into more fantasies with Rory.

To top it all off, Martini Joe's was less than half a block from Dixie Landings. With his string of luck, she and her friends would pop by to check out the action— and he hadn't yet told Rory about his job. The thought of her dropping by and catching him behind the bar as Xander Mann disgusted him. Xander was the man he used to be. Suave, hip, cool. Too slick for his own good. Too aloof for the good of the women around him.

The man he'd been last night—the man Rory coaxed to the surface—now that was someone he'd never met before. Someone he liked. Someone Rory had drawn out from a place inside him he hadn't known existed. Yes, he'd always known he was a skilled lover, but not a self-less one. Holding back, ensuring Rory experienced all the pleasure she could handle before taking any of his own— that was entirely new. Invigorating. Addictive. The min-ute her friend had left, she'd flitted down to his apartment to fill him in with all the exuberance, excitement and naiveté that had brought their lovemaking last night to new and uncharted levels.

He worried for her, but knew Martini Joe's to be a nice place. The crowd outside could be unpredictable, but that was true for any club in the city. He had to trust Rory's ability to take care of herself, no matter how the noble sentiment irked him.

After one night, Rory felt too much like his possession, like his creation, even if he had no basis for this view. She'd blossomed before his eyes last night, and though he'd played a strong part in her transformation from ingenue to seductress, he knew she'd willed her own change, made her own destiny. God, a man like him should consider himself lucky to have had her for one night.

So how come he wanted so much more?

The phone rang at noon, just after he'd dressed and made a list of some errands he needed to run before he went to sleep that afternoon.

"Hey." Rory's voice sounded muted, as if she was in a tunnel. But still, the timbre of her voice danced over his skin, prickling his arms with gooseflesh, arousing his sex with a rush of blood.

"Hey, yourself," he answered. "Aren't you working?"

"Livia sent me to the warehouse to sort through some decorations she needs for a dinner party tonight. I'm all alone in this big, cavernous warehouse."

He shut the door. Tossed his keys on the credenza.

"Is that an invitation to join you?"

She laughed, the vibrations husky, hot. "Some of the boxes are very heavy. I told Livia I couldn't lift them into my car alone, but she can't spare anyone else right now. I told her maybe I could find a friend. She promised to be eternally grateful."

He glanced at his watch. "How much time do you have before you have to deliver your wares?"

"Livia told me to take my time, grab some lunch. Just so long as I deliver the stuff to the client's condo by four o'clock, she said I could arrange my afternoon however I wanted."

His chest tightened with possibilities. When she'd left this morning, he'd resigned himself to the fact that he and Rory wouldn't see each other again until tomorrow, but now...

"Must be nice, working for such generous employers," he said.

"Well, it's not so nice right now in this hot, stuffy warehouse. But it could be. If you're not too busy."

Possibilities danced in Alec's mind. What exactly did party planners keep in their warehouses anyway?

"Just give me directions. I'll be there in a flash."

RORY UNTUCKED AND UNBUTTONED her blouse, then shifted her skirt so her thighs could catch the maximum breeze. Not that much air circulated in this industrial hot box where Divine Events stored their decorations, props, table settings and costumes. But the place was, surprisingly, climate controlled. Cost-conscious Gia, however, insisted they use the air-conditioning system only to control humidity. If the papier-mâché drooped a little, they would replace it. The temperature, somewhere around seventy-eight, was totally safe for the gowns, tuxedos, centerpieces and garlands carefully stored and cataloged in neat, fairly dust-free rows. China in every conceivable pattern style—casual, classy, nondescript—was stacked between bubble wrap. Glassware and silverware, wrapped in tissue or stored in boxes, were lined row upon row upon row. Rory found vases and candleholders in every imaginable color, along with an impressive collection of silk flowers and tulle. Livia's more expensive designs, elaborate costumes and haute couture gowns, were crated in individually cooled trunks along the inner wall, with the contents carefully listed on a manifest posted on the side. Rory explored freely, listening in the cavernous quiet for the buzzer that would announce Alec's arrival.

Her discoveries fired her imagination more than even the *Sexcapades* book, which had fallen victim to at least one curious customer during Rory's brief hour and a half at the reception desk this morning. She'd forced herself to find a reason to linger in the break room long enough to allow the woman—a tough-looking redhead—sufficient time to swipe a page if she wanted to. When she'd heard the telltale rip, Rory squelched a triumphant "yes!" If the woman's fantasy brought her half the pleasure Rory's had, she'd be one happy woman, indeed.

Of course, the redhead wouldn't have Alec. He was her private fantasy man, her temporary lover whose prowess would likely haunt her for a lifetime. On her drive to work, she'd worried that no other man would ever live up to him, in her mind, her heart or her body. She couldn't shake that concern all morning, but finally decided that if her standards remained high, that wouldn't be a bad thing. She deserved the best. If for no other reason than because she'd waited so long.

But the minute she'd alleviated one concern, another popped into her mind and had haunted her since. What if what she felt toward Alec *wasn't* temporary? What if the rare and powerful connection they'd established in just two days didn't bend to the will of their chosen lifestyles, free and independent and relationship-free?

She cared about Alec, she couldn't deny that truth. And everything about the way he treated her convinced her that he cared in return. From what she knew about his romantic past, she might well be the first lover who'd evoked that emotion in him. Would he be able to let her go when the time came? Would she?

The buzzer vibrated through Rory's veins. She dashed to the door, peered through the glass and, catching a glimpse of Alec's casual smile, sighed and unlocked the door.

"Didn't take you long," she commented, pointing him

toward the collection of boxes she'd managed to stack nearby.

"I had the right incentive to hurry." He stepped into the darkness, his eyes squinting.

She shut the door behind him, leaning with the knob pressed into her back, her imagination brimming with sexual scenarios they could make real in the private cavern of the warehouse. They were alone. She was here with permission. She glanced at her watch. Livia didn't need her at the client's condo for at least two and a half more hours.

"Seems to me that nearly every time I need you, I have boxes that need transporting," she said, her tone teasing.

He laughed and grabbed the first of a stack of boxes she'd piled near the door. "That did cross my mind. Reach into my pocket."

The request was matter-of-fact, yet Rory's mind surged with possibilities. She couldn't control how she felt about Alec any more than she could dictate how his emotions ran with regard to her. But she could ensure that the time they spent together brimmed with sensuous games and adventures. She'd invited Alec here on a whim, invigorated by the chance to catch this highly experienced man unaware. But as she slipped her fingers inside his jeans and extracted a foil-covered condom, she wondered if she'd ever surprise him.

"Is this an invitation?"

He shrugged. "If I'm going to work, I'm going to require payment."

13

"TALK ABOUT PRESUMPTUOUS," Rory quipped, palming the condom.

Alec had meant to tease her, challenge her—but he hadn't planned on losing his calling card in the process. Oh, well. He'd get it back soon enough if he played his cards right. From the spark in her crystal-blue eyes, he knew Rory had expected nothing less from him than something completely unexpected.

"Presumptuous? Guilty as charged." He held out his wrists in mock surrender. "Or you could just consider me hopeful."

She fisted her hands on her hips, her eyebrows arched with disbelief. "Hopeful? Or horny?"

"Let's not forget who enticed whom to this hot, humid warehouse, Rory. Besides, just because I ask for payment, doesn't mean you have to give it to me."

Her ponytail flapped as she shook her head. "Yeah, right. Has anyone ever told you no?"

Alec frowned. For a long while, he'd manipulated and charmed and persuaded until he got just about everything he ever wanted. But when the walls of his career came crashing down, reality pummeled him with enough negative responses to last him a lifetime. Luckily, with Rory, he'd retrieved some of his old confidence.

"You're not just anyone, Rory."

The confession caught her attention, and she stared at

him long and hard, as if trying to gauge his honesty. It wasn't a line. He didn't know why or how, but in the span of two days, Rory Carmichael had become very important to him. Not just as a lover, but as a friend.

He wished he could make her promises, offer assurances or, at the very least, take a few moments with her to dream about some sort of future. But how hollow would such a declaration sound after so short a time?

"You keep telling me that," she said, apparently unconvinced.

"Why do you have so much trouble believing me? You'd think that with my vast experience with women, I'd know when one came into my life who was special."

She eyed him skeptically, and he did all he could to keep any visage of his shock from showing on his face. He hadn't said anything that didn't come from the heart, but he hadn't meant to sound so damned *certain* about a topic that bordered on serious. He couldn't make promises to Rory—couldn't even hint at the possibility of a promise—not when he had no idea what his future held.

"You didn't mean to say all that, did you?" she asked.

He closed his eyes and shook his head. "Not quite so emphatically."

She grinned. "I don't mind."

"Why should you?" He matched her confident smile with one of his own. At least when it came to cockiness, he had her outgunned.

She lifted a small flat box from the top of the pile and slid it atop the others he still held.

"Well, keep in mind that if you fall hopelessly in love with me, you'll put a serious crimp in my plans."

He swallowed a chuckle, partly because he was afraid of dropping the boxes and partly because the last thing he wanted to do was insult Rory. Maybe she had meant everything she'd said about wanting to keep their affair brief and discreet. Maybe she wasn't entertaining a secret desire for something more from him than he had a right to give.

But maybe he was.

"I'll try to remember that," he assured her. "Now that we've established the ground rules once again, what's say we get this little moving project completed and progress to the compensation portion of the afternoon?"

Her laugh was light and tinkling, and only after Alec delivered the first stack of boxes to the back of Rory's Jeep did he realize how Xander-like the comment was. In fact, stuffing the condom into his pocket and then inviting her to find it had been classic Xander. Provocative, slick and charmingly demanding. Funny how, at the time, the strategy had seemed playful and adventurous—more like Rory than his former, troublemaking self.

Rory didn't know the guy he used to be and he wanted to keep it that way. He'd been vigilant in restraining himself, allowing only his sexual knowledge amassed in his former liaisons to come to light in Rory's presence. Not the selfish attitude. Not the carelessness. Not the conscious and willing absence of anything remotely resembling emotion.

What he'd done with and to Rory last night felt totally new. Fresh. His body still hummed with the sensations, his libido remained primed, ready for a repeat performance whenever and wherever Rory wanted him. When was the last time the aftereffects of an orgasm had lasted more than ten minutes, much less ten hours?

With the hand truck and Rory's help, he had her car loaded and locked in half an hour. Sweat dripped down his back and when he combed a hand through his hair, salty perspiration dampened the ends of his fingers. He turned back toward the roll-up warehouse door to see Rory standing just inside, in the shadows, tempting him with an iced cold sports drink.

He joined her in the shade, accepted her gift, popped the top and drained half of the neon-yellow liquid.

"Thanks," he said, swiping his hand across his mouth.

"Least I could do," she said with a purr.

She retreated in the shadows to the tiny office tucked in the corner of the warehouse. The window-mounted air conditioner, set at a more comfortable seventy-four degrees, hummed steadily. He whipped off his shirt and stood in front of the vents, allowing the cold stream of air to dry and refresh his skin.

"If you're trying to be sexy, it's working," she commented, still standing in the doorway, her arms crossed over her chest.

"I wasn't trying, but thanks."

"A guy like you probably doesn't have to try. Sexiness comes naturally. Must be nice, to be able to manipulate women so easily."

He shook out his shirt, then laid it over the back of a worn and cracked leather chair. "I haven't manipulated you, Rory, and you know it."

"I didn't say you had. I walked into this…affair…with my eyes wide-open. But I'm not the norm for you, am I?"

"The norm? Hardly."

"So tell me." She cocked her hip against the door-jamb, her arms still shielding her, her gaze intense. "Tell me about your norm. What kind of women used to catch your eye? I don't want details, mind you. Just a general overview. Not the women who got *you* in trouble, but vice versa."

He turned toward the air conditioner again, lifting his

elbows so the breeze cooled the heat beneath his arms. "Getting turned on by my past again, Rory?"

She shook her head. "Not this time. At least, not yet. I'm just genuinely curious about how you've changed. About why you thought you needed to. The loss of the job notwithstanding."

She slipped into the space just behind him and smoothed her hands over his bare back, digging her fingers into the muscular crevices and massaging some of the tension from his tendons.

"I tangled with nearly every kind of woman, Rory. So long as she was looking for trouble, I was her man."

"I was looking for trouble, too. You told me so yourself." She dotted his lower shoulder blade with a feathery kiss. "But now you say I'm different. Why?"

Alec allowed his chin to fall to his chest. He closed his eyes. Thought. Carefully. Rory wasn't that interested in his past, only about how it affected her. What he said next could influence more than just whether or not he got to use that condom she'd confiscated from him. It could determine whether or not she ever spoke to him again.

"You weren't looking for trouble so much as you were looking to experience something new," he answered. "I probably couldn't admit this before today, but I think that's what I wanted, too. Something new."

She smoothed her warm palm down his back, igniting a fire that could potentially sap his ability to think, much less speak.

"Can I ask you about Anne again?"

Despite the continuous friction of her flesh on his, ice seemed to instantly shoot up his spine. "I told you everything there is to tell," he said.

"You didn't tell, you summarized. You were even helpful enough to connect all the right psychological and sociological theories to justify your behavior.'' She ticked his points on her fingers. ''No mother in the house, a distant father, three boys left to their own devices. Too much freedom, too much opportunity to do all the wrong things. But none of that pop psychology answers why going from woman to woman with no emotional connection has satisfied you for all this time.''

Alec's stomach hardened as if she injected him with quick-drying cement rather than food for thought. He didn't like hearing his own words thrown back at him any more than he enjoyed hearing the same question he'd posed to himself a million times. A question for which he could find no solution. At least, not a solution he wanted to accept.

''Men aren't like women, Rory. We don't need emotional connections.''

''That's bull. You tell yourselves that. And, maybe, most of the time it's true. But you haven't told me about anyone, not one woman in all the ones you've made love to, who touched your heart. The tiniest bit. Not one.''

''Do you think I'm incapable of caring, is that it?''

''I know you can care, Alec. Look how you are with me.''

He couldn't deny the truth. ''You're easy to care about.''

She glanced up, surprised. ''I don't want to make you say that.''

''Why not?'' He grabbed her arms roughly, hoping this would end the conversation once and for all. ''It's not a crime to want to feel special, Rory. Especially since you know my history. It's not a breach of our agreement for us to care about each other. If it is, then I've already flunked that part, too.''

She turned away, but he knew he'd not only accurately

assessed her thoughts, he'd at least partially alleviated her fears. He could read so much into the subtle changes in her inflections, in the way her eyes widened, narrowed or blinked. When had this ever happened to him? When had he ever cared enough to watch a woman so closely, to take the time from his own self-interests to truly learn about someone else?

"That's what all of this has been about, hasn't it? You know you're special to me, but you can't really accept the truth until you know why. Rory, sometimes there is no why."

She slipped back into his arms, and Alec didn't know when he'd experienced such a contradictory mixture of excitement and underlying calm.

"I'm sorry. I didn't mean to push so hard."

He kissed her temple, inhaling the sweet scent of her shampoo. "I don't mind. Maybe confession really is good for my soul." He pushed all seriousness from his tone. "But now that we've dismissed all our residual guilt, do we have time to negotiate payment for all my hard work?"

Rory glanced at her watch, grinning. Barely two o'clock. She had a couple of hours before Livia needed her. She also had a stolen condom in her pocket and a half-naked, sensually explosive man in her arms. And an honest one, too. One that didn't blame her for the emotions she'd tried so hard to deny. But as long as they granted each other permission to care, how their affair ended—or when—wouldn't keep showing up as a roadblock to the real reason they'd hooked up. Fun and friendship and pleasure—a powerful combination.

Not that she had any intention of ending anything today. From what Rory could tell, they possessed all the makings of a first-class follow-up to their initial night of passion, right here in the warehouse.

With two fingers, she extracted the condom from her pocket, twisting and turning the square and pretending to contemplate the possibilities even though she knew exactly what she wanted, who she wanted and when. Sex. Alec. Now.

She looked up, basking in the desire sparkling in his earth-toned eyes. Her pulse quickened. Moisture slipped between her breasts, spurring a matching dampness at the base of her thighs. When he unconsciously licked his lips, her temperature climbed a notch. The memory of his mouth on her skin, exploring, enjoying, humming his pleasure at her taste, her texture, spawned a heat she knew no air conditioner could cool.

"I have something to show you."

She dashed out of the office and into the main warehouse before she could change her mind. At first, the combination of her need and the vastness of the building unsettled her sense of direction. Where had she seen it? The crate. The manifest. The fantasy. This time in a box rather than on a piece of paper.

Alec approached her from behind, slipping his hands around her, flattening his palms on her midriff, his fingers spanning her belly, his thumbs teasing the undersides of her breasts.

"You don't need them," he whispered, his breath pure heat against her neck, cooled by his lips and tongue.

She closed her eyes, lost herself in the sensations, the possibilities.

"What?"

"The props. You don't need them."

He undid her blouse, her bra, tossed them to the nearest shelf. With quick hands, he divested her of her skirt, leaving her in nothing but her panties and spiky-heeled sandals, the condom clutched in her palm.

With a quick tug, he spun her around, pulled her close, kissed her long and hard. By the time he finished exploring her mouth, she couldn't remember why she'd left the cool office. She couldn't breathe. Couldn't think. Not with the heat of Alec's kiss and the heat in the warehouse merging into a stifling haze. Why had she come out here again?

Oh, yeah. The props.

"How did you know what I was thinking?" she asked.

"Great minds think alike."

"Then why don't you want to try something new?"

His gaze darkened, his jaw tightened. For an instant, Rory thought Alec might stalk away, angry. Instead he cleared his throat and tightened his hold. "Every minute I'm with you feels new, Rory. Isn't that enough?"

14

ALEC BLAZED A HOT PATH of kisses along her neck, across her shoulder, then back again. He lifted her hair and traced down her spine with his tongue. At the precise spot where the clasps of her bra should have been, he suckled until she was certain he'd left a mark.

His question echoed faintly in her mind, nearly drowned out by the thundering of her heart.

Every minute I'm with you feels new, Rory. Isn't that enough?

"Nothing with you will ever be enough, Alec."

He hesitated, the pause injecting her with an icy fear. Had she said that out loud? Had she said more than she meant to? More than he wanted to hear? They'd agreed in the beginning to keep their relationship simple, brief. Nothing exclusive. Nothing long-term. At the time, Rory had wanted that as much as Alec had. Her body had ached for sensual exploration, but her mind had insisted on ensuring her well-deserved independence. Her heart, so inexperienced, couldn't be trusted in the matter. But here in the hazy heat of the warehouse, Rory didn't know if she could keep her truest desires secret any longer. From him…or from herself.

She hadn't known Alec long enough to love him, but in their fleeting encounters, she'd come to love everything about him. His intelligence. His kindness. His irresistible sexiness. The thought of moving on to someone else, allowing another man to touch her this way, un-abashed, unashamed…she couldn't form even the most misty mental picture. She could only see Alec. Only feel Alec. Only want Alec.

Her words had caused him to stop, but the vacillation didn't last. His mouth lowered to the small of her back, his fingers tugged the silk panties down her legs. The material slipped slowly, a satiny friction arousing her skin. All thoughts beyond this moment fled her brain. What she wanted for the long run didn't matter compared with what she could have in the here and now. Perspiration coated her from head to toe, but a thicker moisture pooled between her legs, flowing from deep within, pushed by a gentle throbbing. Only her mouth felt dry, cottony, as if only his kiss could replenish her there.

Yet, when he turned her around, she realized he didn't plan to be anywhere near her mouth.

He knelt on the ground. The floor was hard, unyielding, a dirty slab of concrete scarred with hand-truck tracks and the scuff of work boots. Yet when Rory closed her eyes, she could have been standing in the middle of a deserted beach. Blood roared in her ears like the waves on the shore. Alec's breath fanned her nudity like a balmy ocean breeze.

With Alec, fantasies came so easily. He was right. She didn't need props or *Sexcapade* pages or anything else to trip into the world of sensual ecstasy. His hands smoothed her skin, igniting her senses, inviting her into the twilight world between reality and their private, intimate desires.

He murmured his delight with each curve he explored, rocking her equilibrium. She grasped sideways, finding a shelf to use as a handhold. When she clutched the metal, a picture formed in her mind.

Alec pleasuring her. Again. Alec learning her body. Again. Alec igniting her body while she did little in return.

Even within a cloud of erotic delight, Rory knew this was wrong. On the brink of making love for the second time, she couldn't allow herself to take a passive role, to lose herself so much in the sensations of lovemaking that she only took and didn't give. Thanks to the instructions on the *Sexcapade,* she'd held some degree of control over last night's seduction, but only on the surface. Alec had taken the role of director, measuring her every move, orchestrating her every sensation. And once they'd reached the bed, she'd lost herself completely in his skilled loving. As much as she'd claimed beforehand that she wasn't going to be submissive in her first sexual experience—she had been.

And enough was enough.

Poised to slip her nipple into his mouth, Alec stopped when she grabbed his cheeks and said, "No."

A dreamy, disbelieving fog had formed over his gaze. She stared at him for a long minute, until the disorientation cleared.

"No?" he repeated.

"That's what I said."

"Why?"

"You."

"What about me?"

"I see what you're doing," she said.

"You should. I'm not exactly hiding." He went for her breast again, but she stepped out of reach.

"What's going on, Rory?"

Desperate to appropriate the upper hand, she slammed her fists on her hips and tried to look as menacing and serious as any naked woman in high heels could.

"What's going on is that I finally see that what kind of man you really are."

That got his attention. He straightened and swiped some of the warehouse dust off his knees. "I'm hoping the punch line here is 'hopelessly sexy and irresistible.'"

She pouted and shook her head. "'Fraid not. You, Alec Manning, are incredibly aggressive."

His shoulders lost an ounce of tension. "Didn't I tell you about that? I could have sworn I pointed this out sometime during our first meeting."

"I don't remember our first meeting that way, but even if you did, to a woman like me, an aggressive lover isn't a good thing."

"Why the hell not?"

Determining that she'd squelched his libido sufficiently to talk to him at close range, Rory sidled back into his personal space, splaying her palms up his bare chest until her fingers curved over his shoulders.

"Because with you taking the lead every time, I don't have anything to do."

"You could enjoy the ride."

She clucked her tongue. "Been there, done that."

"One time doesn't count."

"It does to me, particularly if a few times total is all we'll ever have."

Rory watched Alec swipe his tongue over his lips. Inhale deeply, exhale slowly. He mulled her words. His gaze darkened. His jaw twitched. Briefly she wondered if he regretted placing such a parameter on their affair— or if maybe she was only imposing her own regrets.

"So, what do you want me to do?" he asked, his voice husky, yet honeyed with possibilities that oozed down Rory's spine.

She forced her eyes closed, shutting out as much as

she could of his magnetic power. Long enough to think. She wanted the upper hand and now he was willing to give it. So what the heck did she do now?

Smiling, she stepped back, but kept her hands on his shoulders. "First, lose the jeans. Then, brace yourself. And I mean that literally."

ALEC HESITATED until Rory cleared her throat. The mild reproach pushed all reason, all logic from his mind. He knew what she wanted. To please him. To take the reins of their lovemaking, and perhaps to test her own limits.

How could he deny her? How could he deny her anything? And why would he?

Her body heat taunted him, hovering around his as she explored, her hands grazing over his skin with electric lightness. When her palm smoothed his chest, he made a sizzling noise, a perfect sound effect to the sensations burning over his skin. She explored, touched, tasted. She boldly tweaked his nipple, rolling the pebbled flesh between her fingers, searing the sweet sensation with her tongue. She kissed him higher, on his shoulder blade. Lower, on his navel.

Then she dipped her head below his waist and he couldn't help grabbing her by the cheeks.

"What are you doing?"

"Nothing you haven't done to me," she answered, wide-eyed wonder in her eyes. Not innocence, as he'd seen the first time they'd met. Not naiveté, which he hadn't witnessed once since she'd taken control. She knew what she wanted. Pure need brightened her blue eyes to a most vivid sapphire.

She cupped him, stroked him, banishing his protests to the back of his mind. He closed his eyes, fading into a world where images swirled amid bold colors on the inside of his eyelids, brightening and deepening with each move of her mouth.

He gripped the shelf behind him with one hand, twined his fingers into her soft hair with the other. She had no idea of the madness she'd wrought.

Good God.

Blood surged. His breath rushed out of his lungs. She had to stop. Stop. Before he...

She broke away and in seconds had the condom rolled over his sex. The final snap of the latex was like a starter pistol. He touched her everywhere, kissed her everywhere, twirled her around so that her hands caught the shelf and held her steady as he slipped inside her.

From behind, he could stroke her, arouse her, drive her into the gratifying wave of desire she'd lured him to. She didn't protest, didn't speak. She only moved, arching her back, lifting her hips—her body saying the only things a man wanted to hear.

He drove hard, long, pumping all his passion into her, whispering into her ear sweet nonsense—all of it sincere, all of it meant to soften an act of pure, animal lust.

Or was it?

Panting, his cheek pressed against her shoulder, Alec wondered what the hell they'd done. Rory smiled, sated. She slipped away, but only long enough to turn and snuggle into his arms. He stroked her hair, his heart still slamming against his chest.

She'd been looking for trouble in the warehouse, and he'd given her the full treatment. But a question that had never, ever plagued him after making love to a woman now screamed through his brain.

Now what, hotshot?

He looked around, his throat searing with words he

couldn't say, sentiments he couldn't name. Not admissions of love—he knew he and Rory hadn't known each other long enough for that. But still, something about this sensually guileless woman snared him, activated instincts he'd never felt before. In the past, he would have considered her fierce quest for independence as the best thing about her. She wouldn't want a relationship. She wouldn't want him, at least not for very long.

But Alec had done enough self-examination over the past six months to know when something wasn't right, when his reactions or expectations wandered outside his normal realm. Into the unknown.

He had to decide whether or not he wanted to follow, or if by exploring this new territory, he'd have to let Rory go. Forever.

"What's eating you?"

Alec ran the white rag over the glistening bar for what seemed like the hundredth time. No one had sat at that particular spot all evening, so there was no peanut shell dust or glass rings to swipe away. For the last hour, he'd gravitated to the one undesirable seat at the bar where the lighting and positioning made mate-hunting nearly impossible. Normally he found his most interesting subjects here—the girlfriend dragged along while her buddy stalked the dance floor; the weary Southern traveler braving the club scene in search of a decent mint julep north of the Mason-Dixon. But tonight, the hot seat remained empty. He hadn't met one woman all night that had been interesting enough to interact with. Not one guy worthy of his usual Cupid-playing tactics. Not in that seat or in the whole damned club. Truth was, Alec didn't give a damn who hooked up with whom tonight. He had his own concerns.

However, his disregard for pouring drinks was annoying his boss.

"Sorry, Shaw. My mind is elsewhere."

"I can see that." Shaw Thomas lifted the hinged panel in the bar and slipped to the other side. "Smells like woman trouble to me."

Alec frowned, annoyed. Shaw Thomas was no older than Alec, had never been married and, as far as Alec knew, had rarely dallied beyond flirtation with any one of the beautiful women who slinked across his dance floor every night, despite his ladies' man reputation. Why should he be such a goddammed expert that he could spot Alec's trouble with only a glance?

"Not trouble," Alec insisted. "Just thinking too much."

He pulled a tray of shot glasses from beneath the counter and swiped leftover condensation from the dishwasher with a new towel.

Shaw snatched the rag, then pushed Alec aside, nodding his head sideways to a guy in a Nike T-shirt who looked like he'd been waiting quite some time to order a drink.

Alec inhaled, then quickly mixed the order for a sour apple martini and a Sam Adams draft. The music from a live band, jamming standards from the eighties rockabilly craze, pounded all around him. Normally Alec ignored the music, the clever lighting which swirled and flashed in synchronized rhythm, the assault of odors clashing from the dancing bodies, the kitchen and the bar. Tonight, his entire sensory arsenal seemed on alert, and yet...dulled. Dissatisfied and uninterested in the glowing reds and golds, the relentless bass, the olfactory attack of musk and perfume punching through the down-South scent of fried green tomatoes—Shaw's specialty of the house—Alec had never wanted to quit more than he did right now.

But, instead, he grabbed the towel back from Shaw once the customer paid his tab and returned to twisting the terry cloth into the glasses. Shaw leaned back, his elbows on the bar, the set of his jaw too smug for Alec's liking.

"So tell me about her."

"There's nothing to tell, Shaw. Not every man in your bar has woman troubles."

"Bullshit. If you're a man, you've got woman troubles."

"Not if you don't have a woman."

"Especially if you don't have a woman," Shaw contradicted.

Alec smirked, stacking the dried glasses within easy reach. The band kicked up a particularly popular song and anyone lingering near the bar just behind the dance floor surged forward into the crowd. Shaw Thomas had an incredible eye for musical talent and any time he introduced a new band to his patrons, every club within a mile radius took a hit in their head count. The Stray Copy Cats had only been playing Dixie Landings for a week, but tonight Shaw had had to shut the door when they reached capacity. And yet, despite the thirsty crowd, Alec still found time to be distracted, wondering where Rory was, what she was doing, if she was okay. He'd helped her lug the party supplies to their destination, then had even lent a hand in setting things up. Even he'd been impressed by the way the Divine Events team could transform a smartly decorated condominium into a medieval banquet hall in just under two hours. And though he'd found Gia Divine a little prickly for his liking, he'd watched Rory interact with her as if she'd known her for years.

Rory's ability to creep beneath the surface of someone's chosen veneer apparently applied to more than just him. She was nothing if not genuine, wearing her emotions and her intentions like a diamond choker. Brilliant. Impossible to miss. Everyone he watched her with seemed to sense the same in-your-face honesty, the broadcast message that insisted, "This is who I am. Nothing more, nothing less. You can trust me."

So why was he fighting what he knew to be true?

"She's coming in here tonight, isn't she?" Shaw asked, grabbing a near-empty glass from a girl in a red leather vest whose name escaped Alec at the moment, but who came to Dixie Landings every Saturday night. He topped off her soda, winked, delivered. Even through the cacophony of the club, Alec could have sworn he heard the woman sigh.

"She's interested in you," Alec noted, part of him trying to deflect the topic of conversation, the other part of him slipping into work mode. Until tonight, he'd resisted trying to manipulate his boss for his study. He'd focused more on the women in the club, pointing them toward guys he'd noticed watching them, then observing how the women circled, stalked, then went in for the kill. Most of the men seemed utterly helpless, or were at least adept at appearing so. They practically jumped into the woman's trap.

But not Shaw. He'd never seen a man with more powers of resistance. Nearly every Saturday night, Alec would watch some drop-dead gorgeous knockout approach Shaw with clear, erotic intentions—and just as predictably, the thirty-something club owner would shoot her down. Alec never questioned why—he had his own reasons for redirecting the woman coming on to him toward other guys. He figured Shaw had his own reasons, too.

"You've worked here long enough to know that the women hit on the owner first, then the bartender. Like clockwork."

"So you don't think she's after you, personally?"

The question was almost too inquisitive for a bartender to ask his boss—more like a sociologist intrigued by another prospective theory that he hadn't already noted, researched and proved.

Shaw eyed him suspiciously, but answered anyway in his smooth Southern drawl and overstated humble-pie smile. "It's the hair. They can't resist."

He tore fingers through his blond locks, then shook his head like the lead singer of some eighties hair band. Alec bet the guy could have given Jon Bon Jovi a run for his money twenty years ago.

Shaw rolled his eyes, then tamed his hair with his hand and checked the condiment tray, refilling the olives. Alec chuckled, then turned his attention toward a cocktail waitress who leaned across the bar and shouted a drink order over the din. He mixed and poured the round, then another for the next server, cursing the invention of such drinks as Sex on the Beach and Long Island Iced Tea simply because they required so much damned work. Shaw had already given him permission—facetiously, of course—to shoot the next person who ordered a Flaming Eros, a complicated liqueur mixture currently all the rage in San Francisco. Well, this was Chicago, dammit. Why couldn't people just order a beer?

The song ended and the band took a break, causing a rush for libation that kept Alec distracted and busy for a solid twenty minutes. As usual, Shaw lent a hand behind the bar. By the time the band took the stage again, Alec was convinced Shaw's earlier interest in his mood had waned.

He was wrong.

"So, who is this chick?" Shaw asked.

"What chick?"

"The one who has your boxers in a knot, man."

"I wear briefs," he quipped.

"Pansy."

Somehow, the old-fashioned insult didn't seem so odd rolling off Shaw's Southern drawl. "I'm not the one who's always turning women away, boss man."

"Aren't you?"

Alec shook his head. "You don't know what I do outside this place."

"Right back at you. But I don't come into work with a persistent scowl on my face when things aren't going my way, either."

Aha. Now Alec understood. Shaw, a man's man, didn't pry into his employees' personal lives. As long as they showed up on time and did their job with optimal customer service, he didn't give a damn if your girlfriend just dumped you or if your house caught on fire. Alec hadn't been acting himself all evening—at least, not the self Shaw knew. Not once since coming to work at seven o'clock had he slipped into the role of Xander, his charming, suave alter ego. Not once had he used his charm to pair dance partners, incite conversations and flirtations, which led to more dancing and more drinks being bought. Bottom line was that Xander was good for Shaw's business and, tonight, he wasn't playing the game.

"Sorry, boss. Don't know what's gotten into me."

Alec shook the tension out of his shoulders, rolled his neck until he heard cracks, popped the top two buttons on his shirt. He tugged his pants lower on his waist, then adjusted the wattage on his smile. He scanned the vicinity, instantly finding a pair of twenty-something ladies sucking down Cosmopolitans at the end of the bar. With an equally furtive glance, he saw two college-aged guys throwing back bottled beer and watching the babes as they crossed their path from the dance floor to the bathroom.

Too easy.

In seconds, he'd dispatched the girls toward their intended targets. Zeroing in, the women had the guys out on the dance floor in record time. Older women were always quicker to place with younger guys—and Alec didn't doubt for a minute that the two women—medical interns judging by the badge he'd glimpsed inside the blond girl's purse—could more than handle whatever the college sophomores would dish out.

He'd been halfway toward arranging another pairing when Shaw finally lost interest, left the bar and disappeared into the crowd, heading toward his office on the second floor. Alec turned off the magnetism long enough to wonder...

Rory was at a club much like this one right now. Prancing around in clothes sexy enough to be illegal in some countries, inviting interest from a crowd of men she had no business toying with. He should have been with her instead of here. Protecting her. Looking out for her. She hadn't gone alone—her friend Lisa had arranged a small group to help Rory on her search for her sister. And Rory wasn't stupid. She wouldn't take any unnecessary chances. And yet...

After his liaison with Rory at the warehouse, Alec now understood just how far Rory would go to get what she wanted. Question was, did she know when to stop? And if she did, just where would that leave him?

15

RORY RIPPED OFF HER T-SHIRT, disheartened, exhausted and even a little angry. In a whirlwind she'd gone from knowing nothing about her twin's whereabouts to being so close, the tremors of their genetic connection pulsing and flashing like some sort of internal alarm. She'd paraded from club to club, disguised as her sister, for a week. She'd talked to anyone and everyone who had given her so much as a double-take. *Do you know Micki? Have you seen her? What about her friend, the girl she's always with? Do you know her name? A last known location? A club or parking lot or abandoned building, anything, where the pair would hang out?*

Nothing. Either the down-and-out crowd had an incredibly strong code of silence or they simply didn't know. This afternoon, between her Saturday assignment for Divine Events and her descent into the club scene, Rory had even returned to the homeless shelter where Micki had volunteered. She'd dropped a few precious tens and twenties trying to bribe her way to information, until the shelter's director advised her to stop.

"All you're doing is feeding habits," Deidre had admonished, her fists thrust on her ample hips as she'd stood in the doorway of the building. The old converted church appeared newly whitewashed, but still had plastic buds fading in the flower boxes.

Rory had stepped up from the curb, insistent. "I need to find my sister."

"Maybe she don't want to be found."

"Duh," Rory snapped, her response unguarded, automatic, a testament to her growing frustration. "I'm willing to do anything at this point."

Deidre's face twisted in judgment. "I can see that. Save your money, girl. Word is out on the street that you're looking for Micki. If and when she wants to find you, she will."

Rory hadn't wanted to give up, but Deidre knew the culture better than she did, and while Rory had witnessed the woman impart messages of hope and inspiration to the down-on-their-luck women who came into the shelter, she'd given little to Rory. According to Deidre, Micki was smart and tough. She kept her ear to the ground, knew all the gossip that needed knowing. So far as Deidre was concerned, Rory had been wasting her time.

Yesterday, she would have vehemently argued. Today, she wasn't so sure. She kicked off her boots, then peeled off her skin tight, hip-hugger jeans and flicked off the fake navel ring. She had enough leftover energy to kick her jeans in the general direction of the hamper before she plopped down beside the bathtub and allowed her frustration to bubble to the surface in the form of a good, old-fashioned cry.

God, she wanted her sister back. The emptiness in her chest yawned hollow and deep. It was a void she'd worked hard to banish since the day Micki had failed to meet Rory by the bike rack after school so they could walk to the bus stop together. But it had never fully sealed. The bitterness she hardly ever acknowledged broke through with a vengeance. Dammit, why didn't Micki want to be found? Why hadn't she sought Rory out in Berwyn, where the family had lived for sixty-odd years? Why hadn't she checked in with the shelter or the detective, the only two sources Rory trusted to relay the message that her sister was looking for her. While the tears flowed, the questions ran the gamut from heart-wrenching to ridiculous and irrational, until Rory had had enough of her self-indulgent pity. She was just tired. For God's sake, only ten days had passed since she'd come to Chicago. What did she expect, miracles?

No, she thought, swiping away tears. But she had expected progress. Only in her sex life had anything truly changed since she'd come to the city. And yet she'd searched for Micki every night, no matter how long she'd worked at Divine Events or how many hours she'd spent learning about sensuality and sexuality in Alec's bed. Or her bed. Or the back porch. The attic. The hammock hanging in the small back yard. The adventures had been the ultimate escape and, even now, the memories lifted her mood.

They'd made love in every way she'd thought possible, then she'd learned the truth. With Alec, the possibilities were endless. Unfortunately she knew with each passing night that the end grew nearer and nearer. Particularly last night, when his restlessness had nearly caused their first fight. Rory had had to remind herself that she had no right to place any emotional expectations on him—or vice versa. Couples fought. They weren't a couple—they were lovers. And tensions were running high for both of them, thanks to her bad luck with her search for her twin and Alec's meeting with the review committee, which had been scheduled to happen late that afternoon.

She glanced at her watch before she removed it and tossed it on the ledge above the sink. His meeting should be concluded by now, his future, perhaps, decided. She bit her lip, wondering, hoping. She wanted him to achieve his goals, but couldn't help suspect that the outcome of his bid for his research grant—positive or negative—would somehow affect their relationship in a way she didn't want. Only they didn't have a relationship, did they?

Rory finished undressing, showered, then changed into her favorite Winnie the Pooh pajamas that declared on the pocket that she was now in a Bother-Free Zone. *If only.* She made herself a peanut-butter-and-grape-jam sandwich and a glass of chocolate milk, sat down at her wobbly kitchen table and scanned the newspaper for interesting world events.

She was halfway through her sandwich when Alec called.

"How'd it go with the committee?" she asked.

"It didn't. They postponed. Have you eaten?"

"Just did. Weren't you having dinner with the Yeagers?"

The hiss of Alec's exasperation sparked annoyance in Rory's chest. Closure seemed elusive for both of them today. Over the past week, he'd talked about little else but the importance to his career of obtaining this grant. He needed this nod from the Hensen Foundation to shore up his bid for employment, and, ultimately, tenure. He'd even hinted a bit about the research study itself, something to do with the reversal of roles in dating and how more often women played the aggressor in male-female interaction.

The thought spawned a smile. Even now, Rory couldn't believe how bold she'd been with Alec, with herself. From the moment she'd swiped the page out of the *Sexcapade* book, she'd evolved from passive to active. And she didn't have a single regret.

Analyzing her behavior had led to some very insightful discussions, followed by some incredibly interesting sex. Rory couldn't believe how far they'd come in just ten days' time. She cared for Alec deeply, rooted for his success. She hated to think that neither one of them had had any luck today. Not with so much at stake.

"The Yeagers are stuck at some appointment across town and had to put me off. Our early dinner is now late coffee, and they don't want the official proposal tonight, since time will be short."

"Well, that's not so bad. You can meet with them casually, maybe gauge how to best present your work."

"Good point. And the pressure is off for now."

She wandered into the living room with the portable phone and sat on the couch, kicking her bare feet up on the coffee table. "Don't you have to go to your other job?"

"I called Shaw, told him I'd be late."

She nodded silently, though she still had no idea who Shaw was or what Alec did during his secret second job. Since his study revolved around dating, she figured he worked somewhere very social. A club. A dating service. Heck, for all she knew, he was a gigolo.

She'd made the huge mistake of voicing that supposition and he'd found teasing her so delicious, she hadn't been able to get a serious answer out of him since. But he had promised to give her a big hint tomorrow night, if she played her cards right.

And he'd meant that literally. They were scheduled for a game of strip poker, something she'd always wanted to try. A sensual shiver sizzled up her spine at the thought of winning. Or better—losing.

"So what are you going to do now?" she asked.

"Grab something to eat, and then wait. I'm calling

from a crowded hotel lobby, or I'd suggest something a little more intimate.''

Rory bit her lip, wondering about phone sex. What exactly did you do during phone sex anyway? She made a mental note to ask Alec about this fantasy when he wasn't in a public place.

''What about you? How'd your search for Micki go?''

Rory groaned and the throbbing in her feet from the high heels intensified. ''Nothing new. Lisa took me down to this Southern rock club on Clark Street. The owner keeps the parking lot clear of loiterers, so we went inside and caught the early show. Lisa said she wanted me to experience the impressive manipulations of a certain bartender. I guess he fixes people up or something. He wasn't there.''

Silence ensued, making Rory wonder if Alec had even heard her. ''Alec?''

''Yeah. Sorry. So you didn't find anything more about Micki?''

She chuckled. Either he hadn't heard her or he simply didn't want to talk about this mystery bartender's increasingly infamous reputation. Oh, well. She'd promised Lisa she'd check out the action again sometime, though she couldn't imagine why she should. Who needed a sexy bartender in some club when she had the sexiest landlord in the city at home?

''Micki's elusive—I'll give her that. But I think my questions are making some people uncomfortable. Maybe if they see her, they'll at least tell her I'm looking for her. I don't know. Actually I was thinking about driving out to my grandmother's. Check on things. Seeing if maybe she baked some of her famous chocolate chip cookies.''

She'd called her grandmother twice since moving to

the city and had been surprised about how little Nanna had asked about her new life beyond her job. She suspected her grandmother understood that as long as she didn't push, Rory wouldn't run the way her mother had, the way her sister had. God, if she could only bring Micki home. Heal some of the damage.

"Chocolate chip? We can use them tomorrow night, then," he teased.

Rory smiled. She loved how he always seemed to remember their plans. "No way, buddy-boy. Nanna's chocolate chip cookies are not child's play. This is serious dessert business."

"You're going to hoard them?"

"Oh, I wouldn't say that. But there's no telling what wicked things I'll make you do to earn a taste."

After a few more minutes of banter and teasing, they hung up, with Alec promising to stop by her place if he got home before midnight. She hadn't turned on the light in the living room, so she watched the light fade through the west-facing window, slivers of orange and pink and purple slicing through the shades, half-drawn. She didn't have the energy to lift them, and she wondered if running down to Berwyn after sunset in her state of exhaustion was the right thing to do. Showing up at her grandmother's house in a pensive mood with dark circles under her eyes and blisters on her feet probably wasn't the wisest choice. So after a quick phone call to arrange a dinner the next night with Nanna and Aunt Lil, Rory hunted for the remote control on the television and flipped through the channels until a rockumentary special on Sarah McLachlan caught her interest.

Half an hour later, she'd scooped herself a bowlful of mint chocolate chip ice cream, grabbed a pillow and comforter and settled herself on the couch. She flipped through the channels until she finally convinced herself she was too tired to watch any more TV. She glanced at the clock, noting the time was after nine. Her feet still ached from all day on the job and all afternoon at the shelter and then the clubs. She'd promised Cecily she'd show up an hour early tomorrow morning to coordinate the last-minute details on a rare Sunday wedding, so dressing up again to go out to search didn't make sense, no matter how much she ached for her sister.

She rinsed her dish and returned to the couch, channel-surfed one last time, turned off the television and wandered to the front window. Restlessness battled with her exhaustion as she lifted the shade and stared down into the quiet neighborhood street. Every few minutes, cars cruised to the corner, then turned toward the nearby university. A guy walked his rottweiler on a retractable leash. A trio of young women trudged by, Mizuno sports bags slung over their shoulders, their hair tucked inside ball caps. Rory touched her hand to the glass. Outside, the night was mild. A breeze swept flyers off the windshields of cars parked on the street.

Rory leaned to the left, wondering if some maniac with handbills had found her car. She spied a flash of movement. Solicitors didn't work this late.

Rory unlatched the window and yanked hard to break the humid seal between the frame and the sash. She ducked her head out. Someone was near her Jeep.

Long dark hair.

A miniskirt. Oversize jacket.

A woman.

Though Rory hadn't said a word, the woman by the Jeep spun like a top toward the window. Even from the distance, her eyes, blue as aquamarine, flashed in the light from a street lamp.

Rory's heart froze in her chest, shooting a shaft of ice into her throat, paralyzing her speech.

Micki?

The instant her brain processed the word, Rory managed to shout the namc aloud.

"Micki? Micki!"

She bumped the back of her head on the window, stopped long enough for the stars to disperse, then shot toward her door. She slid down the stairs, barefoot and barely dressed, then dashed into the street, leaving the door ajar behind her. Sprinting to her car, she screamed her twin's name again. Where was she? Where had she gone?

The guy walking his dog stared at her from across the street. Rory yelled again, waited for an answer, then ran toward the guy, paying no heed to the menacing-looking dog growling. He quieted the pooch with a tug on the leash.

"Did you see her? Where did she go?"

"Who? Calm down, lady. What are you talking about?"

Rage and fear and frustration pounded in her ears and pressed her lungs against her rib cage, squeezing out the air. "My sister." She shook her head. This man didn't know her. He was a stranger. *Think, Rory. Think.* "There was a girl—she looked like me. Over by the Jeep," she insisted, pointing toward her vehicle. "I saw her from my window. Did you see her?"

The guy nodded, understanding dawning. "That was you screaming from the window? Yeah. She took off like a bat out of hell."

"Which way?"

"Huh?"

"Which way?" she shouted, wanting to grab the guy by his T-shirt and shake the information out of him.

He pointed down the street, in the opposite direction, toward the train stop not a half block away.

Rory shot down the sidewalk, yelling a frantic thank-you over her shoulder. Questions flew through her mind as she ran, though she couldn't slow down, couldn't stop, couldn't allow this one long shot at finding her sister to slip away. Her gaze darted left and right as she jogged, wondering if Micki was hiding. Wondering to what extremes she would go to evade Rory.

Vaguely aware of traffic, Rory glanced for headlights before darting across the street. Micki couldn't have gone far. But why had she come at all, only to run away again? And how had she found Rory? As a contact number, Rory had left her cell phone, not her address. And she'd just moved here. She wasn't listed in the phone book.

She took the steps to the "L" platform two at a time. When she finally reached the top, her stomach burned from acid and her lungs ached from oxygen deprivation. She threw herself into the crowd, frantically searching for her own face. One by one, the passengers passed through the turnstiles. Rory didn't have a transit card. She couldn't go through. She climbed onto a gate, frantic to find her own face in the crowd.

"Micki! Micki! Please. Don't run from me. Don't run away again!"

Salt slipped into her mouth and she realized tears were streaming down her face. Suddenly someone was behind her, tugging at her elbows.

"Please, miss. You've got to get down from there."

Rory jumped back, her balance off, and slammed into a transit security guard, a black woman with kind eyes.

She grabbed Rory by the arms, keeping her from falling to the ground. "Hey, hey. What's wrong?"

"My sister."

"Calm down, baby. You look like you've seen a ghost."

With a thunderous rumble, the train tore into the station. An automated voice mumbled words Rory couldn't hear. "I need to find my sister."

The guard shook her head, her expression doubtful. The doors to the train hissed open and the people on the platform switched places with the people on the train. The crowd was relatively light, but at least three-dozen men and women headed toward the stairs.

"What was she wearing?"

"She looked just like me. We're twins. Dark coat. Short skirt."

The guard stood up, peered around, genuinely searching. A bell sounded. Rory shot toward the fence again, frantically looking inside the cars for the woman she'd seen by her Jeep.

The guard pulled her back. "Come on now, honey. You don't even know if she's on this train, do you?"

Rory sniffed in the moisture streaming from her nose, then ruthlessly swiped her mouth with her arm. "No. She was next to my car, then she disappeared. The guy with the dog…" She lost her breath, but the guard placed her hand on her arm, calming her. "This guy walking his dog said she ran this way."

"Well, she isn't here now. Maybe you should get back to your place, change your clothes, wait for her to call."

Rory didn't explain that Micki wouldn't call. She never called. She could have posted her phone number at the top of the Sears Tower and her selfish, self-absorbed sister would never call!

Besides, no matter how softly the guard had spoken, she was a stranger. She didn't care about Rory's troubles, though she had just gently reminded Rory that she'd run out of the house in her pajamas. Vaguely Rory recalled that she hadn't shut the front door. And then there was the Jeep. Maybe Micki had left her a note. Maybe the idea of reconciling after all these years had been too overwhelming for her so she'd chosen a more anonymous route.

As quickly as Rory's hopes had been dashed, they surged through her heart again. After an apology to the guard, Rory disappeared down the stairs.

On her way back to the house, she walked slower, avoiding the surprised stares of the pedestrians she met on the street, but looking hard into the shadows. Behind cars and around Dumpsters, into the darkened doorways of homes and apartments and storefronts closed late on a Saturday night. She saw no one dressed like the woman she'd suspected had been Micki, and when she reached the Jeep, she found nothing on the car. She slammed a fist on the hood when a hand gripped her from behind.

"Rory?"

When she swung around and came face-to-face with Alec, she fell into his arms. She didn't care if she was wearing her pajamas, if her feet were black from running barefoot on the street, if her face was streaked with sweat and tears. He was here. Taking her in his arms. Surrounding her with his warmth, his scent.

God, she loved him. She did. Idiot! She should have known she couldn't fight those Carmichael genes—the gullibility. Hadn't that been why her mother had run away? Because she'd loved too foolishly? Because she'd loved a man more than she'd loved her own children?

Rory shoved the thought out of her mind with the same

force she used to extract herself from Alec's embrace. She couldn't follow that path. Playing ''what if'' about a mother who was dead was a lesson in futility. She'd never know why her mother abandoned her life, her twins. She didn't even know if love had anything to do with her selfish choice. Hell, for all she knew, her mother's desertion had been the most selfless thing she'd ever done.

''Rory, what's going on?''

Bending at the waist, Rory placed her hands on her knees, then stood up straight, inhaling oxygen deeply into her lungs and then holding her breath until the act made her dizzy. She exhaled, slowly, calming herself, bringing herself back to a more balanced equilibrium. As awesome as it had felt to collapse into Alec at a weak moment, she couldn't allow her vulnerability to override her good sense. Caring about him and allowing him to care about her was one thing. But falling in love could become the act that drove this one-of-a-kind man right out of her life.

16

"WHAT HAPPENED? Why are you outside? Why is the front door wide open?"

Alec watched, amazed, at how the extreme emotion faded from Rory's face. In seconds, she'd calmed herself. When he'd come down the street from the train stop and seen her standing outside in her pajamas banging on the hood of her car, he hadn't known what to think. The Rory he knew was incredibly rational, determined, single-minded. The Rory pacing around him now brimmed with restless anger, confusion. She had the emotions under control, but just barely.

"I saw her," she answered.

"Who? Micki?"

She nodded. "She was here."

"In the house?"

With her palms, she wiped her face, then rubbed her eyes. "No. Here, by the car." She slammed her open palm on the hood again and cursed. "Dammit! She ran away again. She wouldn't talk to me. But she found me. Why? Maybe someone I talked to today watched me get into the Jeep. Could she track me down that way?"

When her gaze finally met his, her eyes found a focus they hadn't had a moment before. He didn't know what she was talking about, and his expression must have given him away.

She closed her eyes tightly and hissed. "I must look like a total idiot."

"Not exactly, but you do look like you might lose your mind if you don't calm down. Really calm down, as in not trying to act like you've got everything under control when you really want to punch something. Or someone."

"You volunteering?"

He smiled, satisfied when her shoulders relaxed an inch or so. "Why don't we go inside?" He took a step toward the house, but contained his instinct to take her arm. Despite her attempt at humor, he recognized the raging river of emotions sweeping through her. Dangerous and unpredictable, she might strike out at him simply because he was there. And until he knew all the details of what had happened, he wouldn't know how to react, how to help, how to avoid making her distress worse.

"Why are you here?" she asked, still rooted next to her car.

"The Yeagers ended up canceling, but I had to come home first to change before I went to the club."

"The club?"

Alec extended his hand toward the house. "Let's go inside, Rory. I'll tell you about the club and you can tell me about Micki."

The walk to the house progressed in silence, except for Rory's quiet apology for leaving the door unlocked. She hadn't been gone for more than fifteen minutes, tops, but Alec took a look around anyway and found nothing out of place. Once convinced that she'd done no harm, Rory followed Alec, who gently prodded her inside his apartment.

"Maybe I imagined her," she said, sighing as she plopped onto his couch, her hair tangled, her shoulders drooped.

He remained standing. ''In all the years you've been looking for your sister, have you ever imagined her to be somewhere?''

She shook her head.

''Not even when you were young and she was just missing?''

''Never so much as caught a glimpse out of the corner of my eye.''

''Then I don't think you imagined her today, either. Not when you've been out looking. Not when you've been getting the word out on the streets that you want to know where she is. Yeah, I think she could find you through your car. Maybe she has a friend at the DMV. Have you changed your license address?''

She attempted to comb her hair with her hands, but couldn't quite break through the tangle. ''Cecily had me do that Monday. She needed me to have up-to-date identification for when I make deliveries.''

Alec pulled off his sport coat, then his tan polo shirt. ''There you go, then. She could have tracked you down. Let me change. I'll get you a towel, maybe something to drink. We'll figure this out, Rory.''

She didn't respond, just relaxed into the couch cushions and shut her eyes.

Unable to resist, Alec watched her for a minute. Her skin was mottled with dirt and tears and Alec couldn't decide whom he disliked most at that very minute—her sister, who'd inexplicably shown up out of the blue only to make sure Rory relived the horror of losing her, or himself.

He hadn't been honest with Rory. Not entirely. He'd insisted he didn't want a relationship, and yet here he was, injected into her personal life, into her deepest fears, regrets and hopes—and he could think of no place else he'd rather be. Particularly not at Dixie Landing, even though he loved the music, admired his boss and enjoyed the interplay with the patrons he studied.

But Rory wasn't there—she was here. Needing him—and not for sex or escape or revenge or anything all too easy for a shallow man to give. No. Now she needed his strength, support and genuine concern—straight from the heart. Surprisingly, this wasn't as hard to provide as he'd suspected, almost as if he'd saved all his capacity to love for this very moment.

In a lot of ways, Alec realized as he watched Rory's breathing grow steadier and softer, working at the club had been somewhat cathartic. He'd faced down his past, even succeeded in turning his playboy tendencies into something positive. Some of the people he'd played matchmaker to in the bar were still together, a fact he rarely acknowledged since he never pretended to have altruistic motives. But he had made some headway in his own personal quest for self-forgiveness. But enough to justify risking a real relationship with Rory? Someone whose vulnerabilities he was only now beginning to comprehend?

He shuffled into his bedroom, donned his bartender uniform—a soft white button-down shirt and black slacks—then went to the kitchen to check the refrigerator for drink choices. The iced tea pitcher had only a swallow left, so he downed that and tossed the plastic container into the sink. He didn't have time to brew more, or even mix instant, so he grabbed a cold Sam Adams from the top shelf near the back, where they remained icy for moments just like these.

He popped the top, grabbed a clean kitchen towel, splashed it with water and returned to Rory.

She'd curled one of the throw cushions beneath her

head and reclined, but sat up when he approached, shaking away his offer of the beer.

"No, thanks."

"Water, then? It's all I have."

"I should go upstairs, get cleaned up. You obviously have to go to work, wherever that is."

The sound of her sarcasm wasn't the least bit disguised. Just like Rory. Honest, and completely undemanding.

"Come with me," he said, only half-surprised to hear the offer spill from his lips.

"Excuse me?"

"I'm not doing anything I'm ashamed of, Rory. But since I took this job, I've tried to keep that life separate from the new life I've been trying to build."

"Your new academic, professional life?"

He chuckled quietly. "I actually took this job because of my academic, professional life. I meant from my private life. At least, the private life I hadn't intended to have until you moved in. Remember that matchmaking bartender at Dixie Landings? I'm him."

If his moonlighting profession surprised her, she didn't show it. "You?"

Alec sat beside her and took a swig from the beer. "It's for the study. Besides, the club has great music, surprisingly good food and a clientele of singles who don't seem to mind my studying them for my research."

Clearly amused, she knocked him in the shoulder. "Why haven't you told me this before now? I was only half-teasing about the gigolo thing," she admitted.

He rolled his eyes. "Sex for money is about the only thing I haven't reduced myself to over the years. I mean, a guy's gotta draw a line somewhere."

At first, she smiled, but the grin quickly faded to pensive.

"What?"

"Nothing. I was just thinking about Micki again. I wonder what she's had to reduce herself to in order to stay alive all these years."

Dark and ugly images skittered across his brain, like the rats that fed in the Dumpster behind the club, no matter how many traps Shaw set. Everyone knew they existed, were part and parcel of city life, but they still evoked shock when they crossed your path. Alec had seen what desperation had done to the girls who walked the shadowy street corners only two blocks east of the club.

"She's still alive, Rory. That has to mean she's resourceful."

Rory bit her lip. "The Micki I remember could handle anything. Except my grandmother's strict rules and regulations."

He listened as she recounted a sweet story from her childhood, noting the parallels between Micki's troubled tendencies and his own. He'd been a lot like Rory's wayward sister—stubborn, impulsive, angry. He'd turned out okay. Maybe Micki could, too—with some help. Rory's help. She'd done wonders for him without even trying. Little by little, Alec had begun to realize that he couldn't dismiss his playboy tendencies as easily as he'd once thought. He was a sexual creature, plain and simple. Growing up didn't mean chucking the past entirely. Rory kept his sexual hungers well fed and sated, which in turn allowed him to focus on his academic pursuits and emotional needs. She provided balance, something he'd never managed to create for himself.

Question was, what could he give her in return? She'd

asked for sexual knowledge. That, he'd provided. So now what?

"Did you get a good look at Micki?" he asked, determined to help her in whatever way he could.

Rory shook her head. "Only enough to recognize her, if I really saw her at all."

"The guy walking the dog saw her. She must have been out there."

"Why did she follow me home and then not talk to me?" Rory stood and marched toward the window and, despite the battle clearly raging on her face, she pushed the curtains aside and gazed out. After a few seconds, she turned around and stalked toward the door. "I'm sorry, Alec. I didn't mean to drag you into this."

He stood, snagging her by the hand before she could escape. "You're not dragging me into anything. You can talk to me, Rory. About anything."

"No, I can't!" She yanked her hand from his and twisted the knob.

"Look, I should have told you about my job before tonight, but I guess I was so used to *not* telling anyone about it that keeping it a secret was a natural thing."

He wanted to tell her more about Dixie Landing, but preferred to show her instead. She could watch him operate as Xander, witness a first-class retro performance of the man he used to be, then she could make her own decisions and conclusions. Honestly, there wasn't much she didn't already know. But seeing his moves firsthand were night and day from hearing about a past life that seemed further and further away with Rory so near.

"Alec, I don't care about your job. I thought it was cute that you wouldn't tell me. Like a game."

He grinned. It had turned into that, a fun little reason to banter and tease, since the revelation was of no real consequence. At least, not to her. "So why can't you talk to me about your sister all of a sudden?"

She stopped, closed her eyes and took a deep breath. He watched her battle her instincts—watched her automatically honest response get bitten down inside her mouth.

"Because how I feel about Micki is personal. Very personal. The most private feelings I have. I haven't even faced them myself. Not really. I learned that tonight."

Since when could they not discuss or explore the most intimate of topics?

"And you can't talk to me about this? Why?"

Her eyes flashed. "Why should you get involved?"

"Why wouldn't I? What's this about, Rory?"

The look of utter confusion on his face twisted like a knife in Rory's gut. God, she was acting like a child. The child she was. The child she might always be. Mixed up, secretly angry, harboring contradictory and irrational feelings that she could never, ever admit aloud or she might never stop screaming. She loved her sister; she hated her. She loved Alec, but she couldn't fall in love. What did she know about love? They'd been together just short of two weeks. At the same time that she wanted to collapse into his arms and allow him to share her turmoil, she knew that doing so would only dig her deeper into trouble.

"It's about me being very confused, very unsure of what I want anymore. It's about you being the most awesome man I've ever met and how inconvenient that is right now. I'm not making sense, Alec. I'm tired. I'm confused. I'm emotionally wrung-out from my sister being right before my eyes and then disappearing before I could find out what she wanted, or if she'd ever want to contact me again. And you need to go to work, not stick around here and hold my hand.''

Alec listened. With his ears, eyes, mouth. He leaned slightly forward into her space, his palms turned toward her. Every part of him seemed tuned into her needs, her pain. Yet, after a brief hesitation, he pressed his lips together and nodded. "If that's what you want.''

She couldn't move. He reached toward her and gently stroked her arm, igniting an incredibly painful longing. Holding her breath all the way to the staircase, Rory exhaled only after her foot touched the bottom step. She'd escaped without making an even bigger fool of herself, before she'd done something completely insane like tell Alec how much she loved him. Yet just as the pent-up anxiety pushed out of her lungs, Alec grabbed her from behind, spun her around and pressed his mouth to hers.

White-hot need erupted instantaneously. His power injected into her like a liquid drug, his desire snared her like a nylon line—clear, nearly invisible, yet impossible to snap without a great struggle. God, she wanted him. Tonight. Now.

Then he stopped. His chest heaved. Moisture either from the kiss or from exertion pearled on his upper lip.

"Sorry,'' he said, though not an ounce of apology existed in his eyes. "I needed the taste of you on my mouth before I went.''

Unconsciously she drew her fingers to her lips. A buzz zimmed through her, making her forget why she'd left before stealing a kiss as he had.

"Alec, I...''

He shook his head. "No explanations, Rory. We made a clear arrangement when you first arrived. Something about no strings, no expectations. I have no right to push you to tell me anything you aren't ready to tell.''

"Yes, you do. Have the right, I mean."

"How do you figure?"

Because I love you.

"You've been a good friend," she answered.

"That's it? Just a friend?"

She blinked, heat permeating her eyes, her cheeks. "I can't say that."

"Good." He stepped back and hooked his hands in his pockets. "When you do figure out what you *would* say, let me know, okay?"

With a spring in his step, Alec turned around, slipped into his apartment to grab his keys, then disappeared out the front door. Rory remained on the landing the entire time, watching him, wondering what had suddenly lightened his mood. She smirked, speculating on where she could acquire a taste of whatever had injected him with such instant happiness. Then, touching her still-warm lips, she realized she already knew.

"SO THIS IS IT?"

Shaw looked up from the folder Alec had tossed on his desk, a slightly amused tilt to his smooth-as-bourbon grin.

"Might be dry reading for a Sunday afternoon," Alec admitted, "but that's the précis of my study."

Shaw glanced at the byline. "And your name isn't Xander?"

Alec stuffed his hands into his pockets. "Alexander. I had a girlfriend in college who called me Xander. She thought it sounded cool. Everyone else calls me Alec."

"And why are you telling me all this? You could have just given your notice. I lose bartenders all the time."

Alec shrugged, then folded himself into the chair across from Shaw's. After a long night tending bar, Alec had gone home, caught a little rest before his meeting with the Yeagers, then returned to the club to help with Sunday afternoon inventory. As the new recipient of the Henson Foundation's annual grant and with Rory working a wedding in Lincoln Park, he'd had to share his good news with someone.

"Thought you deserved the whole truth. This morning I met with the directors of a foundation that is willing to sponsor a real academic study based on my casual observances while working here."

"And I was the lucky winner of 'whom do I tell first?'"

Alec glanced at the ceiling. "Something like that."

"You need to get a life, man."

"Tell me about it."

"What about that girl who had you so distracted last Saturday night? I never did see anyone show up who caught your eye."

Alec frowned. Despite his invitation, Rory still didn't seem to want to come with him to the club. Before his breakfast meeting with the Yeagers, he'd checked on her. She hadn't yet started dressing for work, and the soft skin around her eyes had been pink and puffy, not so much from crying, he guessed, as from lack of sleep. He wondered how much of the night she'd spent gazing outside her window, wondering, hoping that her sister would return.

As far as he knew, Micki had not come back. And after Rory gave him a rundown of her day—assisting with a big Divine Events wedding followed by a trip to the suburbs to visit with her grandmother and great-aunt—Alec wondered when he'd see Rory again. Of course, seeing her was the least of his desires. He wanted to feel her, touch her. Pleasure her. Wanted to somehow time warp them back to the adventurous, intimate sexual encounters they'd explored just days ago. Before emotions got in the way.

"She's got other things on her mind right now. I guess I have, too," he admitted, gesturing toward the study.

"I get the feeling this is the first time you've ever put your work ahead of a woman."

Alec sat back, thought. "Yeah, I guess it is."

"And she didn't like it?"

"Actually, she didn't seem to mind."

Shaw laughed and for a minute looked every bit his age. Alec knew the man was only five years older than him, but in about every situation he encountered, Shaw had a perennial look in his eyes that said, "Been there, done that."

"Well, either this woman is just yanking your chain or she's the most unique female on the planet. You'd better find out which real soon."

Alec's neck suddenly tightened. His shoulders cramped. Last night, he'd suspected that when he'd planted his parting kiss on Rory, he'd been shockingly close to losing her. But he hadn't thought her sudden reluctance to be with him had anything to do with his career or even her trauma with her sister. There was something deeper, something so personal she couldn't share with him, despite the physical intimacies they'd exchanged so easily over the past two weeks.

Unfortunately, for all his scientific and psychological observational skills and his documented knowledge of the way women operated in relation to men, he had no clue what was at the root of her sudden standoffishness. He'd asked her, but she hadn't answered with her usual aplomb, so he'd backed off. He figured more probing questions would further bolster the wall she seemed to be slowly building between them. But Shaw was right on one point. If Alec didn't want to be fenced out permanently, he'd better figure out what was going on in Rory's head—or, more likely, her heart.

"Good advice," Alec decided. "I'll do that."

Shaw pressed his lips together. "Don't be fooled by how easy that sounds." He turned to the final page of the study, where Alec had listed his reference materials. "I can't wait to dig into this. But you'll be messing me up if you don't at least work tonight. We've got a new band booked. I need a full staff."

"Not a problem. I have a while before I have to return to the less interesting halls of academia. How 'bout I hang out until you find a replacement?"

"Won't take long," Shaw commented, flipping over the cover page of the study outline. "Now get out of here. I've got some reading to do. Might even start understanding the women who come in here."

Alec laughed and stood. "If my study accomplishes that, I'll be famous."

"Yeah, well, just don't forget the little guys who helped get you there."

Relaxed now that he'd come clean to his boss, Alec strode back into the club, thankful the staff was only now arriving and the band was at least an hour short of the sound check and rehearsal. Dixie Landings was quieter on Sunday nights, but still pulled in a decent crowd since other clubs didn't open at all. Maybe some down time in the cavernous bar might just give him a shot at figuring out what to do next about Rory.

He headed first to the bookkeeping office, signed for a cash register till and double-checked the accounting. Once behind the bar, he activated the computer, signed in with his password, then secured the money in the drawer. He inventoried the bottles of well brands first, then the good stuff. Once he'd completed the count, he prepared the bar for opening, refilling the rum and vodka, cajoling one of the waiters into grabbing a case of gin from the back room while he drained a jar of olives into the condiment tray. He'd worked as a bartender throughout college, and while at the time he'd considered the clientele of easy women as the main job perk, he now acknowledged the appeal of a job where he could work hard and earn a buck while chatting with some fairly interesting people. In the classroom, he had to maintain the position as the most educated, most organized, most thought-provoking person in the room. Behind the bar, he could be nearly anonymous, and yet still control the experience of the patrons who paid the cover charge.

"Hey, Barry, where's that gin?" he called out while hunting for the cherries he'd seen yesterday behind the jar of pearl onions.

"You Alec?"

The voice startled him. Where he'd expected a gruff comeback from Barry along the lines of "Keep your pants on," he'd heard the soft, sultry whisper of a woman. He stood and turned, and his lips parted to ask, "Who wants to know?" but he swallowed the question after one glance.

The eyes gave her away.

Micki Carmichael.

17

Rory stood outside Nanna's house, the strap of her backpack purse cutting into her shoulder. The load was heavy thanks to a jar of Gia Divine's specialty chocolate sauce she'd brought as a present. Her eyes scanned the house. All of the bricks were the same shade of red. All of the impatiens in the window boxes bloomed in the same vibrant pinks and snowy whites. The concrete steps with the peeling wrought-iron handrails still looked like she would suffer a serious scrape to the knee if she didn't watch her footing on the way to the burgundy half-moon door with the tired aluminum screen. The screen door had a tear near the latch from the day Aunt Lil had accidentally locked herself outside when she and Rory had run out to catch the ice-cream truck.

The house hadn't changed, but Rory certainly had. She'd been gone just shy of two weeks, but in that nostalgic part of her heart that tended to exaggerate, this homecoming had been a long time in the making. Maybe because before her move to Chicago, she'd never truly left home. Maybe because before last night, seeing Micki again and then losing her so quickly, she'd never realized how much her sister had thrown away.

"Aurora?" Her grandmother appeared in the open doorway, the Kiss the Cook apron Rory had given her once for Christmas wrapped around her five-foot-four-inch frame. Her feet, encased in sparkling white Keds, had no trouble navigating the stairs, and when she placed her aged arms around Rory, vigor and strength anchored the hug.

"What are you doing just standing out here? It's hot as blazes."

Rory gave Nanna a second tight squeeze, then hooked her arm in hers before they walked into the house. "I was just thinking."

"About something serious, judging by the look on your face. Is something wrong?"

Rory's abdominal muscles clenched. She had so much to tell her grandmother, so much to ask. And an equal dose of secrets she had no intention of sharing, mainly about Alec. But she didn't intend to hit her grandmother with the shocking news of Micki's sudden appearance and disappearance before they'd even had a moment to catch up. "Nothing so wrong that we have to talk about it right this minute."

The smell of cinnamon enticed Rory the minute they passed into the living room. With each step across the hardwood floors, her nose twitched, seeking out the distinctive scents of vanilla, nutmeg, toasted oatmeal and piquant, hot raisins. Once in the kitchen, Rory's stomach growled. Her grandmother had indeed baked cookies. Not chocolate chip, but her second favorite—oatmeal raisin. Over ten dozen, if her calorically magnified eyes could be trusted to provide an accurate count.

"Another bake sale for the church?" Rory asked, her mouth pooling with moisture, her mind forming an image of exactly which delicious task she'd invent for Alec so he could earn a taste of confectionery heaven.

"Fourth of July picnic. And I thought you'd like to

take some back to your apartment, maybe share with the neighbors.''

Rory glanced at her grandmother, but Nanna innocently opened the refrigerator, removed a jug of milk, then shut the door. Nothing in her expression indicated that by "neighbor" she meant "Alec." She snagged the closest cookie and took a bite, hoping that, for the time being, she could put all thoughts of him aside. She wanted to focus on her grandmother. She wanted to make this visit count, perhaps in more ways than one. She desperately wanted to tell Nanna that she'd seen Micki, that her runaway twin was alive, though she'd vanished as quickly and mysteriously as she'd appeared. But she needed fortification, courage.

A warm raisin melted sweetly in her mouth and she couldn't help but close her eyes while she savored the flavors of nutty oatmeal, caramelized brown sugar and sweet, creamy butter. The taste of comfort. The taste of home. Once the initial euphoria waned, however, she finished the cookie in two quick bites, then noticed more of them cooling on racks all around the kitchen. In a tall Tupperware container, she spied what had to be several dozen more cookies, ready for delivery or freezing.

Nanna loved to bake, but unless she planned to provide inventory for bake sales for every church in the Diocese of Chicago instead of just for St. Leonard's, the sheer number of cookies was alarming.

"You've decided to start a home business, haven't you?" she guessed, not entirely joking.

"Don't be a tease," her grandmother said, smiling. She scooped another tablespoon of raw batter onto a cookie pan. "I overbaked a bit, I'll admit. But it's not like they'll go to waste."

Wait. Batter? Rory beelined across the room in seconds, just in time to get her fingers smacked with the spoon.

Nanna didn't have to ask Rory if she'd washed her hands first. They'd played out this scene too often. Instead Rory grumbled, but headed straight to the sink.

"How long can you stay?"

"A couple of hours," Rory answered. "I'm meeting a friend later tonight."

"A boyfriend?"

That came from Aunt Lil, who shuffled into the room in pale pink slacks, blue Keds and an oversize white T-shirt with yellow baby chickens parading over the slogan, Chics Rule.

Rory almost choked on her cookie.

Her gaze darted back to her grandmother. Beneath her apron, she wore blue jeans. Jeans? Denim? Wait…pants? Nanna never wore pants unless they were part of one of her famous pastel pantsuits she wore to church on the coldest days…and even that had been a radical change in later years after decades of wearing only dresses and thin hose, no matter the weather.

"Nice shirt, Aunt Lil," Rory said, crossing the room to peck her great-aunt on the cheek.

"Ain't it the pip? I saw it at the store and had to have it."

Lil was the queen of the impulse buy. A retired nun, Lil had conservative views offset by a streak of radical behavior that had convinced Rory that her own genetic propensity for trouble went back several generations. Even the Catholic Church hadn't been able to spirit the sass out of Lil, and the rumor whispered among extended family had always been that she'd moved back in with

Marjorie so she didn't stir up too much dissent at the home for retired sisters. Even at eighty, she worked a part-time job answering phones for a local lawyer, earning just enough money to satisfy her need to buy something frivolous for one or another of the kids in the neighborhood. Or, every so often, for herself.

"It's a great shirt. But the fact that Nanna's allowing you to wear it in public? That's throwing me for a loop."

Her grandmother's sigh was wholly exaggerated. "I'm too old to argue anymore."

Rory sidled up behind her grandmother and gave her a hug. "You don't look old. In fact, you look particularly spry."

Nanna tilted her head against Rory's. "You're a sweet girl, Aurora."

"Yes, I am."

"And I am feeling good," Nanna confessed.

"I can tell."

"I've been fortunate."

"You've been exercising and following the doctor's rules and not eating any of these cookies," Aunt Lil explained, snagging a handful of treats for herself.

The mention of the word "doctor" spawned a hitch in Rory's heartbeat. "What rules did the doctor give you?"

Nanna patted Rory's arm before returning to her stirring, scooping and plopping. "Nothing he hasn't told me before. I'm fine, dear. It's just that Lil's all hyped up over the exercise regimen we started this week. We're walking a mile a day."

"Might be up to two miles by next week," her aunt added.

"We won't push it."

Rory wasn't satisfied. Dr. Manning had put her grandmother on regimens before, but usually they included drugs like Cytoxan and Adriamycin. "But the cancer? It's still gone?"

"Won't dare come back," Lil said, popping another cookie over wizened lips. "Don't hold dinner for me. I'm going down the street for a bit. Jessie Hopper is doing a report for her college class on the Depression and I told her she could interview me."

"What do you know about the Depression?" Rory's grandmother asked, incredulous. "We were poor before and poorer after. Not much to tell, if you ask me."

Lil shook her head, her short white hair catching the last light from the setting sun through the window. "That's my Margie, always so darned pragmatic. Do you have no sense of drama? Don't you remember the time…"

Rory tuned out the story she'd heard a thousand times before, smiling, certain Miss Jessie Hopper was going to get more than enough material for her essay, though she wouldn't vouch for the authenticity. Lil was good and kind and full of fun, but she often had trouble separating fact from fiction, particularly when the fiction proved more entertaining.

Her grandmother, on the other hand, was sensible and sweet and sometimes even indulgent—something Rory hadn't thought about in a long time. How could she? Ever since she'd made the decision to move out and build her own life, she'd thought of little but her own independence. Finding a job. An apartment. She'd spent hours wrapped up in her concerns about leaving her family, living in the city, searching for her sister…and finding a lover.

She'd been so concerned that she'd stolen a few pages

from the *Sexcapades* book and then approached a virtual stranger to share the fantasies with her. Yet she hadn't been nearly concerned enough. Because she should have been afraid that her deepest fear might come true. And it had. She'd fallen in love.

She'd fallen in love with the first man who'd shown her a good time. It hadn't just been good, though. It had been awesome. Better than she'd ever imagined possible in her lifetime. She tried to convince herself that her connection to Alec was nothing more than friendship laced with gratitude because he'd introduced her to an orgasm, but she knew their connection was much, much more. Lust, desire and honest affection fortified the layers of trust and need that Rory undeniably felt for Alec. Unfortunately she had no idea if he was similarly afflicted. And she had only one way to find out.

As much as she hated confrontations, Rory knew today would brim with them. First, with her grandmother. Then, with Alec. But, luckily, not right this minute. In silence, she set the small round table in the corner of the kitchen, then popped open the Crockpot beside the stove to find it simmering with a rich vegetable soup.

"There's fresh bread in the breadmaker. You can eat now if you're hungry. I've just got this last batch."

"I'll wait."

Rory grabbed a tablespoon from the drawer next to the sink and proceeded to help Nanna space out the dollops of dough on the glossy cookie sheet.

"So, you're going to make me pry, aren't you?" Nanna asked quietly.

"Pry?"

"About your job, your apartment?"

"That's not prying. My job is fantastic. The Divines

are the coolest. They've only been in business for a little over two years and the operation is booming.'' She proceeded to tell her grandmother about the dinner party at the Plaza 440 building—one of the most exclusive in the city—skipping, of course, the part where she asked Alec to help her at the warehouse.

"Big changes," Nanna commented, sliding the last cookie sheet into the oven and setting the timer. "But you're happy. Aren't you?"

Rory licked the last of the batter off the spoon, then tossed it in the sink. "Don't I look happy?"

"Frankly, no.''

Rory pursed her lips, wondering how her grandmother had honed her observational skills so keenly. She decided there was no use trying to hide the truth. Two troubles weighed heavily on Rory—her twin's sudden appearance and disappearance, and her deepening feelings for Alec. Since she didn't want to talk about one, she had no choice but tackle the other.

She took the plate out of her grandmother's hand, relatively certain she shouldn't have anything breakable around when Rory dropped her bombshell.

"I saw Micki.''

"Micki who, dear?''

"Michaela, Nanna. I saw Michaela.''

As expected, her grandmother's balance faltered. Rory grabbed her elbow, but the older woman shook her away. "Where did you see her?''

"Outside my apartment.''

"She found you? How?''

"I'm not sure. But I've been looking for her.''

Nanna shuffled to the table and sat down. Desperate to help, Rory grabbed her bowl and ladled in a serving of soup, then did the same for herself. She tossed the crusty bread in a dish towel-lined basket, then sat down, hoping the cozy setting might take some of the edge off this particular conversation.

"Are you mad? That I've been looking?"

"Of course not. I knew you'd look. That you'd been looking for quite some time."

Nanna patted her hand, but Rory hardly registered the sweet gesture. "You knew?"

"Rory, you're a good girl. But you don't lie well. Besides, you've always been curious by nature…a trait you got from me."

Nanna leaned around to the wooden rack Rory had made once at summer camp that was now the final resting place for expired coupons, clipped newspaper articles and recipes. She extracted a copy of the police report Rory had found on the Internet, detailing Micki's arrest.

"I found this."

Rory took the paper, but didn't need to read it. "I don't know how that's possible. My copy is still at my apartment."

Nanna frowned and chose that moment to take a hearty spoonful of soup.

"Nanna?"

"Rosemary at the library found it on the printer. She said you must have hit Print one time too many, whatever that means."

Rory rolled her eyes. She should have been more careful. Nanna had been friends with the local librarian for years, and while she'd been vigilant about surfing the Internet from a corner cubicle where no one could see over her shoulder, had cleared the cache and cookies from the computer she'd used and had rushed to the printer to snag her printout before anyone could see what she'd found, she hadn't lingered. She might have double-clicked the print command by accident.

"So if you knew I was looking all this time, why didn't you ask me about it? Why didn't you try to stop me?"

"I tried, actually. Before you moved into your apartment, I asked Dr. Manning to talk to his son, try to get him to discourage you from your search. He refused to stand in your way. So, I accepted the inevitable. She's your twin. How could I stop you?"

Rory pushed a carrot and stewed tomato around in her soup bowl, smiling softly at the thought that even before they'd met, Alec had stood up for her right to make her own choices.

She looked up at her grandmother. "I always thought that once you and Aunt Lil gave up hope of finding her, you didn't want anyone else to look anymore, either."

"It's not that I didn't want anyone to look, sweetheart. I simply didn't need them to."

Rory paused, the spoonful of soup halfway to her mouth. "You knew where she was?"

Her grandmother placed her spoon directly beside her bowl, fiddling with the handle until it was perfectly straight. "Not exactly."

Heat boiled in Rory's stomach, and she'd yet to take a steaming bite. "What exactly?"

"I knew she was alive and that she had no interest in coming home again."

"And you knew this how?"

"She told me so herself, four years ago. She came home, high on something, on your birthday, no less."

"She came home to tell you she wasn't coming home?"

Rory pushed her food away, her appetite lost, her stomach churning with anger, rage. Just what was Micki up to anyway? Torture? And why hadn't her grandmother told her this before today?

Nanna pushed her bowl aside as well. "I think she might have wanted to come home for a little while, but I'd just found out about the cancer. I told her she was welcome to stay as long as she cleaned up her act. She said I couldn't tell her what to do. Defiant until the end, that one. You have to understand, Rory. I couldn't have her here if she was going to bring added stress. I had to focus on recovering my health."

Rory did understand. But she still would have wanted to know. Maybe she could have helped Micki without involving her grandmother, though, at the moment, she couldn't have imagined how. "Why didn't you tell me?"

"I was afraid you'd follow her. Go after her. End up like her."

Tears glistened in Nanna's eyes and, despite her rage, Rory reached out and gently laid her palm over her grandmother's hand, which shook softly.

"I couldn't end up like her, Nanna. You didn't raise me that way."

"I didn't raise her that way. I didn't raise your mother that way!" A dollop of moisture dropped from her pale blue eyes, and Rory choked back her regret.

"I'm sorry. You're right. Mom and Micki were restless souls. There wasn't anything you could have done to keep them here."

"I could have tried bolts and chains."

Rory laughed, despite her suspicion that her grandmother hadn't been joking. At least, not entirely. "They would have escaped eventually."

"You did."

"I didn't escape. It was just time for me to move on, make my own way. I have you to thank for the fact that I'm not screwed up. I'm confident. I know I can take care of myself."

Her entire life, Rory's family had never been overly demonstrative. They kissed and hugged, sure—but they didn't cry jags together or shout when they were angry. Emotions simmered, warm and steady. How her mother and her twin could have run away from such reliable love, she'd never understand.

But she did have a clue as to why Micki took off last night. Maybe she was still a junkie or a drunk or both. Maybe she was embarrassed to reveal herself to a sister who, despite her sheltered upbringing, had a strong handle on her future. Maybe she was afraid, as Rory had been, to confront her true self.

Like the aroma from the soup, Rory's fears seeped out of her in a curling mist, disappearing into the spicy air. The timer on the oven dinged, sending her grandmother for the oven mitts. Once the cookies were on the cooling rack, she returned to the table, where Rory had pushed both their plates back into place.

"I'm glad I came home today, Nanna."

She slipped into her chair and sipped a spoonful of soup. "I'm glad, too. I was afraid that once you left, you'd never come back. Frankly I'm surprised you stayed around here so long."

"You could have kicked me out," Rory joked.

Nanna almost spit out her soup at the ridiculous suggestion. "Don't you think I've driven out enough of my girls?"

"You didn't drive my mother out," Rory insisted, regretting her choice of quip. "She chose to go. All you ever did was love her."

"I was too strict. But there weren't many single mothers when I was trying to raise her. God bless your grandfather, but his dying young caught me so off guard. I didn't have any friends to talk to, to emulate. Not ones that didn't have a husband. I knew your mother needed a firm hand, but I think I went too far."

Rory had once thought this way, once blamed her grandmother for her mother's wayward wanderings. But Micki's leaving had changed her mind. Rory had grown up in the same house, with the same rules—with the same love. Her sister's restless spirit simply couldn't stand the same confines that made Rory feel loved, safe. From that moment, she'd decided her mother had suffered the same affliction—a need to go out on her own that Rory had managed to ignore until very recently.

"I'm not here to judge you, Nanna. But you and I both know that if you'd loosened the reins on my mother, she might only have self-destructed sooner. Then you wouldn't have had me."

"Or your sister. I love her, Rory—you know that."

"Of course."

"That's why I couldn't help you look, but why I couldn't stop you from looking, either. How could I? I'm so ashamed."

"Ashamed? Of what?"

"Of how I drove Micki away, how I kept the two of you apart."

Rory twisted her mouth, then covered her regret with

a few spoonfuls of soup. She wished she'd known about Micki's visit, but she'd been living near the junior college at the time, and that night she'd likely been out celebrating with her friends. And her grandmother had been terrified when she'd first received her diagnosis. And rightly so. She couldn't judge her grandmother for putting her health first, possibly for the first time in her life.

"Micki could have found me a million times, Nanna. She found me last night, and I still don't know how she did it. Or why."

Nanna tore her bread into bite-size pieces, but made no move to put one in her mouth. "Did she look okay?"

"She looked fine."

"Not drunk? Not high?"

She wished she knew, but Rory's glimpse hadn't lasted that long. "I'm not sure."

"But you'll find out."

The hopeful gleam in Nanna's eyes solidified Rory's resolve. She would find Micki, as soon as she could. Life was too short for less than total honesty and complete disclosure.

So she wasn't going to waste any more time dancing around her feelings for Alec, either. Maybe his initial reluctance to try anything long-term had melted away just as hers had. Maybe it hadn't. But she wouldn't know until she confronted him, which she'd do. Tonight.

"I will find her, Nanna. Don't worry about me."

Nanna's smile sparkled. "I don't worry about you, Aurora. You know what you want from life and you don't jump in without looking first."

Rory couldn't contain a laugh. "Depends on what I'm looking for."

If only her grandmother knew how she'd gone looking

for trouble, she wouldn't be so certain of her ability to emerge from the search unscathed. She'd found her trouble in the form of Alec Manning. Now, the question remained of what she was going to do to keep him.

18

RORY DROVE UP AND DOWN the street four times before she found a parking space near her apartment, her gaze alternately seeking out a curbside opening or anyone who resembled her sister. Was Micki out there, waiting for her, watching her? Why had she come looking for her the night before only to run away? And why had she gone to their grandmother's high when past experience should have told Micki that her appearance in such a condition would not be welcome? Maybe under other circumstances, Marjorie Carmichael would have opened her heart, offered to help her troubled granddaughter in whatever way she could. But Nanna had just found out about her cancer, and by the time she'd been clearheaded enough to react with compassion, Micki had disappeared yet again.

Rory couldn't help but be angry and scared for her sister at the same time. Was she still addicted? Neither Detective Walters nor the woman from the shelter had mentioned such problems. Either way, Rory didn't care. Micki could be a strung out junkie, for all she cared. She just wanted her sister back. They could deal with her problems once they were reunited.

Sitting in the parked Jeep, she scanned the faces of the trio of girls jogging down her street. She watched a middle-aged man with a newspaper under his arm, then followed the movements of the man she'd seen the night before walking his dog. She peered at hedges, watching for any sign of movement. But emotional exhaustion cut her stakeout short—that and the smell of fresh-baked cookies her grandmother had loaded onto her back seat. Luckily Gia had given her two jars of her famous chocolate sauce. One, she'd given to Nanna and Aunt Lil. The other remained on her kitchen table, a planned gift for Alec.

Multiple uses for the rich cocoa concoction eased into her mind, giving her good reason to jump out of the car and hurry up the steps. She'd had enough angst for one day. She wanted Alec. She wanted no expectations, no strings. Nothing but complete and utter sexual satisfaction with a man who wanted only what she wanted to give him.

Trouble was, she wanted to give him a whole lot more than she thought he'd want. Her heart was his. Her soul, too. She loved him, wanted to make a life with him, embark on a real relationship. She still wondered if she wasn't naively reacting to the glorious freedom of their sexual interactions—but she'd decided she didn't care. If things didn't work out, she'd have a broken heart. So what? Broken hearts healed. She'd had enough what-ifs in her lifetime. Enough what-could-have-beens. Living meant loving and, sometimes, losing.

She wasn't afraid to lose, not when she knew that not playing was infinitely worse. She accepted the inherent risk, but would Alec? He'd played fast and furious with his career and his reputation, but from what he'd told her, his heart had never been part of the mix. With the other women in his life, he'd protected his emotions by leaving them unengaged. But Rory knew he hadn't done that with her. Yes, she was inexperienced, but she wasn't completely unaware. Alec cared about her, just as she cared about him. But to what degree? And would what he felt be enough?

She unlocked the front door, then knocked at his apartment without hesitation. She checked her watch. Ten-thirty. Darn. She knocked again. "Alec?"

She couldn't remember if he had to work at the club tonight. But when he hadn't answered her third knock and her ear to the door didn't reveal the sound of a running shower or his adorable snoring when he napped on the couch, she figured he must have been out. She was halfway up the staircase when she heard the door creak open. The sound of shoes—decidedly female—echoed behind her and stopped her cold.

Rory's breath hitched, and she swallowed to press down the unease burning up her throat. Who was there? Who had been in Alec's apartment? She stood perfectly still, her presence hidden by the curve in the landing, but she'd already revealed herself to whomever had come out of Alec's apartment when she'd called his name.

The footsteps were tentative, light. Unable to tamp down her curiosity, she poked her head around the corner. The minute the woman walked into the light, Rory dropped the metal key ring to the floor, making them both jump at the clang.

"Micki?"

Her twin's smile raised only on one side. "Hey."

Air pressed out of Rory's lungs. Dizziness wobbled her stance, but she regained her equilibrium the minute she dashed down the stairs, her purse thudding on the floor, her mind focused on nothing but wrapping her sister in her arms. Micki smelled like cigarette smoke and hair spray. Her fake leather jacket crinkled beneath Rory's arms, but Rory'd never felt anything so rich, so fine. She pulled back long enough to look into mirrors of her own crystal-blue eyes, lined with kohl just as Lisa had described. Micki's raven hair was tinged with streaks of midnight blue and her grin was nothing less than sardonic, but Rory instantly recognized the clarity in her sister's expression.

She wasn't on anything. She was here. She was sober. She was the most beautiful woman she'd ever seen.

Tears splashed down Rory's cheeks. She had never felt so tired and emotionally spent—and yet she brimmed with energy and could barely hold still in Micki's arms.

"Why'd you run away last night?" She gripped her sister by the elbows, so she couldn't leave. Not now. Not ever.

"It was stupid. I got scared, seeing you. I didn't expect—"

"How'd you find out where I lived?"

Micki rolled her eyes. "Remember that phone call from the cable company, verifying your address?"

Rory shook her head. No, she didn't remember. She'd taken and made dozens of move-in calls over the past week or two.

"Well, you should be more careful with your personal information. I got your number from someone at the shelter. You left a card. I called you at work about the cable and you gave me the address yourself."

Rory couldn't believe she'd fallen for such a ruse or that she'd failed to recognize her sister's voice. Never mind that she hadn't heard it in nearly ten years. Or that Micki's voice had a raspy depth that hers lacked. After a minute without her chest pressed against Micki's, she decided she didn't care. She pulled her sister into another hug.

"So I'm gullible. Sue me. But you're brilliant. Let's just leave it at that. Come upstairs with me. Please. We have so much to talk about."

She hated letting her twin go long enough to walk upstairs but she did, though she held tight to her hand, pulling her behind her like she'd done when they were children. With giddy excitement, she showed her sister her apartment and, surprisingly, Micki didn't seem to mind her silliness. She was acting like a fool, but her sister understood. Of course, she understood. They were sisters. Twins. Separate, but never quite separated. Even after all these years.

"It isn't the Taj Mahal, but it's mine. As long as Alec keeps renting it to me, I guess. Speaking of which, you were in his apartment when I came in. How did that happen?"

Rory adjusted her tone, hoping her sister would admit to breaking and entering if that were the case. She figured her sister had a complete range of survival skills that would at the very least include the ability to pick a lock.

She hadn't figured on her possessing a key.

"Alec gave me this," she said, producing Alec's leather-strapped key ring from her pocket. "I tracked him down at Dixie Landing."

"You tracked *him* down? Why?"

"I guess I wanted to know what you were like, if you really wanted me back or if you were looking for me out of some sense of duty or because Nanna had died or something."

"Nanna's fine."

Micki shrugged and Rory knew this wasn't the time

for her twin to deal with her feelings for her grandmother. Nanna and Micki had their own baggage to lug and unpack. For now, Rory was only concerned about Micki and herself.

"That's good."

"What did Alec tell you?"

Micki strolled toward the window, but not toward the door. Rory exhaled, easing her instinct to grab on to her sister just to make sure she didn't escape again.

"He was cool. Gave me the key, told me to quit being a coward and find out what you wanted for myself."

Impressed, Rory sat down on the couch and watched her sister pace. Micki brimmed with nervous energy, just like she usually did, though Micki was obviously more effective at keeping her anxiety contained. Rory's twin possessed a wariness in her eyes, constantly darting her gaze from corner to corner, even in a room with a closed, locked door. Rory figured her sister had a very limited capacity for trust, but with the way she'd lived her life the past ten years, this trait had probably kept her alive.

"How'd you find Alec?"

Micki grinned. "The old-fashioned way."

"The phone book?" Rory asked, skeptical.

"I followed him. He takes the "L" to the club, so I just hopped on behind him."

"What's the club like?"

"Haven't you been there?"

"Not when he was working."

"Does he have a honey there?"

Rory smirked. She doubted this scenario and was pleasantly surprised that not even an inkling of jealousy seeped under her skin.

"He could have a hundred honeys there for all I know."

"And this doesn't bother you? How long have you two been together?"

"He's my landlord. How do you know if we're 'together' or not?"

Micki matched Rory's earlier smirk, then added a sardonic tone of voice. "I thought he was going to beat his chest when he saw me. You should have heard him. He told me off with words I still need to look up in a dictionary, if you have one handy. He's a sophisticated caveman, I'll give him that."

"Caveman, huh?"

Rory couldn't help grinning from ear to ear. Caveman meant possessive. And possessive meant... Well, she wasn't sure what that meant, but her instincts told her it had to be good. Men didn't beat their chests for women they didn't deeply care about. Did they?

"So I return to my first question," Micki said, triumphantly. "How long have you two been together?"

"Shouldn't we be talking about you? Like why you ran away, why you stayed away, where you've been for, oh, the last ten years?"

Micki shook her head, plopped down on the couch beside Rory and kicked her high-heeled boots onto the edge of the coffee table.

"Why I ran away? Because I was a stubborn, smartass kid. Why I stayed away? Because I am a stubborn, smart-ass adult. Where I've been the past ten years? Nowhere."

Rory took her sister's hand. "It's not that simple, Micki. You know it."

Micki relaxed into the couch. "I know. I'll give you

the short version for tonight, okay? I was a dumb kid who ran away, then got too scared of the consequences to come home."

"That's a little too simple, don't you think?" Rory ventured, wondering if she should confront her sister so soon. She didn't want her to run again. But she also thought she deserved the whole truth. "You haven't been a kid for a long time."

"No, but I had one to look after."

Rory gasped.

Micki clutched her hand tighter. "Oh, jeez. No! I didn't mean I *had* a kid. There's this teenager, Danielle. Danielle Stone. I met her five years ago on the street. It was rough for me, but nothing compared to how it was for her. I cleaned myself up so I could help her out. I've been keeping an eye on her ever since."

Rory squelched her instinct to point out the irony of that situation, figuring Micki was quick enough to see the obvious. "Is she okay? This Danielle?"

"Actually, no. But she will be, as soon as I get her real treatment. She's an addict, Rory. Not like me who just drank and partied because I could. She may have started that way, but now she can't stop. At least, not without professional intervention."

"Doesn't she have a family?"

"Yeah," Micki said, her face twisting with distaste. "But I don't know how much I can count on them to help me."

"I'll help you," Rory said, knowing she'd do anything to make sure her sister stayed in her life. She'd found her, finally found her—she wasn't going to allow even a noble cause to separate them again.

Micki pulled her into a hug. "I know you will. And I

may need you to, really soon. But for tonight, let's stop worrying. Now that I'm here, I don't plan on leaving. At least, not permanently. So we don't have to fill in all the blanks tonight. Let's just enjoy hanging out, maybe dissect your love life, the way sisters are supposed to. The people I hang with don't really have love lives.''

"Neither did I until two weeks ago," Rory quipped.

Micki leaned her head on her shoulder. "Aw, how sweet. You waited for me?"

"Yeah, that's what I did!"

They dissolved into girlish giggles, a sound that echoed loudly for all the years that had been silent of the sound. Rory gripped Micki's hand tightly and recounted the secrets of the past two weeks, all the way down to the stolen pages from the *Sexcapades* book.

"*Sexcapades,* huh? I'm going to have to check that sucker out.''

"I'll try and grab a few pages for you, if there are any left. One of these days, I'm going to ask my boss if they purposely put the book on the table as a lure for customers. Best marketing technique I've seen in years."

"I don't know about that, but I'm glad to hear my Goody-Two-Shoes twin isn't beyond a little thievery from time to time. I'd hate to think I inherited all the negative Carmichael genes.''

Rory shook her head. "I think mine just took a little longer to reveal themselves."

"But they're hitting you full force now, aren't they? Thanks to this Alec dude."

With a sigh, Rory stood up and went to the kitchen to grab two sodas from the refrigerator. Micki followed behind her, leaning on the doorjamb. Rory thought her face would permanently freeze in a smile if she continued to grin any longer, but she couldn't help herself. Especially not when she spoke of Alec.

"I have a lot to thank him for."

"He sounds a little too good to be true, if you ask me."

Rory tossed her twin a can of soda, then pulled out a small plastic tub filled with her favorite cheese spread. After snagging some crackers from the cabinet and a knife from the drawer, they returned to the living room for a snackfest.

"He *is* too good to be true. He's been very careful to tell me all about his negative qualities and his sordid past, but I haven't seen a hint of anything that worries me."

"Maybe that's why he kept you away from that club. Maybe that's where he shows his true colors. Maybe that's why he didn't want you to go there."

Her twin's theory seemed too simple, but Alec had recently changed his mind about her going to Dixie Landings. Before she'd met Micki on the stairs, she'd been too exhausted to think about going anywhere other than to bed. Preferably with Alec. Now, she was invigorated—antsy, even. And more anxious than ever to pour her heart out to Alec and see what happened.

"Will you stay at my place tonight?" Rory asked.

"I have somewhere to go, Rory. I'm really not on the streets anymore. I mean, it's not as nice as this, but it's a roof and a floor, and it's pretty much bug-free."

"How are you paying for it? Do you need money?"

"Who doesn't need money?" Micki joked, but Rory couldn't find the humor. "Don't worry. I'm not currently footing the bill. I'm staying with a friend who has more money than she should, if you ask me."

"She? No boyfriend, then?"

Micki laughed and shook her head, spreading the jalapeño cheese spread over her cracker. "Unlike you, sis, I've had my fill of men. Remember how we used to speculate about the losers mom hooked up with?" She popped the circle into her mouth whole.

Rory frowned for the first time since Micki's return. "Yeah."

After she chewed and popped open her soda can, Micki took a dainty sip. Rory realized her sister was a mixed bag. Coarse, yet intelligent. Honest, but shrewd.

"Let me just say that, in my experience, those assholes outnumber the cavemen like your Alec about one hundred to one. I quit looking for a prince a long time ago. I'm making it on my own. It's slow, but I think I have my priorities straight now. But my cynicism doesn't mean I don't think you should hold on to your Alec with both hands."

"I may have no choice in the matter. He was pretty clear up front. He didn't want a relationship. And when we first hooked up, neither did I."

"And I take it you've changed your mind?"

"It's a woman's prerogative, right?"

"That's what I've always heard. You should go for it."

"I will."

"Tonight. Now would be good."

"But you just got here!" Rory protested, despite the fact that she wanted nothing more than to leap over the obstacles between her and Alec right here and now.

"And I'm not going anywhere, I told you," Micki reassured. "I'm done running, Rory. We have a lot to catch up on, a lot to deal with. I admit that. But I have a feeling you'll be much more agreeable to forgiving my missteps if you're happy with your man. Come on," Micki said, sandwiching two crackers and cheese together before grabbing Rory's hand. "Go brush your teeth and put on something trashy."

"Then what?"

"You tell me."

"Alec won't expect me."

"That's a bad thing?"

Rory grinned. No, unexpected wasn't bad. Not at all. She'd come into Alec's life that way two weeks ago, and she really hadn't heard him complain. All she wanted from him tonight was an agreement that what they'd started was worth exploring further, deeper. They'd agreed on a no-strings, no-expectations affair, but she was about to break that pact. And no matter how he reacted, she promised herself she'd have no regrets. She'd come looking for trouble with Alec, and what she'd found was love.

"Unexpected has actually worked very well for us so far."

Micki pushed her toward her bedroom. "It usually does, sis. It usually does."

19

THE COCKTAIL NAPKIN WAS halfway to the garbage pail before Shaw grabbed Alec's wrist.

"I wouldn't toss that if I were you," his boss warned. His lopsided grin took the sting out of the admonition, but spawned a prickle across the back of Alec's neck nonetheless.

Alec glanced down at the paper. Just after ten o'clock, the dance contest was about to commence. With half the crowd vying for first prize—dinner for two and a round of drinks on the house—and the other half circling the dance floor to watch, Alec had been using this lull in orders to clean up. He'd figured Shaw had handed him the napkin for disposal.

Apparently, he figured wrong.

"What is this?"

Shaw clucked his tongue. "Something interesting, if I'm a good judge of women—which, lucky for you, I am. And the one who asked me to deliver that note to you was very interesting."

Alec scanned the crowd, but saw no one he recognized beyond the club regulars. For a moment, he thought Rory had finally taken him up on his invitation to stop by the club, but he couldn't imagine that she and her sister had parted ways so soon. Unless Micki hadn't followed through with her plan to wait for Rory in Alec's apartment. He'd wring her slim neck himself if she dashed Rory's hopes and hurt her twin again. Maybe Micki had written the note—some lame excuse for why she'd deviated from their plan.

He unfolded the paper, but the fuzzy, bleeding ink made the letters unreadable in the dim light.

"Where is she?"

Shaw tilted his head toward the stairwell leading to his office, then grabbed an extra apron from a hook and wrapped it around his waist. "You need a break. But read the napkin first. She insisted. You have no idea how hard it was for me not to peek."

"But you didn't?"

"I'm a gentleman and a man of my word," Shaw insisted, his drawl only slightly exaggerated. "I'm also a man who appreciates a woman with an imagination. So get the hell out of here."

After wiping his hands, Alec ditched his dish towel and ducked out of the bar, taking the most direct route through the dance floor to the black door tucked on the other side of the bathrooms. He leaned into the empty men's room, where the light allowed him to read.

Tonight, one dream came true, thanks to you. My turn to reciprocate. Didn't have the Sexcapade *book handy, so I'm writing one of my own. I'll call it "Hide and Sleek."*

Alec's blood surged. Apparently Micki hadn't chickened out. And Rory, aware of his part in reuniting the sisters, was planning on thanking him in some inventive way. She was nothing if not creative. And fearless. And fun. How could a man like him possibly resist a woman as ideal as her? Try as he might to contain his libidinous ways, he realized now what a fruitless, ridiculous quest that had been. Sex hadn't been his downfall. His attitude had. Pursuing women that would stir his lust but not his emotions—that had caused the destruction in his life that he'd finally started to repair.

Rory, on the other hand, appealed to him on so many levels, he didn't know where one desire ended and another began. Yes, he wanted her physically. His groin tightened and his cock hardened with the simplest thought about what wicked possibilities she had in store for him. Yet, at the same time, his heart warmed with knowing that whatever fantasy they indulged in tonight was rooted in the genuine trust and affection they'd developed over the past two weeks. Hell, they'd gone beyond trust and affection. They shared love, plain and simple.

Alec followed a set of written directions that led him to Shaw's office, where beside the desk lamp, he discovered a manila envelope with his name written in bold letters.

Inside, he found her bra. Black and lacy, he remembered the first time she'd worn the sexy lingerie, the night they'd rented a movie and ordered in. Her air conditioner had refused to cool the living room and while Alec had instantly suspected sabotage on her part, he hadn't complained when she'd slowly stripped down to the underwear he now held in his hand, the satiny black cups contrasting with the light flesh of his palm, just as it had her pale skin. Complaining about the heat, she'd lured him to the window in her kitchen, the one that faced the back of the house. With no lights behind them, they'd made love with his bare ass on the sill and her sweet bottom writhing on his lap. Her thighs flush to his. Her breasts aroused by his hands. Her neck and shoulders bare to his lips, tongue and teeth.

His mouth dried. His sex throbbed. Every detail in the memory made him harder, hotter.

The tiny tag stapled to the back of the bra kicked the heat up even more.

There are no sills in this kitchen, but there is another clue.

Alec raced down the stairs, then through the hall that led to Dixie Landing's kitchen. Steam from the stoves slapped him in the face, clouding his vision. The industrial-size kitchen teemed with cooks, waiters and staff shouting orders, telling jokes, moving with the same frenetic precision as the dancers in the club. Where was he supposed to look?

"Yo, Alec! Got something here for you!"

The head chef waved his spatula in his direction, then handed him a small pastry box, taped securely at every corner.

Alec didn't wait to interrogate the cook; he knew who'd prepared the box. He thanked the man and dashed back into the private hallway, nearly giving himself a paper cut in his hunger to open Rory's next clue.

Inside, he found her panties. Not the ones she'd worn with the bra—those had been black thongs he'd easily hooked aside with his finger before he'd pulled her down atop his sex and buried himself inside her. No, these were the sapphire-blue ones he'd bought for her himself. The ones she'd yet to wear. The ones she'd been teasing him with for days.

Below them, the note read, "I'm still not wearing these. I'm saving them for another special occasion. But the good news is, I'm not wearing any panties at all. Find me.''

Alec cursed at the lack of a specific clue to guide him to his next destination, until he heard the box rattle. At the bottom, he found the automatic locking mechanism Rory used on her car. After a quick dash back into and out of the men's room, he tore into the lot behind the building.

He scanned the tightly parked collection of cars, fighting the urge to climb on top of the nearby Range Rover to get a better view. Instead he maneuvered atop a stack of crates and spotted the Jeep in the back row.

Impatience ruled as he tore through the nearly nonexistent space between the cars. Only the valets used this lot and with the capacity crowd on the verge of hearing the band's last set for the night, Alec knew they'd have at least a modicum of privacy. On such a hot night, no one lingered by the cars, not even the valets, who were likely smoking cigarettes by the curb up front and catching a cool breeze whenever the front door opened.

Lord, he had so much he wanted to tell Rory, so much he wanted to say…all of which could be said after he made love to her. She'd taken great pains to whet his appetite with lingerie, memories and hot promises. He'd never met a woman who could spark his flame so easily and he wasn't about to let her go.

The front seat of the Jeep was empty, but the engine hummed. A dark cloth, nearly unnoticeable in the unlit corner of the parking lot, blocked the view of the back seat. The side door was locked. But when he squeezed around to the back, the hatch was up enough for him to climb underneath. He was halfway in when Rory stopped him.

"What's the password?"

She'd lowered the back seat, doubling the size of the cargo area. Alec climbed in, the gentle blow of the air-conditioning fluttering her makeshift curtain.

Light from a street lamp slashed into the car. He couldn't see much, but his eyes instantly focused on her tight tank-top, her nipples erect, inviting—unhampered by a bra. With her legs pulled beneath a long, soft skirt, he had to wonder if she'd told the truth about the panties, but figured he'd find out soon enough.

"The password? Should I know this?" he asked, trying to push past his hot desire to remember if they'd established some secret code over the last few weeks. *Sexcapade* was too obvious.

His eyes adjusted further to the darkness and he watched her snare her bottom lip with her teeth. "You should, but I'm not sure if you do. It's a word we haven't spoken to each other. Or to anyone else. Not like this."

The waver in her voice instantly clued him in on her meaning. On what she wanted him to say. On what she needed to hear. He and Rory were so different, yet so alike. "You mean something like I love you?"

"Something like that."

He crawled over the blanket. "How about exactly like that?"

"Only if you mean it."

"I do. I love you, Rory Carmichael. I'd like to say I tried really hard not to, but that would be a bald-faced lie."

He folded his body into the cramped space as best he could, then jiggled the dome light so he could see her face completely.

"You didn't want a relationship," she reminded him.

"Neither did you."

"Apparently I didn't know what I wanted. Well," she amended, "I knew I wanted sex."

"Tell me that's still on your list," he said hopefully.

She tugged down one stringy strap off her shoulder. "Oh, yeah."

"So why the makeshift *Sexcapade?* All you ever have to do is look at me and I'll want you. Hell, you don't even have to be around and I'll want you."

She glanced aside, but he spied how her eyes lit with pleasure. "Well, I've been watching you work for the past hour. The way you flirt and smile and entice all those women without ever wanting them. I could tell, you know. I know what you look like when you see a woman you want."

"Like the way I'm looking at you right now?"

"Exactly. Makes me pretty hot, knowing I'm the only one."

Alec shifted in the cramped space, his body growing harder with each word she spoke. Apparently she, too, had finally come to terms with his past.

"Wait. You were watching me work?"

"I sat in a corner where you couldn't see me. You're so smooth. I can see why all those women in your past found you irresistible."

His exasperation flowed out in a sigh. "I've come to terms with that past, Rory. Thanks to you."

She snuggled closer, smoothing her hand over his chest. Before he knew it, she had the shirt unbuttoned and tugged back over his shoulders. "Oh, I have, too. That's why I wrote the *Sexcapade* and convinced your boss to help me lure you outside. I've realized something about us and I wanted to show you what it is. So I thought I'd build the anticipation, remind you of some of our naughtiest adventures, make you hot for me before you finally found me," she said, reaching between their tight bodies and unbuckling his belt. "What I realized was that these sexy fantasies are what's special between us. You've never explored this way with any other woman, have you?"

"I've never loved any other woman, either."

She grinned, then nipped a kiss on his earlobe at the same time she tugged down his zipper. "Yeah, that, too."

She gasped when his sex unfolded into her hand.

"If you weren't wearing panties," he explained, "I decided there was no point to my wearing briefs."

"You're bad, you know that?" she chastised, unwrapping a condom and sheathing him quickly.

"Yes, I do. And you do, too. Are you sure you still want to risk your heart with me?"

Just as boldly as she'd lured him outside—hell, just as boldly as she'd enticed him with that first *Sexcapade*—Rory straddled him. The minute she positioned her warm, moist flesh at the tip of his erection, Alec knew she could risk anything so long as he was her man. Anything. He'd move heaven and earth to give her everything she wanted. For the first time in his life, he was completely, utterly and entirely whipped. And, damn, it felt good.

"I've already risked my heart, Alec. When I first came to town, I thought I could keep my heart and my body separate, just as you thought you could separate who you'd been with who you wanted to become. But I couldn't satisfy either my heart or body without engaging both. Not with you. I love you. I want to make a life with you."

Alec forced himself to swallow, his brain singling out the sensations of her sweet wetness against him over anything else. Knowing he might not be able to form another coherent thought until he buried himself inside her, he shifted until he did just that.

Rory moaned softly as Alec slipped inside her, filling her with his delicious flesh. She braced her hands on his shoulders, lifting slowly, then pressing down inch by inch so each and every nerve ending could sing with the hot, lubed friction.

He lifted her shirt, then devoured her breasts with his hands, his tongue. Sparks of insatiable need flew from her tight nipples to her hot center. She moved faster, unable to fight the overwhelming battle for climax.

Alec stilled her movements by bracing her buttocks with his strong hands. "Not so fast, Aurora Carmichael."

She blinked. "Hm?"

"What do you mean, make a life with me?"

Shaking her head, she fought beyond the streaks of fire licking her from the inside out. "Talk later."

She tried to move again, but he held her fast.

"Talk now. When we burst over that edge, I want to know what's on the other side. Not so long ago, you told me you wanted to be on your own. Now you want a life together. What does that mean?"

Rory didn't know. What was the question again? His chuckle at her confusion caused another wave of pleasure to vibrate through her. She milked the tiny movement by clenching her muscles around him. He groaned.

"You're torturing me," he warned.

"You deserve it. Make me come, Alec. Then we'll talk."

He moved ever-so-slightly to his right, igniting a

quiver inside her she knew would soon build to an incredible explosion. "Sorry. I'm looking for some reassurances here."

"Well, I'm just looking for trouble, remember?"

He punished her wicked tease by shifting to his left. She cried out when the tip of his cock touched her clit in the precise spot that only he knew, the one that drove her utterly insane with wanting.

"You've found more than trouble, haven't you?" he goaded.

He released her buttocks, and she slid fully over him, every inch of him filling every inch of her. "Yes!"

He pumped, driving upward, loving her body with the same care that he adored her with his eyes. "And you want to marry me?"

She pressed downward, her mind lost in a swirl of explosive need, yet totally aware of what he asked. She'd wanted to build her own life, but knew without a doubt that doing so with Alec by her side would be even more triumphant.

"Yes!"

With a growl, he accepted her answer and pulled her mouth down on his. They'd both been looking for trouble—and they'd found it. With each other and the explosive love they'd share for now, and for always.

Epilogue

"WHAT'S THIS?"

Rory grinned at her twin's wary expression. In just one month of being reunited with her sister, she'd become incredibly accustomed to that look, so dissimilar from any expression she ever wore on her own face. Unlike Rory, Michaela Carmichael was wary about nearly everyone and everything. Her inherent distrust made her incredibly street smart, but also isolated. Something Rory wanted to help her change. Among other things.

Thanks to Alec, Micki had a job lined up at Dixie Landing as the new bartender. She'd learned to mix drinks with ease and flair and had an incredible head for measurements and numbers, making her a real whiz on the computerized tab system. She'd soon move into the unfinished third-floor apartment over Rory's, rent-free, until she was securely on her feet. Actually, Nanna had paid three months rent to Alec on Micki's behalf, but no one was stupid enough to tell Micki that. She didn't take charity well.

And Rory wasn't offering her charity now. She was offering her a gift. Such as it was.

"It's a book," Rory answered.

"I can see that," Micki said, doubtful. She flipped open the red leather cover, fanned through the few remaining sealed and perforated pages, then eyed her sister with hesitant humor. "I can read, you know. Big words, too. If you want to give me a book, you can include all the pages."

"I would if I could, but those pages seem to be worth more than gold."

"Ah! This is the notorious *Sexcapades* book," Micki guessed.

Rory sat down on the floor beside Micki, where she was packing for her trip. "None other. This little book has generated quite a bit of interest from its perch on the lobby table at Divine Events. So much interest that most of the pages have been stolen. But there are a few really good ones left."

That sparked Micki to open the book again. "Stolen, huh? That's right up my alley."

Rory laughed. "Yeah, mine, too."

"Why are you giving it to me? I don't have a man in my life."

"Neither did I until I stole my first page."

Micki nodded, her lips pressed in a tight-lipped grin. "Ah, yes. But you were actually looking for a man. I, on the other hand, have had my fill of losers."

"Alec isn't a loser," Rory insisted.

Micki held her hands up in surrender, then pointed sparkly-tipped fingernails in her direction. "He used to be. You just reformed him. I don't want to work that hard."

Rory eyed the book dreamily. "Trust me. The work wasn't bad. Isn't bad. And I did not reform him! He reformed himself. Besides, I like tempting the bad boy out of him every so often."

"Every so often? From the look on your face, I'd bet you're tempting the bad boy at least twice a day."

Rory laughed, but didn't deny her sister's bawdy claim. Since she and Alec had become engaged, their wild sex life certainly hadn't waned. And she'd decided that if it ever did, she had the perfect means to reignite the fire.

"As penance for stealing the pages, I bought a new copy of the book for the office," Rory explained, keeping to herself that she'd also bought a copy for her bedside table. "I thought you might get some use out of what was left of the first version."

Micki sighed and stuffed the book into her backpack. "Yeah, well, the table up in the attic has a wobbly leg. I'll put this to good use, I promise."

Rory swallowed a grin and shrugged, knowing there was no use in arguing with her stubborn sister. Since they'd reunited a month ago, they'd talked at length about Micki's past, sexual and otherwise. Rory realized that what Micki needed was something new, something exciting, something to shake up and destroy all the negative associations she had with men and sex. The *Sexcapades* book had come immediately to mind.

Right now, though, Micki had to concentrate on packing so she could deliver her friend, Danielle Stone, to a rehab clinic in Paris. Her twin shuffled the airline tickets, tore off a copy of the itinerary to give to Rory, then zipped the tickets inside the bag.

Rory scanned the travel plans. "How exciting. Paris! But wait." She looked at the arrival and departure dates. "You're barely going to be there for two days."

"Once Danielle gets to the clinic, I won't be able to see her or talk to her for thirty days. No use in my hanging around. Besides, her brother didn't volunteer to spring any of his millions for a hotel room."

"Did you ask?"

Micki leveled Rory with a wry glance. Of course Micki hadn't asked. Micki never asked for anything. She took or she did without.

Except when it came to Danielle. For her, she'd asked for help. Over the past five years, Danielle and Micki had been surviving on the streets together, though Rory suspected Micki had been more a protector than anything else to the younger Danielle, the daughter of wealthy, but cold parents who'd ignored their daughter's depression, drug addiction and loneliness. Micki had filled in the gaps, doing her best to keep Danielle out of trouble when she indulged in another binge or tried to kick her habit on her own. But now that she was on the brink of finally getting her life together, Micki had decided that Danielle needed intense professional help for her problems. She'd gone so far as to track down and contact Danielle's brother, Sebastian, a world-renowned venture capitalist who'd been completely in the dark about his sister's demons.

So he'd sent her two tickets to Paris, as well as a brochure detailing the top-notch treatment Danielle would receive. He promised to meet them in France and take up the mantle of Danielle's care. And once Micki delivered Danielle to Sebastian, she'd be free of her past, free to pursue a brighter future. A future that Rory, high on the incredible power of passion, had decided to inject with *Sexcapades.* The seductive book had done wonders for her life. She could only imagine what the naughty fantasies could do for Micki.

"Promise me you'll read that," Rory said.

"Promise me that by the time I get home, you'll have overcome your desire to meddle in my life."

Rory shook her head. "No can do. You're my sister. You chose to stay out of my life for ten years, now you have to pay the price. I've got a lot to make up for."

Micki frowned. "Maybe I won't come home right away."

Rory laughed. She knew her sister wasn't serious. They'd made a pact to stay with each other—a pact Micki had promised not to break again. "You've got two weeks until you start your new job, until the attic apartment is completely ready for habitation. In the meantime, you can come stay with me or you can hang out in Paris."

"Only two choices?"

"You have something else in mind?"

Rory watched Micki glance around the dump she'd called home for the last while. The apartment she'd taken with Danielle wasn't much, but according to Micki, she and Danielle had shared some good times here, along with the bad. Once she deposited her friend into the care of a brother who claimed to love her and professionals who knew how to address her problems, Micki would be free to focus on herself—something Rory knew she hadn't done in a long time.

"Nothing in particular. Just don't get too bored while I'm gone," Micki warned, wiggling her eyebrows before leaping off the floor to grab the jacket she'd left hooked over a rickety chair.

Rory patted her pocket. What had that last stolen *Sexcapade* been titled, the one she'd grabbed just before meeting Micki this afternoon? Ah, yes. "Hot for Teacher." With Alec finally back on the rolls as a professor, how could she have resisted the little role-playing game? She could only imagine what delicious delights he'd create as her first assignment. Or even better—homework.

A trickling thrill shot through her. "Me? Bored? With Alec?"

Not in a million years.

*   *   *   *   *

For more Sexcapades *check out*
INVITATIONS TO SEDUCTION,
the Blaze collection, available next month.
Then come back to Blaze for Micki's
story in UP TO NO GOOD
Harlequin Blaze 100, August, 2003

HARLEQUIN® *Temptation*®

*Legend has it that
the only thing that can bring down a Quinn
is a woman...*

Now we get to see for ourselves!

The youngest Quinn brothers have grown up.
They're smart, they're sexy...and they're about to be
brought to their knees by their one true love.

Don't miss the last three books in
Kate Hoffmann's dynamic miniseries...

The Mighty Quinns

Watch for:

THE MIGHTY QUINNS: LIAM
(July 2003)

THE MIGHTY QUINNS: BRIAN
(August 2003)

THE MIGHTY QUINNS: SEAN
(September 2003)

Available wherever Harlequin books are sold.

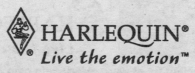

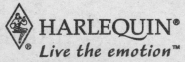

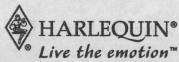

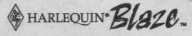
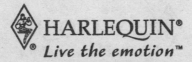